WHIPLASH

WHIPLASH

Graham Ison

This first world edition published in Great Britain 2004 by
SEVERN HOUSE PUBLISHERS LTD of
9–15 High Street, Sutton, Surrey SM1 1DF.
This first world edition published in the USA 2004 by
SEVERN HOUSE PUBLISHERS INC of
595 Madison Avenue, New York, N.Y. 10022.

British Library Cataloguing in Publication Data

Ison, Graham
    Whiplash
    1.   Brock, Detective Inspector (Fictitious character) - Fiction
    2.   Poole, Detective Sergeant (Fictitious character) - Fiction
    3.   Murder - Investigation - England - London - Fiction
    4.   Police - England - London - Fiction
    5.   Detective and mystery stories
    I.   Title
    823.9'14 [F]

    ISBN 0-7278-6073-9

Typeset by Palimpsest Book Production Ltd.,
Polmont, Stirlingshire, Scotland.
Printed and bound in Great Britain by
MPG Books Ltd., Bodmin, Cornwall.

One

I was not in the best of moods at being called out to a road traffic accident. At least, the phone call had implied that it was an accident, but I later learned that the crew of the traffic car thought there was a bit more to it than a straightforward RTA. Or, to put it another way, they thought it was a bit 'iffy'.

They'd sent for the 'feet' – as traffic officers are prone to call ordinary policemen – from the local nick, who in turn had called the CID. But the CID obviously thought it came into the MTD category: *much too difficult.* The natural corollary to that was to send for the Serious Crime Group.

And, as I happened to be the next detective chief inspector on the list, it was me who was lumbered with it.

So, as it was a traffic unit that had called me – indirectly, of course – I thought it only proper that they should be saddled with the responsibility of getting me, as quickly as possible, from my home in Wimbledon to Richmond Park, it being a sod of a journey during the morning rush hour. Or, for that matter, at any other time.

With the aid of flashing blue lights, a siren and a great deal of swearing and caustic comments from my highly skilled driver, I arrived at Pembroke Lodge – just inside the park's Richmond Gate – in record time. It did, however, cause me to reflect, once again, that I seem to be in the gravest danger of serious injury only when I am being conveyed anywhere by the police.

The crime scene – for that, regrettably, is what it turned out to be – was crowded. Not with the general public, but

1

with coppers. Three or four members of the Royal Parks
Constabulary, led by a sergeant, were standing around looking
important. The traffic car that had been called by them was
there, messing about with tape measures, watched by the
crew of the immediate-response car from Richmond nick,
who, apart from admiring the scenery, appeared to be doing
little else.

As I got out of the car, I was met by the local Metropolitan
Police duty officer, an attractive lady inspector who looked
young enough to be my daughter. *God forbid that I should
ever have offspring who want to join the police!*

'Who's in charge?' I asked her, a question guaranteed to
sort the women from the boys and girls.

'Er, well, I suppose I am,' said the inspector hesitantly,
looking round to see if there was anyone else brave enough
to take the risk. 'From Tango Romeo,' she added, explaining
in copper's jargon that she was attached to Richmond police
station. 'And who are you?'

'Detective Chief Inspector Harry Brock, Serious Crime
Group West. And what's so special that my expertise is
required to deal with a traffic accident?'

'They're not called accidents any more, sir,' the inspector
said smugly as she wrote down my name. 'The Yard's
directed that they're to be called collisions from now on.'

*Oh my God, the boy superintendents up at the dream
factory have been at it again.*

When the inspector had finished writing, she drew me
gently to one side, some distance from the blue-clad
onlookers. 'I'm afraid it's a bit more complicated, sir,' she
said.

'Isn't it always?' I said, speaking rhetorically.

'According to witnesses, sir, the vehicle was obliged to
swerve to avoid a motorcyclist travelling in the opposite
direction and on the wrong side of the road. It finished up
down there.' The inspector gestured towards a dip in the
ground, and then paused.

'Do go on,' I said. 'I can hardly contain my excitement.'

'The driver was rendered unconscious, sir, and, by the time he came round, police were already on scene.'

'What police?'

'The Parks Police, sir.'

'I hope you're going to get to the point of this, Inspector.'

'The impact caused the front passenger door to fly open and the body of a young woman was thrown out. She's dead, sir.'

'You still haven't convinced me that my presence here is a necessary charge on the police fund.'

'She was naked, sir.' The inspector smiled as if she had just scored match point in a hard-fought game of tennis. She looked the type to be terrifyingly good at tennis.

'Oh, I see.' Be fair, what the hell else could I say? 'Have you questioned the driver of the vehicle?'

'Briefly, sir. He denies all knowledge of the woman.'

'Don't blame him. I think I would in the circumstances.' It is a fact of life that any man accused by the police of a public association with a dead, naked woman generally denies knowing her. 'So, how d'you know the woman was thrown out?'

The inspector paused long enough for me to know that she had jumped to a conclusion. 'Well, I imagine that's what happened, sir.'

I, too, paused. Long enough to let it sink in that she'd committed the police officer's cardinal sin of supposition. 'Have you called the pathologist, crime-scene examiners, photographers . . .?' Which she should have done anyway for a suspicious death.

'No, sir. I called the local CID and they said they were calling you.'

And you promptly washed your hands of it. That was par for the course: when in trouble or in doubt, wave your arms and run about, *but for God's sake don't do anything useful.* 'Where is the driver of the vehicle?'

'Gone to hospital. There didn't seem much wrong with him, apart from a bang on the head, but best to be on the safe side, eh, sir?'

'Oh, indeed. Very wise.' I got the impression that this was an inspector who would always err on the side of safety. 'He is under police guard, I presume? Being a *material* witness, if not a suspect.'

'Oh, I, well . . .'

'Arrange it, Inspector, if you please.' I was never happy at having to do other people's work for them. 'Immediately.'

'Yes, sir.' There was more dedicated scribbling on the clipboard, a PC was summoned and told to get to the hospital urgently. The inspector had the earnest look of someone who hoped the driver hadn't already discharged himself.

'Has the vehicle been reported stolen, by any chance?' I enquired blithely. *Nothing like piling on the agony.*

'No, sir, we've checked.' The inspector gave me another smug match-point smile.

'I'd better have a look at the body, then,' I said.

A Vauxhall, the front of which was now firmly attached to a tree, had veered off the road and down a slight incline that was just steep enough to shield all but its roof from the road and, more importantly, as it transpired, the deceased's body.

As the inspector had said, the victim was naked, but what she hadn't mentioned, or perhaps had not noticed, were the marks across the dead woman's back and buttocks: marks indicating that she might have been beaten quite severely. There were also chafe marks on the wrists and ankles, and a broader one around the neck.

I made a decision, something that I do only if forced into it, like now, when confronted with prima facie evidence of a sex crime. 'Well, it seems that I *shall* need a pathologist, CSEs, photographers . . . the whole works. And I want this area cordoned off from there, all round there, to there.' I indicated with a sweep of the hand exactly where I wanted the tapes to be put.

The inspector wrote busily on her clipboard again before shouting to the crew of the immediate-response car to string out blue and white tapes around three or four conveniently sited trees.

'And one other thing, Inspector . . .' I said when she had
finished her call to the police station.

'Sir?'

'Ask the nick to get on to Curtis Green. I want Detective
Sergeant Poole down here like yesterday.'

'Curtis Green, sir?' The inspector raised a quizzical
eyebrow. 'Where's that?'

Heaven forfend! 'Curtis Green is where my office is . . .
in Whitehall,' I explained patiently. 'It used to be called New
Scotland Yard North before somebody decided to move the
Yard to Victoria Street. Doubtless before you were born,' I
added testily. I ask you, what chance do the public stand if
the police don't even known where Serious Crime Group
West has its office, *and* the responsibility for investigating
all serious crimes from there to Hillingdon? Of which the
naked lady was about to become the latest. 'And where are
the witnesses?'

'Witnesses, sir?' The inspector looked up from her obses-
sive scribing.

'You mentioned witnesses who saw the accident.' I refused
to go along with this nonsense of calling it a collision.

'Oh yes. Actually, there was only the one, sir. The traffic
officers took his statement and sent him on his way.
Apparently he was already late for work.'

'Oh dear! We can't have him being late for work, can we?
Tell me, during the brief moment he did grace police with
his presence, did he say whether he saw the woman in the
passenger seat before the accident occurred?'

That disconcerted the inspector. 'I'll find out,' she
muttered, and beckoned to one of the white-capped traffic
officers.

'The only witness, sir,' said the PC as he joined us, 'was
travelling behind Vehicle One—'

'By which you mean that one?' I gestured at the Vauxhall.

'Yes, sir.' The PC, an ambling sort of fellow in his forties,
gave the impression of having seen it all, that there was now
nothing left to surprise him. 'It seems that a solo motorcyclist

5

came towards Vehicle One on the wrong side of the carriageway' – policemen always call a road *the carriageway* – 'and, in attempting to avoid him, he went off the road and collided with a tree. Unfortunately the driver didn't get the index mark of the motorcycle.'

'How very remiss of him,' I murmured.

'Indeed, sir,' said the traffic officer earnestly. I suppose that to him it was a serious failing on the part of a driver who was throwing his car all over the road in a desperate attempt to avoid a collision himself, not to make a note of the number on the rear of a motorcycle vanishing at high speed in the opposite direction.

'And I don't suppose he was able to say how many people there were in the ... er ... in Vehicle One.'

'No, sir.'

I moved closer to the body and confined my initial examination to placing a finger on the carotid artery, just to satisfy myself that the woman was dead. She was, but I've known coppers to make mistakes before. Standing beside the body was a Royal Parks policeman, looking frighteningly officious.

'What are you doing?' I asked.

'Preserving the scene, sir.' The constable drew himself briefly to attention.

'Well, I've got a better idea. Rather than contaminating the scene any more than it's been contaminated already, why don't you go back up to the road and get that lot moving before you have another accident on your hands?' I waved at the two lines of cars that were crawling in opposite directions, the drivers peering out of their windows to see what the police were doing. Presumably it added a little excitement to their usually mundane journey to work. And would give them something to talk about when they got there.

'Morning, guv.'

I turned. Detective Sergeant Dave Poole was standing behind me, attired, as usual, in such a way as was unlikely to win him a best-dressed-man award. 'How did you get here, Dave? Charter the job's helicopter, did you?'

'No, sir.' As usual my black sergeant ignored this lame attempt at humour. I knew he didn't find it funny: he had called me 'sir'. 'I was in the office when the original call came in, so I got straight down here. I thought you might need me.'

'How very conceited of you.'

'So, what have we got, guv?'

I outlined what was known so far and explained that we were awaiting the arrival of the pathologist and the rest of the circus that forms part of a suspicious-death enquiry.

'Henry Mortlock's on his way, guv, and the supporting cast should be here soon. I rang them before I left Curtis Green.'

'Thank God someone's got their act together,' I said.

'And who's the dolly bird in the policeman's costume, guv?'

'That, Dave, is the duty officer.'

'Blimey! She's a bit of all right.'

'I don't think Madeleine would like that,' I said.

Madeleine was Dave's wife, a gorgeously petite principal ballet dancer who, it was rumoured, occasionally beat him up. Having met the girl, I had great difficulty in believing that particular snippet of canteen scuttlebutt. She was a twenty-five-year-old, slender five-two of vibrant sex appeal, whereas Dave was six feet tall and fifteen stones of solid muscle.

I took one of Dave's cigarettes and searched my pockets for my lighter.

'I see you're still giving up giving up, then,' Dave said spitefully. He produced a box of matches, lit both our cigarettes and replaced the dead match in the box. Dave knew all about scene contamination.

'I will, one day,' I said. I'd been trying to give up smoking for ages now, ever since a schoolmaster had caught me smoking behind the bike sheds and told me a horror story about his brother dying of cancer.

Suddenly there was action. A couple of white vans

containing the technicians of murder arrived, followed minutes later by a black car from which the portly figure of Dr Henry Mortlock emerged.

'Got some business for me, then, Harry?' asked Mortlock, briskly rubbing his hands together as, doubtless, he calculated his call-out fee.

Mortlock, an exponent of a black humour that rivalled that of most detectives, strolled across to where the body lay and walked slowly round it. 'Mmm!' he said eventually. 'Where did she come from?'

'I was hoping you'd tell me, Henry.'

'I'm a pathologist not a soothsayer, dear boy,' said Mortlock, opening his bag of tricks and preparing himself for his preliminary examination. After a few minutes of medical hocus-pocus, he stood up. 'When did this accident occur, Harry?'

I glanced at the traffic-division PC. 'Well?'

'Zero–eight–zero–five, sir,' said the PC after briefly consulting his clipboard.

'That's five past eight in English, Henry,' I said.

Mortlock put his hands in his pockets. 'The cadaver's been here longer than that,' he said. 'At a guess I'd say at least twelve hours, maybe a touch less.'

'So, there was no chance that she was thrown out of the car . . .'

'She may have been thrown out of *a* car,' said Mortlock, 'but not that one.' He gestured towards the Vauxhall attached to the tree. 'Not if that's the one that left the road at five past eight.'

The traffic-division officer looked disappointed and began to rewrite his report.

'And the cause of death?' I asked, knowing full well that I was not going to get a definitive answer.

Mortlock scoffed. 'I'll tell you that when I've done the post-mortem, Harry. Maybe.'

It was the reply I'd expected. 'OK to shift the body?'

'Sure. And get them to take it to Horseferry Road. I don't

like messing about in these local mortuaries. Incidentally, she appears to have been subjected to some physical abuse.'

'Yes, I noticed,' I said.

As Mortlock departed, the photographers started to record the scene for posterity and, I hoped, for the Crown Court. A passing taxi driver, presumably thinking we were doing a fashion shoot, shouted some obscene witticism and promptly had his name and address taken by a Royal Parks constable.

Finally, the crime-scene examiners, attired in white boiler suits and latex gloves, began the business of collecting such evidence as might eventually help me to discover who had murdered this young woman if, in fact, she had been feloniously killed. But, at this stage, I have to say that accidental death did not look a promising option.

At last the white suits completed their examination of the scene. The body was removed, the tapes taken down; the car was winched on to a flatbed truck and Richmond Park resumed its normal bucolic tranquillity. It was now eleven o'clock and Dave and I retired to the tea rooms in Pembroke Lodge for coffee and a discussion.

'What d'you make of that lot then, guv?' Dave nodded towards the window that faced the road near where our body had been found.

'It's obviously unconnected with the traffic accident,' I said. 'It looks as though some bastard ventured in here during the night and dumped her there.'

'Park's closed at night,' said Dave helpfully.

'As you're obviously a parks expert and know about these things, find out at what time it was closed last night and when it opened this morning.'

'Yeah, right.' Dave scribbled a few lines in his pocketbook. 'Anything else?' He looked up expectantly.

'Yes, get on to Mr Mead and ask him to liaise with the Parks Police to run a roadblock this evening and tomorrow morning – at all the gates – and question regular drivers as to whether they saw anything suspicious.'

Contrary to television mythology, it isn't just a DCI and his sidekick who investigate murders. There's a whole team of detectives, fifteen at least. And Detective Inspector Frank Mead, an ex-Flying Squad officer, was in charge of them. It was they who did all the mundane, but essential, legwork arising out of a murder enquiry.

And I was pretty sure that's what I was dealing with.

Dave scribbled some more. 'Be a waste of time,' he said.

'Yes, I know, Dave, but if we don't do it, someone will ask why we didn't. Like the Crown Prosecution Service or the judge or the commander.' The commander, whose distinguished career in the Uniform Branch had carefully skirted around crimes of any significance, had been placed in charge of Serious Crime Group West. I think it was someone's idea of a joke. Unfortunately, just because some administrative order had, theoretically, made him a detective, he thought he was one.

Dave finished his coffee, smoked one of my Marlboros and stood up. 'Where to now, guv?'

'The office, and we'll wait until after lunch to go to Horseferry Road. It'll give Henry time to assemble his tools. I hope you brought a car, because the bloody traffic lot have long gone.'

Dave waved the car keys. 'Of course, sir.'

He was calling me 'sir' again. He always did when I asked what he thought was a stupid question.

'Ah, you've got here at last,' said Henry Mortlock, glancing at his watch. 'Now I can begin.'

'It's only two o'clock, Henry,' I said. 'And I have had a rather busy morning,' I added caustically.

Mortlock ignored my attempt at sarcasm. 'Time's money, Harry.' He strolled casually around the body, humming a theme from Rachmaninov's Second Piano Concerto – which even I recognized, courtesy of Classic FM – before peering into the body's mouth and carefully examining the teeth. Slowly he went over every part of the body from the top of the head to the soles of the feet. He turned the body over and started again. All the time he spoke into the microphone that was suspended from the ceiling, commenting in detail about the marks on the woman's back, neck, wrists and ankles.

With a sigh, he turned the body over again, picked up a scalpel and began the task of dissection, interspersing his findings with more hummed snatches of classical music.

'Good,' he said. Eventually.

'Well?'

'I'll let you know, Harry. Got to run a few tests.' Mortlock yawned and then enigmatically added, 'There's something not quite right about all this.'

But he always said that.

'When are you going to let me in on the secret, then?'

'Should be able to tell you something later today.'

And with that, I had to be satisfied.

Dave and I went back to Curtis Green.

Detective Sergeant Colin Wilberforce, our efficient incident-room manager, looked up expectantly. 'We up and running on this one, sir?' he asked.

'Looks like it, Colin.'

'The commander would like a word, sir.'

'Thought he might,' I said, and made my way to his office.

'Ah, Mr Brock. This body in Richmond Park. Is it a murder enquiry?' The commander tipped his glasses forward and peered at me over them.

'Remains to be seen, sir. Depends on what Dr Mortlock has to say about it, but, on the face of it, it looks like a runner.'

'A runner?' The commander made it sound as though I was talking about a bean, but he knew exactly what I meant. Unfortunately he was one of those men who deplored slang of any sort. It made life difficult, having to explain my every action in plain English.

Two

There was a time when investigating officers had to wait forever and a day to get the result of a fingerprint check. But nowadays, with all this high-tech computer gismo, it can be done in minutes. Not that it did me any bloody good in this case.

One of the CSEs had taken the dead woman's prints at the scene – a standard procedure – but the victim had no criminal record. And that begged the question: who the hell was she?

The moment Dave and I had returned to Curtis Green, Colin Wilberforce had fed the dead woman's description into the Police National Computer and produced three possibles: women who had been reported missing by their family or friends.

Six months ago, Daphne Wainwright had walked out of her home in Durham leaving her husband and two young children, and had not been heard of again. At least, not according to the computer. Two years ago, Sandra Bellamy had vanished without trace from Romford after a row with her live-in boyfriend and, finally, an Alexandra Forbes had gone missing three weeks ago from the marital home in Battersea. Each of the missing women was in the mid-twenties to mid-thirties age bracket and had long black hair. Henry Mortlock had estimated that our victim was about thirty, and she certainly had black hair, hair that almost reached her shoulder blades.

Colin telephoned the police in Durham and Essex. Daphne Wainwright had returned home after a week, but no one had thought to cancel the entry on the PNC, idle bastards. As for Sandra Bellamy, well, she was still adrift, but I knew damned well that if she'd been murdered two years ago, her body wouldn't have been in the comparatively pristine condition in which we'd found the one in Richmond Park.

'Where in Battersea did this Alexandra Forbes live, Colin?' I asked.

'Number sixteen Crouch Road, sir.'

We should be so lucky. In my experience, abandoned corpses usually originated in some faraway place like Manchester. And so did all their family and friends. And probably their killer too.

'Any progress, Mr Brock?'

Oh Jesus, the commander! All I needed now was him interfering yet again. 'We have a tenuous clue to the victim's identity, sir,' I said, trying not to let my impatience show. 'DS Poole and I are going out to check. This evening probably.'

'Good, good. And who is this woman?'

'We have an Alexandra Forbes reported missing from Battersea three weeks ago. She fits the description and it may be her. Of course, Battersea's on SCG South's patch,' I added, hoping to offload the enquiry even at this early stage.

'Yes, but she was found in our area, Mr Brock, so we'll deal with it,' said the commander, smiling archly. And when he said *we* will deal with it, he meant that *I* would deal with it.

Well, it was worth a try.

Allowing for the fact that Maxwell Forbes, the person who had notified police of Alexandra Forbes's disappearance, probably worked during the day, Dave and I waited until gone six o'clock that evening to pay him a visit.

Crouch Road was one of those streets off Lavender Hill that had been gentrified by people with more money than the sense not to live in Battersea, and number sixteen was no exception. The windows were what estate agents call 'replacement UPVC double-glazed' and had been specially designed – no doubt at great expense – to blend in well with the Victorian façade of the house, the brickwork of which was in excellent condition.

Immediately outside was a fairly new, top-of-the-range Mercedes, but it didn't necessarily belong to the occupant of number sixteen. One thing was sure: I wouldn't have left it in a Battersea street if it had been mine. Not if I'd wanted to see it in the same condition the next morning. Or, come to that, to see it at all the next morning. Nevertheless, Dave made a note of the car's number; he tends to collect snippets of seemingly irrelevant information. Just in case.

The man who answered the ornate front door appeared to be in his fifties – we later found out that he was fifty-seven – and was casually attired in a check shirt, well-tailored chinos and brown leather loafers. His grey hair was neatly trimmed – at a guess by a West End barber – and gently waved. I was cynical enough to think he might have had it permed. He was, I suppose, about six feet two inches tall and slim enough to suggest that he took regular exercise. It did cross my mind that he might be our victim's father.

'Yes?' The man stared at us, apparently mystified as to the reason two strange men were standing on his doorstep. He already had double-glazing, so that was out. Maybe he thought we were about to give him a quick reading from the Bible as a precursor to telling him that everyone loved everyone else, and that the world really was created in seven days. But then all manner of weirdos call at people's doors these days, especially in Battersea.

'Mr Maxwell Forbes?'

'Yes, I'm Max Forbes. What is it?'

'We're police officers, sir. I wonder if we might have a word.'

He looked doubtful and I produced my warrant card, which he examined carefully. But then you can't be too careful if you're unwise enough to live in Battersea.

'You'd better come in,' said Forbes, and led us into an

14

expensively furnished sitting room on the front of the house. 'Do sit down,' he added, and sat down opposite us. 'Now, what's this all about?'

'I understand that you reported an Alexandra Forbes missing from home, sir, about three weeks ago,' I began.

Forbes sat forward in his chair, his interest immediately aroused, and concern etched on his face. 'That's correct. Why, have you found her?'

This was always the difficult bit. I have discovered, over my twenty-odd years' service, that there is no easy way to tell anyone that their nearest and dearest has been murdered.

I remembered the first time. It wasn't a murder, but, as a young constable, I'd been sent in the middle of the night to tell a man that his father was dangerously ill in hospital. All the way there, I'd been framing in my mind the most sympathetic way of breaking the news. But the moment the man saw me on the doorstep, he'd said, 'Oh no, the old bugger's not at death's door *again*, is he?'

Mind you, the woman we'd found might not have been Alexandra Forbes.

'We have found a body, sir,' I said slowly.

'Oh God!' Forbes let out a long sigh before speaking again. 'And you think it might be Alex?'

'We don't know as yet,' I said. 'The woman we found fits the description of your . . .' I paused, unsure of the relationship between Max and Alexandra Forbes.

'Alexandra is my wife, Chief Inspector. She is twenty-six years younger than me.' I don't know why he found it necessary to tell me that.

'I see. Well, as I was saying, the woman we found fits the description of your wife, but until—'

'But until I come and look at her you won't know for sure, is that it?'

'Precisely so, sir.'

'What happened? Was it suicide, or an accident of some sort?'

I paused. 'It would appear that she had been murdered,

sir.' I wondered what had led him to think she might have committed suicide.

'Murdered, you say?' Forbes sat back in his chair, a blank expression on his face.

'Yes. But we don't know that it's your wife,' I emphasized.

'When would you like me to view the body then?' Forbes had obviously been stunned by what we'd told him, and the question was completely devoid of emotion.

'Now would be ideal, if you're free to do so.'

'Certainly I'm free to do so,' said Forbes, with just a trace of impatience. 'I'll get my jacket.' He paused. 'Is it cold out?'

What, in August? Strange that, being more concerned with the weather than with the violent death of someone who may be his wife.

'No. I was warm enough in just a suit. But we do have a car.'

'I won't keep you a moment then.' And, with that, Forbes rose and went upstairs.

'Doesn't seem too put out, guv, does he?' whispered Dave.

'You got him down as a suspect already?'

'Haven't you?' Dave asked in reply.

'We don't even know if it's Alexandra Forbes yet,' I said. 'Let's not jump to conclusions.'

Our whispered conversation was cut short by the return of Forbes, now wearing a denim bomber jacket that would have looked good on a man thirty years his junior, but was faintly ridiculous on him: the pose of a man trying to re-invent his vanished youth, I imagined.

I'd alerted the Horseferry Road mortuary to stay open and we drove there in silence. The keeper, with a felicitously contrived air of sympathy, doubtless born of years of dealing with the bereaved, ushered Forbes into the viewing room as an assistant removed the sheet just enough for Forbes to see the face of our victim. It took only a moment.

'That's her,' said Forbes. 'That's Alex.' And he turned away, not a trace of grief evident on his face.

'You're sure, Mr Forbes?' I asked.

'Of course I'm sure.'

We took Max Forbes back to Crouch Road, and Dave took a formal statement of identification from him.

'I have to ask you some questions, Mr Forbes,' I began, once Dave had finished, 'and I appreciate that it may be painful for you.'

'You have your job to do, Chief Inspector,' said Forbes blandly.

'When your wife's body was found there was evidence that she had been beaten, possibly with a whip.' I decided against mentioning the other marks at this stage. 'I wondered if you might be able to offer any explanation for that.'

'No, I can't, I'm afraid.'

'Have you any idea why your wife left home?'

'None at all.' Forbes appeared perfectly relaxed and apparently unaffected by having just viewed the murdered – and possibly tortured – body of his wife. 'I can't offer you a drink,' he continued. 'I'm an alcoholic. I don't keep anything in the house. Too much of a temptation. Being policemen, I imagine you'll understand.'

I wasn't sure whether Forbes meant that all detectives were alcoholics – there was a day when he could have been right, nearly – or whether he had assumed that we were accustomed to dealing with such people.

'What happened, then? She just upped and left?'

'That sums it up rather neatly, Mr Brock, yes.'

'When exactly was this?' I knew from the entry on the PNC, but I wanted to hear what Forbes had to say.

For a moment or two, he gazed pensively at the ceiling. 'Ah, yes, it was a Monday.' He stood up and walked across to a davenport that stood against the wall opposite the window, opened the lid and thumbed through a desk diary. 'It was Monday the fifteenth of July,' he said, speaking over his shoulder. He sat down again. 'I'd been to a livery dinner in the City and when I got home – it must have been just after midnight – she was gone.'

'Had she taken any clothes with her? Any personal belongings?'

'No, nothing.'

'And you've no idea where she went?'

'None whatsoever, no. Not then, anyway.'

'And so you reported it to the police.'

'Of course. She still hadn't returned by the following evening, so I told your people at Lavender Hill police station.'

'But from what you said just now, I gather that you did hear from her.'

'Yes, I did. We'd arranged to go on holiday on the Wednesday: that would have been the seventeenth of July. There seemed little point in cancelling it, so I went by myself.'

Well, well, what a callous bastard. His wife buggers off, but he still goes on holiday.

'For how long?'

'A fortnight.'

'And where did you go?'

'Germany. To the Black Forest, not far from Karlsruhe, as a matter of fact.'

'So when did you hear from her?'

'When I got back there was a postcard waiting for me, a short scribbled note from her to say that she wasn't coming back.' Forbes stood up and crossed once more to the davenport. 'I've got it here, if you want to see it.'

It was the usual sort of photograph of a beach, and the postmark indicated that it came from Ostend. I spoke the name aloud.

'It's on the Belgian coast,' said Forbes in a way that suggested I might never have heard of it.

'I know. And you've heard nothing more?'

'No, nothing. I thought I'd seen the last of her.'

'May I keep this?'

'If you wish.' Forbes waved a hand of dismissal.

I handed the postcard to Dave, who shrouded it in one of the little plastic bags he seemed always to carry.

'Was your marriage a happy one, Mr Forbes?' I asked.

'Yes, idyllic.' Forbes spoke without hesitation.

'Did it cross your mind to go and look for her?'

'No. If she wanted to leave me, there was no point in my trying to persuade her otherwise.' Forbes shrugged dismissively, as though it was a pointless question. 'I realized that marrying a much younger woman was risky, and I knew that, if one day she decided to leave me for a man more her age, there wouldn't be a great deal I could do about it.'

'And did she? Leave you for a younger man, I mean.'

'Your guess is as good as mine. I really have no idea.'

'Was there anyone you might have suspected she would leave you for?'

'No.'

'Did she have any friends who may be able to help us, Mr Forbes?'

'I suppose you mean men-friends,' Forbes said acidly.

'Anyone,' I said, but I'd meant men.

For some time, Forbes gazed unseeing into the middle distance. 'There was a Mike Farrell who was a friend of hers,' he said at last. 'I agreed that she would be free to visit him any time she wanted to.'

'What was the purpose of those visits, Mr Forbes?' For all I knew, Alexandra Forbes might have been taking piano lessons. *Like hell she was!* Detectives, however, have to get answers; mere supposition is not enough in a case of murder.

'For sex, for Christ's sake. What d'you think it was for, man?' shouted Forbes, his reserve at last breaking down, and he stared at me, a sullen expression on his face. He was quiet for a moment or two, and then said, 'I'm sorry, Mr Brock, that was unforgivable. As I said earlier, Alex was much younger than me and her sexual appetite was unabated. Regrettably, I was unable to satisfy her any more.' He spoke quite calmly now, as he explained in a matter-of-fact way the problem that he and his late wife had apparently resolved amicably.

So the marriage hadn't been that idyllic.

'Do you know where this Mike Farrell lives, Mr Forbes?'

19

For a moment Alex's husband looked perplexed. 'Er, Thames Ditton, I think. Just a moment, I came across her address book here after she'd left.' He stood up and crossed to the davenport again. 'Yes, here we are.'

'I should like to take that if I may.' I held out my hand.

'Why d'you want it?' Forbes placed one hand over the other and held the small book close to his chest.

'It may contain names of people who can assist me in my enquiries.'

'Very well.' Reluctantly, Forbes handed over the book. 'But you will return it, won't you?'

'Of course. What is your occupation, Mr Forbes?'

'I'm an artist and I run an advertising agency. In the West End.'

'And Mrs Forbes? Did she pursue a career?'

'She was with a Central London estate agent. She was rather good at it by all accounts.'

'The Mercedes outside . . . is it yours?'

'No, it's Alex's. That was a strange thing. It disappeared the night she went missing, but when I got home about a week later, there it was.'

'What about the keys?'

'I've no idea what happened to those.'

'We'll need to examine it, Mr Forbes. I'll arrange to have it removed to the laboratory as soon as possible.'

'As you wish,' said Forbes and shrugged.

'He's a cold bastard, guv,' said Dave, as we drove back to the office. 'He couldn't give a toss, could he? He never asked when and how she died, or where she was found. In fact, he wasn't the least bit interested in what had happened to his wife.'

'It's certainly not what I expected, Dave.' Over the years I'd seen a wide variety of reactions to the murder of a loved one: uncontrollable grief, stunned disbelief, anguish, fury tinged with a desire for revenge, but never had I seen the calm, cold indifference that Forbes had displayed. It made me suspicious. Very suspicious indeed. Max Forbes claimed to have raised no objection to his wife having an affair with a younger man, but had he been as complacent about it as he'd suggested?

Admittedly my ex-wife, Helga, had done a similar thing, but the doctor she'd jumped into bed with was only a year younger than me. And he had a hell of a lot more money. What, I wondered, had Mike Farrell got? Apart from the obvious.

On our return, I handed Alex Forbes's address book to Colin Wilberforce and asked him to check out the names and telephone numbers it contained. I toyed with the idea of ringing Sarah Dawson, my girlfriend, and inviting her out for dinner, but realized that there was too much to do. Like interviewing Mike Farrell, the man with whom Alex Forbes – according to the woman's husband – had had a sexual relationship.

'What's Madeleine doing tonight, Dave?' I asked.

'Dancing, guv. Finishes about half ten.'

'You won't mind a trip to Thames Ditton, then. See if we can find this Farrell guy.'

'Want me to ring him?'

'Yeah, but do the wrong-number trick. Don't want to forewarn him of our interest.'

'He's probably read about it in the papers,' said Dave.

'But we haven't released a name. We've only just found out ourselves who she is.'

Dave dialled Farrell's number, got a reply and apologized. 'He's in, guv.'

We drove to Thames Ditton and eventually found Barge Court, a block of modern service flats overlooking the river. Number eleven was on the second floor.

It was now nine o'clock. Such is a detective's life.

Three

'Mr Farrell, we're police officers.'
'Oh Christ! It's not the bloody boat again, is it?'
'The boat?'
'Yeah. I've got a small boat moored down near Raven's Ait. The damned thing's been broken into twice already this year. What's happened now? Have they sunk the bloody thing?'
'No, Mr Farrell, it's not the boat,' I said, after I'd introduced myself and Dave. 'It's a little more serious than that.'
'Oh! Sounds ominous. You'd better come in, then.'
Farrell ushered us into a plushly furnished sitting room that had a near-panoramic view of the river. A floating gin palace was making its leisurely way downriver towards Teddington, the beat of its amplified music plainly audible through the open windows. 'Pleasant, isn't it?' he said, as he turned off the television.
He was about thirty-eight, forty maybe, and was smooth, muscular and good-looking, with a neatly trimmed moustache. He wore light-coloured slacks and a turquoise silk shirt, cuffs turned back to display a gold Rolex wristwatch.
'Drink?' Farrell opened a cabinet alongside the television set and looked up expectantly.
I shook my head. 'No thanks.'
Farrell shrugged and closed the cabinet without pouring anything for himself. 'So, what's this serious business you want to talk to me about?' he asked.
'Alexandra Forbes.'
'What about her? Haven't seen her lately.'

22

'She's dead, Mr Farrell. Her body was discovered this morning in Richmond Park.'

Farrell sat down, suddenly, his face white. 'My God! Surely not. What the hell happened?'

'She'd been murdered,' I said.

'Jesus! I don't believe it.' Farrell was visibly shaken by what I'd told him. 'Alex was a lovely girl. Who would want to do a thing like that?'

'That's what I'm trying to find out,' I said. 'When did you last see her?'

'Hey, now just hold on a minute.' Farrell shot forward in his chair, a look of alarm on his already distressed face. *Perhaps he was a good actor.* 'You're not suggesting that I had anything to do with this, I hope.'

'Well, did you?' Dave spoke for the first time since our arrival.

Farrell cast a dismissive glance in Dave's direction. 'Of course not.'

'When did you last see her?' I asked again.

'About three or four weeks ago, I suppose.'

'Where? Here?'

'Yes, here.'

'Did she come to see you often? It's quite a long way from Battersea.'

'About twice a week, I suppose. Sometimes more often, sometimes less, but never less than once a week.'

'Why? Why did she visit you so often?' I sat back in Farrell's deep sofa and crossed my legs. I knew the answer – at least I did if Max Forbes had been telling the truth – but was mildly interested to see what this obvious ladies' man would come up with.

Farrell glanced at Dave and then back at me. 'You having me on?' he asked.

'It would be helpful if you'd just answer the question,' I said.

'We were having an affair, of course,' said Farrell, as though that was blindingly obvious. He relaxed and played a brief tattoo on the arm of his chair with his right hand. 'I don't know how much you know about Alex, but she was in a loveless marriage. Her husband Max – he's getting on for sixty apparently – was bloody useless in bed, so she said, and she needed a man, a real man.' He smiled conceitedly and brushed his moustache. 'Simple as that.'

'And how long had this affair been going on?'

'About a year, I suppose. With Max's consent, I may add. Incidentally, he was a reformed drunk, which probably accounts for his lack of performance.'

'But after seeing her every week over that period, suddenly she didn't turn up. Didn't you find that strange?'

'Sure I did. After a week I telephoned her, both at home and at her office. There was no answer from the house and the office told me that she'd taken leave. They didn't know where she'd gone. Either that or they wouldn't say.'

'How often did you try to contact her?' I asked.

Farrell paused for a few seconds. 'God, I don't know. Perhaps four or five times. That was during the second week.'

'Did you know she was supposed to be going on holiday with her husband on the seventeenth of July?'

'No, I didn't. She never said anything about that, although, as I said, her office told me she was on leave. But then I got a postcard from her, from Belgium of all places, with the usual sort of wish-you-were-here message scrawled on it.'

'Do you still have that postcard?' asked Dave.

'No, I chucked it away,' said Farrell. 'Thought to myself, well, that's the end of that. Despite her wishing I was there,' he added with a wry smile.

'So you gave up trying to contact her?'

'Yeah, I gave up. I assumed that she'd found someone else.'

'Did you ever get in touch with Max Forbes, to see if he knew what had happened to her?'

'I left messages on their home answerphone, but she never

rang back, so I didn't bother any more. There was no point. To be honest, I thought she'd ditched him – not before time, either – found someone else and pushed off to the sun with him. That was definitely her scene: sun, sand, sea and sex. Oh yes, lots of sex. She was a pretty demanding lady, I can tell you.'

'Demanding? In what way demanding?'

'She was a bloody nympho. Unfortunately she wasn't deaf and dumb and she didn't keep a pub,' Farrell added, forcing a laugh as he rehearsed the old joke. He was speaking quite openly now, jocularly almost, about his sexual relationship with Alex Forbes. 'I reckon I've got an appetite, but there were times when I had one hell of a job keeping up with her. Maybe she found someone else,' he said again. 'But if she did, he must have been an Olympic-class stud, believe me,' he added.

'Was there ever any talk of her divorcing her husband and marrying you?'

'No, but I wouldn't have wanted to know about that even if she'd suggested it. It was purely a physical arrangement, nothing more. It suited her and it suited me. I'd already been in one disastrous marriage and I had no desire to repeat the experiment, thank you very much. You get a bit cautious: once bitten and all that.'

I certainly knew all about disastrous marriages. When I married a German girl, Helga Büchner, some seventeen years ago, following a whirlwind romance, it had all seemed so wonderful. Then, due entirely to Helga's selfishness – that, at least, was my view – our son Robert had drowned in the swimming pool of a friend with whom Helga had left the boy while she was pursuing her career. That was the beginning of the end. Row followed upon row and we divorced a year ago. Mind you, Helga's 'friendship' with a doctor hadn't helped.

Now I was in a fairly stable relationship with Dr Sarah Dawson, a gorgeous, thirty-year-old forensic scientist on the staff of the laboratory at Lambeth. But whether either of us was prepared to take the big step into marriage was something yet to be resolved.

'Did you ever meet Maxwell Forbes?' I asked.

'No. I had no reason to. I was borrowing his wife, and Alex had told me that it was OK by him. No sense in complicating things.'

'But presumably you spoke to him on the phone occasionally?'

'Oh sure. But only when I rang Alex and he answered. He knew what Alex and I were up to and that that's why I wanted to talk to her. He seemed quite resigned to the arrangement. He was always very pleasant to me on the phone.'

'What do you do, Mr Farrell?' asked Dave, looking up from his pocketbook.

'Do? What d'you mean, what do I do?' The change in questioning seemed to catch Farrell wrong-footed and he looked puzzled.

'What is your occupation?'

'Oh, I see. I'm an interior decorator.'

'Really?' Dave glanced around the opulent sitting room, clearly surmising that there must be money in painting and decorating.

'And before you say it,' said Farrell, reading Dave's mind, 'I'm a consultant interior designer. I'm retained to advise on the decor of restaurants, offices, shops and large houses.'

'Jolly good,' said Dave, smirking.

'Just now you described Mrs Forbes as sexually demanding . . .' I began.

'I called her a nympho,' Farrell cut in.

'Well, whatever, but you also said that there were times when she only visited you once a week. That doesn't accord with your version of her sexual appetite, surely. Do you think that she was also seeing someone else?'

Farrell shrugged. 'Your guess is as good as mine, old boy,' he said, 'but I suppose it's possible. If she was, I wasn't really in a position to argue.'

'Do you know of anyone who she might have been seeing?' I asked.

'No.' It was starting to get dark. Farrell stood up and switched on a couple of table lamps, but left the curtains open.

'Mr Farrell,' I said, once he'd sat down again and I'd got his full attention. 'When Mrs Forbes's body was found this morning, there was evidence that she had been beaten.'

'Beaten?'

'The pathologist is of the opinion that she'd been tortured, whipped perhaps.'

'Oh, I see.' Farrell sounded relieved.

'You don't seem surprised,' I said.

'I'm not. Alex was into that sort of thing. Being chastised turned her on. She was a masochist.'

'And did you ever whip her?' I prayed that Dave would not choose this moment to explain that it was a principle of English law that technically no one can give permission for an assault upon themselves, no matter how pleasurable they might find it.

'Yeah, sure, but only when she wanted me to. It wasn't every time.'

'When would have been the last time you beat her?'

Farrell frowned, obviously not liking that word, and hesitated before answering. 'The last time she came here. That would have been about four weeks ago, I suppose.'

I glanced at Dave, who was scribbling furiously. 'Do you know the exact date?' he asked.

'It was a Wednesday.' Farrell reached across to a side table and picked up a pocket diary. 'Hang on a mo', I can tell you.' He thumbed through the small book. 'Yes, it was Wednesday the tenth of July.' He shut the diary and tossed it back on to the table.

'Did you always keep a record of when she came here?' I wondered if there were other women's names in the book, and perhaps a score of between one and ten against each. Farrell looked the type who would do that.

'Yes, I did.'

'Why?'

'I don't know. It's just a habit I got into.'

'Did you ever use any sort of restraints on Alex Forbes?'

That clearly disconcerted Farrell. 'Look, what the hell is all this?' he said, his voice rising. 'I had nothing to do with her death, if that's what you're driving at. All right, I didn't love the girl, not in the sense that I wanted to marry her, but I enjoyed her body and she enjoyed mine. It was pure sex. What the hell would I have wanted to kill her for?'

I could think of a few reasons, but then I'd investigated murders before that had motives of sexual jealousy. I waited until Farrell had cooled off. 'Did you ever use restraints on her?' I asked him again, calmly.

'Sort of.'

'Meaning?'

'I've got a couple of pairs of handcuffs that she liked me to shackle her to the bed with.'

'And where did you get those from?' asked Dave, obviously wondering if some leery copper had done Farrell a favour by parting with some of the job's ironmongery. It had happened before.

'Alex gave them to me. It was a jokey sort of birthday present. Want to see them?' Without waiting for an answer, Farrell left the room. 'There you are,' he said, returning a minute or two later.

The handcuffs were of the sort that are easily obtainable from the sex shops of Tottenham Court Road. I'd only ever seen similar ones in a police station when they'd formed part of a prisoner's property.

'Thank you, Mr Farrell,' I said. 'It's possible that we shall want to interview you again.'

'Don't you want to ask me where I was when she was killed?'

'We don't know when she was killed, Mr Farrell.' And that turned out to be more prophetic than I realized.

*　　　*　　　*

I dropped Dave off in Kennington at eleven o'clock, just in time to wave to Madeleine as she opened the front door.

'See you in the morning, Dave,' I said. I had a feeling that tomorrow was going to be a long hard day.

I arrived at Curtis Green at a quarter to nine, but Dave was already in, appearing in my office with the usual tray of coffee in one hand, and a sheaf of papers in the other.

'You're not going to like this, guv,' he said, dropping the papers on my desk. 'It's Henry Mortlock's report and, apart from telling us that the cause of death was strangulation with a fairly wide ligature, it buggers things up a treat.'

'I can't wait,' I said, and took a sip of coffee.

Dave wasn't wrong about the report. The telling paragraph leaped out of the page at me: *The deceased's body had been preserved in a freezer for some indeterminate time following her death.*

The corollary to this damning statement was that Mortlock was unable to assess, with any degree of accuracy, when the girl had been murdered. And it therefore followed that he could not say when the weals and other marks on her body had been inflicted.

I grabbed the phone and rang him. 'Henry, what's this all about? How d'you know she was kept in a freezer?'

'Are you questioning my professional expertise, dear boy?' asked Henry impishly. 'It's all in the report.'

'Yes, I know it is, but I can't understand a word of it. Just explain it in words of one syllable, will you. I'm only a simple policeman, after all.'

There was a scoff from the other end of the phone. 'The short answer, Harry, is that the young woman was killed and her body was stored in some sort of freezer. Other than to say that she was murdered between the time she was last seen alive and when you found her yesterday morning, I can't tell you when she died. And if you want to know how I know, read the damned report.'

'And thank *you* very much, Henry.'

'What d'you think, guv?' asked Dave, throwing me a cigarette as I replaced the receiver.

'I think that might just put Mike Farrell in the frame, Dave, but how we can prove it is another matter altogether. He said he last saw her four weeks ago – but he could have been lying – and it was three weeks ago that Maxwell Forbes reported her missing.' I leaned back in my chair and sighed. I knew it wouldn't be as simple as that. Why the bloody hell did I always get stuck with murders that were complicated right from day one? Why could I not, once in a while, have a nice simple domestic killing? The sort where a brutalized housewife, after twenty years of marriage, suddenly stabs her husband to death and then calls the police? Or a street fight where there are fifty witnesses who all point to the killer and say, 'He did it.'

'I've done the checks on the phone numbers in Alexandra Forbes's address book, sir,' said Colin Wilberforce, appearing in the doorway of my office.

'Sit down and tell me the worst, Colin,' I said gloomily. 'I have a feeling it's going to be one of those days.'

'I've traced the subscribers to the five telephone numbers that had a man's name against them, sir.' Colin placed a computer printout on my desk. 'All are living in the greater London area, and within a reasonable distance of Battersea.'

'Well, that's something, I suppose. Do we know anything about these men?'

'I've done an electoral roll check, sir, and they all appear to be single. At least, there's no one else shown on the voters' list for their addresses.'

'Bloody marvellous,' I said. 'And I bet they're all out at work during the day. Any joy with CRB?'

CRB was the abbreviation that the Metropolitan Police uses for the Criminal Records Bureau, which contains details of all convicted persons in the United Kingdom, although it's probably got a different name now. CRB that is, not the United Kingdom. Oh, I don't know though. But one thing's sure, the whizz-kids at the Yard can't resist changing things once we at the cutting edge have just got used to them.

'There's no trace of any of them, I'm afraid, sir.' Colin looked as disappointed as I felt.

If only the list had contained a convicted murderer, or at least someone with previous for violence, it might have helped me to reduce the odds.

I glanced down the list. 'At a rough, cynical guess,' I said, 'it seems likely that this young woman was spreading her favours fairly evenly around the Metropolitan Police District.'

'I reckon we're looking at an eternal polygon here, guv,' said Dave, carefully surveying a banana he had taken from his pocket. 'So where do we start?' he asked, already resigned to a lot of late evenings spent knocking on doors.

'I think we'll try the nearest, Dave. There's a Bill Griffin who lives on a houseboat on Chelsea Reach.'

'I doubt if you'll get a body-sized freezer on a houseboat,' said Dave. 'On the other hand, he might work in a butcher's shop.'

'Do me a favour, Dave,' I said. 'Wind your neck in.'

Four

The consultant graphologist who had been retained by the forensic science laboratory was no bloody help at all. Having compared the handwriting in Alex Forbes's address book with that on the postcard that Max Forbes had received from Ostend, this so-called expert eventually decided that he was not prepared to commit himself. 'It could be the same hand, Mr Brock, but then again, it may not be. There isn't sufficient of a sample on the postcard to make an accurate comparison.'

'Thanks very much,' I said sarcastically.

'Not at all. Any time,' said the expert, obviously thinking that I was delighted with his professional opinion.

I spent quite a while going over the detailed statement that Dave had taken from Mike Farrell about his liaison with Alex Forbes, but there was nothing that I could read into it that helped. He'd admitted to whipping the girl and he might well have been her killer, but on the basis of what we had learned so far, there was absolutely no proof.

Yet.

There was no doubt in my mind that this enquiry was going to be a long, hard grind.

The postcards from Belgium that both Max Forbes and Farrell had received from Alex intrigued me. If she really had gone to Belgium, whom had she gone with – or had she gone by herself – and when did she come back? And I hadn't overlooked the fact that her husband, on his own admission, had been in mainland Europe at the same time, although he claimed that he was there alone. Furthermore, the handwriting, purporting to be that of Alex, could have been penned by Max and posted by him in Ostend. He was, after all, an artist.

And in my book, for artist read forger.

Added to which, Max Forbes had displayed absolutely no emotion on learning of the death of his wife, and that made me wonder whether he qualified as our Number One Suspect.

'Alex Forbes's Mercedes was taken into Lambeth late last night, Harry,' said DI Frank Mead, appearing in the doorway to my office.

'And?'

'There is no evidence that it was driven other than with the keys,' continued Frank, dropping into my armchair. 'And there were no identifiable fingerprints, only smudges in all the usual places. She was probably the sort of woman who wore gloves when she was driving. The boffins have also collected a few hairs and fibres from inside the car and the boot, but they'll probably show positive when compared with Alex Forbes's body.'

'One bloody brick wall after another,' I said.

'Looks like it,' said Frank, and smiled. 'But it's early days yet.' A great optimist was Frank. 'Incidentally, I've been trying to make contact with the Forbeses' next-door neighbours: the Madisons at number eighteen and the Websters at number fourteen, but no luck so far. I'll keep trying.'

'Yes, good. This guy Max Forbes worries me, Frank. He was as cold as could be when he viewed his dead wife. Doesn't seem to be in the slightest cut up about it.'

'Delayed reaction, perhaps,' said Frank.

'Or guilty knowledge,' I said.

Dave and I had an early lunch. 'Oh, to hell with it,' I said. 'Let's get down to Chelsea and see if this Griffin guy is at home. For all we know he may work from his boat.'

Bill Griffin's houseboat was moored on the Thames embankment just above where the Chelsea Flower Show is held every year. I rang the brass ship's bell at the cabin door, but got no response. The door was unlocked and we went into the main cabin: there was no one aboard. Some people are so trusting. Idiots!

The vessel was furnished in the way that one imagines most Chelsea houseboat dwellers would furnish their floating homes: an attempt at the nautical without sacrificing creature comforts. Along both sides of the long cabin, beneath lockers set into the wood-panelled sides of the vessel, were built-in sofas that converted into bunks. Over one of them was a small brass plaque that said *Captain*, and over the other, one that said *First Mate*. Original! A widescreen television on a stand against a bulkhead, a state-of-the-art hi-fi unit, and what, to my unqualified eye, appeared to be an expensive Persian rug completed the furnishings. And, just to remind you that it was a boat, a yachting cap on a shelf, and an ornamental ship's lantern suspended from a large hook in the centre of the deckhead.

I was immediately drawn to a framed photograph on a ledge. It was of a girl standing on the deck of a yacht, right arm hooked around the mast and left hand attempting to control her long black hair in the face of what must have been a strong breeze. She was wearing a string bikini that left little to the imagination. It was not a particularly good photograph, but even with the sunglasses she was wearing, I was fairly sure it was Alex Forbes.

'That's pretty scanty, even for a bikini,' I said, admiring the picture for longer than was professionally necessary.

'It's called a tanga, guv,' said Dave.

'How d'you know that?'

'Madeleine's got one.'

'Really?' I said, trying unsuccessfully to put from my mind a vision of the delectable Madeleine in such a brief outfit.

'If this guy's got this much cash, why doesn't he live in a proper house?' asked Dave, casting an appraising glance around the cabin. There were times when Dave displayed a very suburban view of life. He pushed open a door at the far end of the main cabin. 'Shower, washbasin and chemical loo,' he said before opening the adjacent door. 'And a kitchenette, of sorts. Not enough room to swing a cat.'

'As in cat-o'-nine-tails?' I asked, mindful of Alex Forbes's sexual proclivities.

'Not even that,' said Dave. 'And no chest freezer either, but then I did say there wouldn't be, not on a houseboat. And you couldn't even get a dead cat in the fridge.' Dave reappeared from the kitchenette. 'As in dead furry animal,' he added.

'Who the hell are you?' There was a clatter as the cabin door crashed back on its hinges. I turned sharply to see a man standing in the doorway that led from the after deck of the houseboat. He was about thirty-five, was wearing a pair of black leather trousers, a black shirt with a Paisley kerchief at the neck, and a tan-coloured suede jacket. What hair remained on his otherwise bald head was cropped close to his skull. He took off his sunglasses and stared at us.

'We are police officers.'

'So? What are you doing here?' He cast an unbelieving glance at Dave Poole.

'Mr Griffin, is it?'

'Yes, but you still haven't answered my question. What are you doing here?'

I suppose he was sceptical because Dave was black. Even in this enlightened age there are some people who find the idea of a black police officer hard to accept.

'I'm Detective Chief Inspector Brock and this is Detective Sergeant Poole, Mr Griffin, and we're investigating the murder of Mrs Alexandra Forbes. Her body was found yesterday morning in Richmond Park.' I gestured at the girl's photograph. 'I understand that you knew her.'

'Yes, I read about it in this morning's paper. It was a terrible shock.' Griffin waved a hand at one of the sofa beds. 'Do sit down,' he said as he opened one of the cupboards. 'I think I need a drink.' He poured himself a stiff Scotch, which he downed in a single swallow. 'Sorry, damned rude of me. Can I offer you something?'

'No thanks,' I said, speaking for myself and Dave.

'Ah, not on duty, eh?'

I didn't bother to refute that widely held myth. Most of the coppers I'd grown up with would never refuse a drink. But I drew the line at drinking with suspects, and Griffin might yet come within that category.

'Just how well did you know Mrs Forbes, Mr Griffin?'

'How did you know I knew her?'

'Your telephone number was in her address book. And you have a photograph of her.' I pointed at the picture again.

Griffin poured himself another Scotch before sitting opposite us, cradling the tumbler in both hands. 'I think you could say that I knew her intimately,' he said, smiling. 'She used to come here for the specific purpose of getting laid. But what the hell happened? Who'd want to murder her?'

'At the moment I've no idea, but it's my job to find out.'

'Jesus! The poor little bitch.'

'When were you last in Belgium, Mr Griffin?' asked Dave suddenly.

'In Belgium? God, it must have been years ago. Why, does that have something to do with this?'

'When did you last see Alex Forbes?' I asked, ignoring his question.

'The day she left Max.' Griffin answered without hesitation.

'Which was when?' I knew what Max Forbes had told me, but wondered whether Griffin's version would accord with it.

'I can't remember the exact date, but it was about three weeks ago, I suppose.'

'Did she come here?'

'Yes, she did. Bloody embarrassing it was too.'

'In what way?'

Griffin took a sip of his whisky. 'She turned up here at about eight o'clock that evening. Just burst in without knocking or anything, and announced that she'd left Max and wanted to stay here with me.'

'Did she say why she'd left him?'

'Yes. She said he was gay.'

Well, that was a revelation, but hardly a surprise. I'm not easily surprised after years in the CID.

'And you weren't in favour of that sort of permanent arrangement, I take it.'

'I might have been, but she didn't exactly choose the most propitious moment to arrive.'

'Oh?'

Griffin laughed. 'You see, I was stark naked and so was Caroline, and we were, er . . .'

'I think I get the picture, Mr Griffin.'

'Should have locked the door,' commented Dave drily. 'It's called crime prevention.'

'So, what happened next?' I asked.

'She slagged me off, shouting and screaming. Quite hysterical, she was. I'd never heard her use language like it before. For a moment, I thought she was going to attack Caroline, so I got between them, but I have to tell you that a naked man trying to stop a cat-fight doesn't have much clout.'

'But she eventually left, did she?' I realized that was a stupid question; of course she'd left.

'Yes, once I'd calmed her down. But I was in a difficult position. I couldn't very well tell her that Caroline didn't mean anything to me, because Caroline was right there. Anyway, I said I'd ring her – Alex, that is – but she told me not to bother, and muttered something about there being plenty more fish in the sea, or other fish to fry. Something trite like that, anyway. And then she went.'

'And I suppose Caroline didn't think much of it either,' said Dave, his prurient interest, as usual, getting the better of him.

'No, she didn't,' said Griffin ruefully. 'As soon as she'd got her kit on, she was out of the door and I've not seen her again since.'

'Not having a lot of luck, are you?' said Dave.

'Where was the photograph taken?' I asked, nodding towards it.

'Isle of Wight, Cowes Week last year. I was crewing for a mate of mine and he invited me to bring a girlfriend. In fact, we all brought girls. I asked Alex and she jumped at it. It was a swan really. No one was interested in the sailing. It was just an excuse for an almighty piss-up, and swapping girls as often as we could.'

'Didn't Caroline take exception to the photograph?'

Griffin laughed. 'Give me some credit. I always put it in a drawer when I entertained.'

'Then why is it on display now, if Alex ditched you?'

'Sentiment, I suppose. I'd hoped to see her again, despite what she'd said. She was some performer, that girl.'

'But you didn't see her again.'

'No, but I heard from her.'

'What, a phone call?'

'No, a postcard. From Ostend and—' Griffin broke off. 'Ah! Hence the question about Belgium.'

'Do you still have that postcard?' I asked.

'Yes, it's here somewhere.' Griffin stood up and opened a drawer that was part of a unit on the bulkhead. 'Here we are. Just the usual sort of picture and a scribbled note. Here, take it. Keep it if it helps.'

The postcard was brief: *Wish you were here – A*. No doubt the graphologist would say it was insufficient for a comparison.

'Didn't you find that a strange sort of message, given that she had flounced out of here swearing never to see you again?'

'Women are fickle creatures, Mr Brock, and she thoroughly enjoyed what we got up to.'

'And what did you get up to?'

'Are you joking? I told you, it was for sex, pure and simple.'

'Was it really pure and simple? I've a special reason for asking that question.'

Griffin paused, clearly embarrassed. 'She did like a bit of kinky variation,' he said, his voice barely above a whisper. 'Sado-masochism, bondage, all that stuff.' He pointed at the brass lantern. 'I'd take that down and tie her wrists to the hook, and give her a whipping. She was like a bloody animal after that, I can tell you. It really turned her on. Me too.' He sighed, presumably a lament for pleasures never to be repeated. 'The first time I suggested it to Caroline she accused me of being a sex maniac.'

I was beginning to think that the unknown Caroline was quite a sensible sort of woman.

'And that's the last time you heard from Alex, is it?'

'Yes.'

'And when did you last whip her?'

'What sort of question is that, for Christ's sake?' asked Griffin.

'When her body was found yesterday morning, there were weals on her back and buttocks consistent with having been beaten.'

'Really? Well, she must have found someone else willing to do the business for her. The last time we indulged in that sort of fun must have been four or five weeks ago.'

Is that so? Or was it really three weeks ago and you killed her and put her in a freezer someplace?

'You say you tied her up. What did you use?'

'A couple of leather straps with rings on them. Want to see them?'

'Please.'

Griffin returned to the drawer from which he had taken the postcard and produced two small straps. They looked like the collars that doting owners impose on their small dogs.

'And you used these on her wrists, did you?'

'Yes.'

'Did you ever use straps on her ankles? Or put anything around her neck?'

Griffin frowned. 'Good God no, never.'

'You said just now that Alex told you her husband was a homosexual. Did you ever meet him, talk to him?'

'No, never,' Griffin said. 'In fact, I did wonder if she really was married, or whether it was just a story. Some girls like to pretend, reckon it turns the man on. Personally, I couldn't have cared less, one way or the other. As I said, she came to Cowes without any talk of having to make excuses. She just said OK and turned up the next morning in white trousers and a Breton sweater.' He paused as if relishing the memory. 'And an overnight bag containing that bikini' – he gestured at the photograph – 'and very little else. Not that she needed it. The weather was fabulous.'

'What is your profession, Mr Griffin?' Dave asked.

'I'm a photographer.'

'Paparazzi?' Dave always enjoyed reducing the vain to ground level.

'Hell no! Do me a favour. I take portraits, fashion plates and stuff for adverts, all that sort of thing. I've got a studio just off Sloane Square.'

'Take any risqué ones of Alex Forbes?' asked Dave, getting to the nub of the matter again.

Griffin paused for long enough to suggest that Dave had scored. 'As a matter of fact, yes.' He paused again. 'Oh well, I suppose I'd better show you.' I was fascinated that he was able to reach down and extract a folder from beneath the bunk he was sitting on without even looking. I assumed he studied the photographs often. 'They're not porn, if that's what you're thinking.'

The portfolio consisted of half a dozen tasteful nude poses, certainly nothing that even the keenest Porn Squad detective could interpret as a contravention of the obscenity laws, if in fact there are any obscenity laws left.

'And that's Alex Forbes, is it?' I asked. The poses were such that none of them showed Alex full-face.

'Yeah, that's Alex. Great, isn't she?' Griffin paused before correcting himself. 'Wasn't she?' he said, a sad expression on his face.

'Do you know of any other men with whom Alex was friendly?' I asked.

Griffin shook his head. 'No, I don't, but I'm pretty bloody sure there must have been some. She used to come here about twice a fortnight and, knowing her as I did, I'm bloody sure she couldn't have gone that long without getting laid.' He shrugged. 'So what? I had other girls, so why shouldn't she have had other men?'

Five

'The road block in Richmond Park was a complete blowout, Harry,' said Frank Mead as I walked into the office on Thursday morning. 'We ran it on Tuesday evening and from when the park opened on Wednesday morning. Nobody saw anyone dumping a body where Alex Forbes was found.' And then, with a laugh, he added, 'Or dumping one anywhere else, for that matter.'

'No more than I expected, Frank.' And it was true. We often spend God knows how many man-hours running these things and only rarely do we get a positive result.

'What's next?'

'Keep trying the neighbours and, in the meantime, I shall visit Alex Forbes's employers.'

The estate agency where Alex Forbes had worked was in that part of Mayfair where shop rents were so exorbitant that the asking prices of the properties they handled had to be equally exorbitant.

A smooth young man greeted us warmly and rose from his chair with a cheerfully expectant expression on his face, obviously hoping that we were passing millionaires. But he became openly crestfallen when I told him who we were, and that I wished to speak to whoever was in charge.

The manager's spacious office was oak-panelled and furnished with an antique desk and a leather three-piece suite. The manager, whose name was Skinner, wore an expensive suit and shoes that were, I suspect, hand-made. But, given the outrageous commission that estate agents charge, he would be able to afford good suits and hand-made shoes, wouldn't he?

'How may I help you, Chief Inspector?' asked Skinner urbanely, having sent his secretary for coffee.

'Mrs Alexandra Forbes.'

'Ah! I thought so. A very sad business and a great shock to all the staff here, I can assure you.'

The sofa emitted a squeal of undoubted quality as Dave and I sat down. 'I'm told that Mrs Forbes left home on the fifteenth of July,' I began. 'Presumably she had taken leave.'

'Yes. Yes, she had. She asked me on the preceding Friday if it would be convenient for her to take a few of the days that were due to her.' The manager smiled. 'We had a little joke about it. I told her that it was never convenient for her to take leave. She was one of our senior negotiators, you see, and she was extremely good at her job. Her sales record was most impressive, and her skill at assessing the value of a property indicated that she was very much in tune with the market.'

'I presume that her job entailed showing prospective purchasers over property from time to time.'

'Yes, of course. We did have a rule about that, though. I'd never allow her to show anyone over an empty property unless accompanied by a male member of my staff. I'm sure you know the reason for that.'

'Yes, of course.' Every policeman knew the reason, but there was nothing, so far, to indicate that Alex Forbes might have fallen victim to a potential purchaser. However, I was keeping an open mind.

'Was there any property that she recently visited more than once?' asked Dave.

I wasn't quite sure why Dave had asked that question, but he's an intuitive detective and I'd had reason to be grateful for that intuition in the past.

'I'll have to check on that,' said the manager, clearly a little puzzled by the question.

Skinner's secretary appeared with a tray of coffee and

poured it. I noticed that the coffee set was of bone china. Naturally.

'Fiona, would you get me Alex's diary, please.'

'How much leave did Mrs Forbes take on that occasion?' I asked, while we were waiting for the secretary to produce the answer to Dave's question.

'She said she wanted a week.'

'And did she say where she was going?'

'Yes, as a matter of fact she did. I believe she said that she was spending the week touring in France, with her husband.'

Interesting. That's not what Max Forbes had said.

'As a matter of fact, I think we had a postcard from her.'

'Do you still have it, Mr Skinner?'

'It may be here somewhere. I'll get Fiona to see if she can find it. I don't allow the staff to pin them up on the wall as they do in some firms. Looks unprofessional.' I wondered what the staff thought of their Mr Skinner. Bit of a stuffed shirt probably.

'And did she come back at the end of her week off?'

'No, she didn't. In fact, her husband telephoned on the following Monday – the day she was due to return to work – to say that she'd been taken ill whilst in France. Some continental tummy bug, I think he said.'

'Had you ever spoken to her husband before?'

'No, never.'

'So you can't be certain that it actually was her husband who rang you.'

'Er, well, no, I suppose not. But why should it not have been him?' It was obvious that Skinner was having trouble following my line of questioning, but he didn't know what I knew about Alex Forbes, or the complications surrounding her death.

I saw Dave making a note, probably to check Max Forbes's telephone account.

The secretary returned and put an A4-sized book on the manager's desk. 'Alex's diary, Mr Skinner,' she said.

'The chief inspector would like to see the postcard we got from Alex, Fiona. See if you can find it, will you?' said Skinner, and then spent a few moments riffling through the diary. 'In the last eight weeks there was only one property she visited more than once, Chief Inspector,' he said eventually. 'Number nine, Drovers Lane, Hampstead. She went there three times.' Then his professional interest took over and, taking off his glasses, he added, 'A very well-appointed property just off the heath, complete with three reception rooms, six bedrooms, each with an en-suite bathroom and an indoor swimming pool. On the market with a guide price of three-and-a-half.'

'That would be three-and-a-half *million*, would it?' I asked. I hoped that Dave, an English language graduate of London University – and purist when it suited him – would forbear from asking if Skinner really had meant that each bedroom had an indoor swimming pool.

'Of course,' said Skinner with a condescending smile. It was apparent that anything valued at under a million would not interest him.

Fiona returned with a postcard and handed it to me.

Once again the message was terse: *Having a great time – A*. And again it was postmarked Ostend.

'May I keep this?' I asked the manager.

'Of course. Is it important?'

'Possibly,' I said and gave the card to Dave. 'Any idea why she visited that particular property three times?'

The manager shrugged. 'Not really. Once was usually enough for Alex, but it may have been that she was unhappy about her original valuation. Either that or the client was unhappy with it. It happens occasionally. Some of our clients have an optimistic view of their property's value.'

'And has it now been sold?'

'No, it's still on the market.' Skinner afforded himself a brief chuckle. 'Why, interested?'

'Yes, but only in the present owner. D'you have a name?'

Skinner jibbed at that. 'It's not our practice to disclose details of our clients, Chief Inspector. I, er—'

'I can get a warrant if you prefer, Mr Skinner,' I said. Not that I'd need it. The name would be on the electoral roll. Client confidentiality is all very well, but with an estate agent? I ask you.

'It's a Mr Clive Parish. But if you're going there, I hope you won't mention us.'

'Wouldn't dream of it,' I lied, waiting while Dave made a note. 'Did Mrs Forbes ever talk about her married life, Mr Skinner?'

The manager pondered my question for a moment or two. 'No, I don't ever remember her doing so,' he said. 'As far as I know she was happily married. She never gave cause for me to think otherwise. I seem to recall she said something about her husband being in advertising, but I don't think she mentioned anything else about him or their life together.'

And there we left it. For the time being.

In our search for a cab, Dave and I walked towards Park Lane. A mistake. Anyone with the bearing and confidence that indicates he may be a native Londoner will be stopped by traipsing tourists who expect him – or her – to be fully conversant with the most obscure facts about the capital. The first questioner, a German holidaymaker, wanted to know if the Marble Arch really was made of marble. I assured him it was.

'Why did you ask that question about any properties Alex may have visited more than once, Dave?' I asked during a brief cessation of inane tourist enquiries.

'Knowing that she's a devotee of sex games, guv, it's possible that this guy Parish was a practitioner too, and, for a bonus, had a big house in a fashionable part of London and a lot of money into the bargain.'

'You're a bloody cynic, Dave,' I said, 'but you could be right. We'll have a chat with him. But I do rather think we're clutching at straws.'

'Right now, guv,' said Dave, 'there ain't much else to clutch at.'

A bit of a homespun philosopher is Dave.

*　　　*　　　*

The house in Drovers Lane was as grand as Skinner had said it was, its façade shielded from the road by a high, dense screen of leylandii: perfect cover for a burglar.

The door was answered by a curvaceous Filipina girl of about twenty. At least, I think she was about twenty. It's not always easy to guess the age of Eastern women. But one thing was certain: she wasn't too clued-up on security. I told her we were police officers wishing to see Mr Parish and she let us in. Just like that.

'This way. Misser Parish in swimming pool,' she said in barely intelligible English.

'Wonderful,' murmured Dave. 'Just like the best television dramas.'

'What the hell are you talking about?' I asked as we were led through a magnificent entrance hall that would have done credit to the Royal Opera House, and down a passageway on the far side.

'The number of times I've seen that on TV,' said Dave. 'The Old Bill turn up at some expensive drum and the owner of the place is always in the swimming pool. Although it's usually a good-looking bird wearing next to nothing. Or even nothing at all,' he added, an element of disappointment in his voice.

The Filipina girl opened a door at the end of the passage, beckoned to us to follow her through and pointed to a man doing a lazy breaststroke in a fair-sized pool.

'Misser Parish!' she shouted, waving her arms. 'Policemen come see you.'

Clive Parish swam to the side of the pool nearest to us. Placing his hands on the edge, he hoisted himself effortlessly on to the wide surround and grabbed a towel. Walking the few steps to where we were standing, he held out a hand. 'Clive Parish. What can I do for you?'

I told him who we were and then said, 'We're investigating a murder, Mr Parish.'

'Really? Sounds serious.'

'It is. All murders are.'

'Yes, I suppose so. Sorry, didn't mean to sound flippant.' Parish glanced at the Filipina girl. 'Conchita, some tea, eh?' he said slowly. 'Tea. OK, Conchita?' He repeated the instruction, enunciating each word carefully, and then muttered, 'God Almighty!'

A sudden look of comprehension crossed Conchita's face and she nodded and disappeared.

'Now, what's this about a murder?' Parish said. He waved at a group of stainless-steel chairs. 'Do sit down.' He took a few moments to towel himself dry and then sat down opposite us. I reckoned he was about forty and, from the state of his sun-tanned body, devoted a great deal of time to regular exercise, when he wasn't reclining on a sunbed, that is. His stomach was flat and taut, and his shoulder and thigh muscles were well developed.

'I understand you knew a woman called Alexandra Forbes, Mr Parish.'

'I did?' Parish appeared puzzled. 'Should I have done?'

'She worked for an estate agent as a negotiator. I believe she valued your property for you a few weeks ago.'

'Oh, yes, of course. I do remember her. A very attractive girl, very personable, came here two or three times. Don't really know why, because I was quite satisfied with her valuation. Not that it did me any good. I still haven't sold the place.' Parish glanced around the pool with a dejected look. 'It always seems to be a good time to buy property, but never to sell it,' he said. 'Mind you, I think the pool puts people off, oddly enough. Costs a fortune to maintain.' He suddenly realized why I'd mentioned Alex Forbes's name. 'Good God! D'you mean she's been murdered?'

'Exactly so, Mr Parish. You didn't see it in the paper?'

'No, I must've missed it. When did this happen?'

'Sometime in the past three weeks.'

'You don't sound too sure.'

I wasn't going to tell him that her body had been kept in a freezer for up to three weeks. 'The pathologist is still

48

running tests,' I said. 'She was only found the day before yesterday.'

'What happened?'

'She'd been strangled.' In view of Henry Mortlock's reservations, I wasn't too sure about that, but it would do for the time being.

'My God! That's awful.' Parish appeared genuinely distressed. 'It seems worse when it's someone you know,' he said.

'How well *did* you know her?'

'Only from when she came here. That's all. I didn't know her socially. We only met the three times. I think it was three.'

'And you've no idea why she found it necessary to come here three times?'

'No, not really.' Parish glanced at the door. 'Where's that damned girl with the tea?' he muttered.

'Is she your housekeeper?' asked Dave, obviously thinking that she fulfilled an additional role.

Parish glanced sharply at Dave. 'That's what the job specification says she's supposed to be,' he said, 'but she's worse than useless. Pretty to look at, I'll grant you, but that doesn't get the housework done. She doesn't know a fridge from a freezer from a dishwasher from a washing machine. I've got all this expensive equipment and she hasn't got a clue how to work any of it.'

'And you saw Alexandra Forbes on each occasion, did you?' I asked, steering him back to the purpose of our visit.

'Yes, that's right.'

'Did your wife meet her at all?'

'I don't have a wife, Mr Brock. Not any more.'

'I'm sorry.'

'You needn't be. We were divorced a couple of years ago. The settlement cost me a small fortune.'

But still left you enough to scrape by on, I thought.

'So you live here alone.'

'Apart from Conchita, yes. But why all the questions?'

'I'm trying to piece together her last movements, Mr Parish. She left her husband on . . .' I glanced at Dave.

'The fifteenth of July, sir.' Dave was always formal in the presence of the public, or, as he usually regarded the public until proved otherwise, suspects.

'Husband! I didn't know she had a husband.'

Now why should that worry you? Or even surprise you, I wonder.

'Didn't she introduce herself as Mrs Forbes, then?'

'No, she gave me a card with just her name on it: Alexandra Forbes, and the address of the company. Seems that businesswomen are a bit coy about telling you too much about themselves these days. But why all the questions?' Parish asked again. 'You're not regarding me as a suspect, surely?'

'Not at all,' I said, not meaning it, 'but Mrs Forbes was known to have a number of men-friends.'

'Aha! I see. And you wondered if I happened to be one of them, is that it?'

'Knowing what we've learned about her, it did cross my mind, yes.'

'Well, I can assure you that our brief relationship was a purely professional one. The manager of the estate agents – Skinner, I think his name was – assured me that she was one of his best people.' Parish gave a mirthless laugh. 'But she didn't manage to sell this place for me.' He waved a hand around the pool.

'Do you work from home, Mr Parish?' I asked, given that it was three o'clock in the afternoon and we'd found him in the pool.

'I don't work at all, old boy. Not in a way that gets my hands dirty, if you know what I mean.' Parish smiled diffidently. 'I suppose I'm what you'd call a playboy. The old man left me extremely well off. Poor old bugger worked his socks off creating the family fortune, but I wasn't going to do the same. I play the stock market, make a few clever investments here and there and, lo and behold, the pile keeps growing.' He laughed, obviously at his own cleverness.

And there we left it. On the way out we met Conchita carrying a tray of tea. 'You want tea, misser?' she enquired.

'Next time,' I said. I had a feeling that there would be a next time.

'OK.'

We drove back to Westminster. 'And what d'you make of him, Dave?' I asked.

'Dodgy, guv. Definitely dodgy,' said Dave.

But then Dave is one of those people who's imbued with the work ethic. He just can't fathom how it's possible to survive without working for someone else.

'And,' he continued, 'we know he's got a freezer.'

Six

I was not very happy about Clive Parish. Not for the same reason that Dave was worried by him, but because I have an inherent distrust of suave playboys who are frittering away their father's hard-earned money. And that's probably because my old man was a motorman on the underground all his life, and when he died left me nothing but a pile of porn magazines and his slate at the local boozer: a debt of thirteen pounds and twenty-three pence. Such is life.

However, I determined that it might be revealing to have a few discreet enquiries made about Parish, and next morning I set DI Frank Mead and his team the task.

The one thing that really bothered me was that Parish had seemed unduly interested – concerned even – that Alex Forbes had been a married woman. Knowing what we did about her, the possibility of an affair was quite on the cards, but I wouldn't blame Parish for denying it. He might well be innocent of her murder, but prefer not to get involved in any nastiness that might come out in court. Anyway, I was sure that he was screwing the gorgeous Conchita, otherwise why would he keep her on as a housekeeper if her domestic skills were as poor as he said they were. But then, as I've said before, I'm a cynic.

'I've been going through Max Forbes's statement again, guv,' said Dave, swanning into my office in his usual insubordinate way, that is to say, without knocking.

'Anything interesting? And do your bloody tie up.' If there is one thing guaranteed to annoy me, it's the sight of a detective with his tie slackened off and the top button of his shirt undone.

'Right.' Dave attempted to do as I'd asked, dropping the papers on the floor in the process and swearing an obscene oath.

Sitting down uninvited, he shuffled the sheaf of statement forms into some semblance of order. 'He says he went on holiday on the Wednesday, for a fortnight in the Black Forest near some place called Karlsruhe, but later on he said that he found that Alex's car had reappeared outside his front door.'

'So?'

Dave found the place on the page. 'What he actually said was: "When I got home a *week* later, there it was." So, which was it? He says he went for a fortnight and then talks about finding the car a week later.'

'Well spotted, Dave,' I said. 'I didn't pick that up at the time.'

'Nor did I, guv, and it wasn't until I'd read his statement about three times that I realized what he'd said. D'you think he used Alex's car to go abroad? And, if so, why didn't he say so?'

It was an interesting conundrum, but, in all fairness, Max Forbes might have been in shock at hearing of the murder of his wife, even if he hadn't displayed any signs of it at the time. But grief takes people in many different ways.

'Time to have another chat with Mr Forbes, I think, Dave,' I said. 'Give him a ring at work. See if he's free.'

A receptionist conducted us into a large studio that contained two or three drawing boards. Max Forbes, wearing a white overall coat with paint stains on it, sat at one of them, putting the finishing touches to a storyboard.

'Ah, Mr Brock,' he said, carefully replacing the cap on his pen as he got off his stool and wiped his hands on his overall.

'I thought this was all done with computer graphics now,' said Dave, nodding towards the drawing board.

'I'll be using a computer later on, but I still prefer to do the draft by hand,' said Forbes. 'Come into my office,' he added, and opened a door on the far side of the studio.

'I'm sorry to have to bother you again,' I said, once Max Forbes had seated himself behind his desk, 'but there are one or two inconsistencies in your statement. I'm sure you'll be able to clear them up for us.'

'I'm sure there are, Mr Brock,' said Forbes, 'but the day I spoke to you – the day you found Alex's body – I wasn't really thinking straight.'

Really? You could have fooled me, sport.

'Of course not, sir. I quite understand,' I said.

'So, what d'you want to know?'

Dave thumbed through the statement and repeated to Forbes what he had said about the reappearance of Alex's car.

'Did I say that, Sergeant Poole? I'm sorry, I obviously got it wrong. I was away for a fortnight and it was when I got back that I saw it there.'

'And you went to the Black Forest, I believe you said.'

'Yes, I did.'

'In your own car?' Dave queried.

'I don't own a car. I went by train. I'm terrified of flying, you see.' Forbes gave a diffident little smile.

'So am I,' I said. 'So, you went by, what, Eurostar?'

'No. As a matter of fact, I took the train to Dover and went across to Calais as a foot passenger. I caught a train on the other side down to Karlsruhe. Well, two trains in all. Then a taxi to the nudist colony in the Black Forest: the Beck *Nacktkulturlager*.'

'You're into that sort of thing, are you?' I asked.

'Yes, we both were, Alex and I.' Forbes smiled wistfully. 'It's very relaxing, being completely free and uninhibited. You ought to try it, Chief Inspector. I've even met policemen there, you know.'

'Yes, well, I don't seem to have much time for holidays at the moment, dressed or undressed.' I glanced at Dave. He was smirking again. 'There's just one other thing, Mr Forbes,'

I continued. 'When I spoke to Mr Skinner, the manager at the estate agency where Alex worked, he said that he'd received a call from you on Monday the twenty-second of July to say that Alex would not be returning to work, because she was sick.'

'But that's absurd,' protested Forbes. 'She'd been missing for a week by then. I'd no idea where she was. Anyway, I was still in the Black Forest.'

'So, it wasn't you who made that call?' I forbore from pointing out that there were telephones in Germany. Anyway, he could have had a cellphone. A lot of people have.

'Certainly not.'

'D' you reckon he's kosher, guv?' asked Dave, once we were back at Curtis Green.

'Probably, but that doesn't mean we're not going to check his story. For a start I'll get the German police to make an enquiry at this nudist colony. In the meantime, Dave, ask Mr Mead to get the team started on doing a check to find out if Alex's car travelled abroad on a ferry, and if there's any trace of Max Forbes having crossed as a foot passenger to Calais. Oh, and one other thing: see if you can trace that call that Skinner said he'd received from Forbes about Alex being sick. Start with the director of security at British Telecom. He's bound to be an ex-copper.'

One of the few benefits, if not the only benefit, I derived from having been married to Helga Büchner was that I spoke fluent German. After a few false starts, I eventually found myself speaking to *Hauptkommissarin* Heidi Stolpe of the Karlsruhe Police. She sounded delightful on the phone, but I've been caught like that before. She was probably a humourless, middle-aged, ugly *Hausfrau*. And I knew what they were like: I had one for a mother-in-law.

Be that as it may, I explained my enquiry and, without even a titter that a nudist colony was involved, the *Hauptkommissarin* promised to ring back as soon as she had something to tell me.

The upshot of the enquiries into Max Forbes's movements, however, was disappointing, not that I should have been surprised at that. None of the Dover–Calais ferry companies had a record of him crossing as a foot passenger on the seventeenth of July, but that wasn't to say that he hadn't. Foot passengers often turned up at the last minute, I was told, and paid their fare on board. In such cases, paperwork is rarely held at the company's offices.

I suppose I should have expected that. In all honesty, people don't usually ensure that records are kept of their movements on the off chance that they may become involved in a murder enquiry at a later date. Mind you, if ever I pay cash for my petrol I always get a receipt, just in case some goon later accuses me of making off without paying. You can't be too careful these days.

The enquiry about Alex's car was, however, a little more promising, but only slightly. It revealed that her Mercedes crossed from Dover to Calais on Tuesday the sixteenth of July and that two passengers were paid for, but the company couldn't say what their names were, or even confirm that two passengers actually travelled. Disappointingly, there was no record of the vehicle's return but, as the company's representative pointed out, millions of people cross the Channel at that time of year. Sometimes they arrive early – or late – and board a different ferry from the one they were booked on. Often, she added apologetically, paperwork wasn't always as accurate as it should be. However, that seemed to bear out that Alex Forbes, and perhaps one of her men-friends had gone to Calais. And the postcards had come from Ostend, not a million miles away from their port of arrival.

This time I telephoned Max Forbes and apologized for troubling him yet again. He said he didn't mind if it meant catching Alex's killer, but he denied knowing anything about the movements of Alex's car and repeated that he'd only found it outside his house when he returned from his naturist holiday in the Black Forest.

But even that piece of his story was thrown into doubt by

the call I received from *Hauptkommissarin* Stolpe in Karlsruhe.

'I have visited this nudist camp, *Herr* Chief Inspector,' she began, 'and they do not know this name Maxwell Forbes as someone who stayed there recently. But the director told me that often people give false names to protect their identity. It seems that some of these people are ashamed at going to such a place in case their friends find out. You understand?' And then she laughed. 'I don't know why they should be,' she added. 'I go quite often.'

Oh well, perhaps the Hauptkommissarin *was human after all.*

'Yes, I can believe that they might be embarrassed,' I said. 'The English are like that.'

'Yes, I think so,' said Heidi Stolpe. 'But the director said that he doesn't worry about it so long as the guests pay their money. So, it is possible that your Maxwell Forbes was a guest there, but was using another name and paid in cash. Now that we're all in the European Union, passports don't have to be produced for registration.'

I thanked the *Hauptkommissarin* and put the phone down. But it would be interesting, I thought, to discover whether Max Forbes's neighbours knew that he pranced about in the nude playing volleyball at some German retreat. Not an edifying sight, I'd've thought.

Frank Mead dropped into the office when Dave and I returned from a scratch lunch – a pie and a pint at the Red Lion – to tell me that he'd finally contacted George Madison, who lived next door to the Forbeses, and had made an appointment for me to see him and his wife at six that evening.

George and Stella Madison lived at number eighteen. They were probably in their early fifties and George Madison told me that he worked as a senior manager in a bank in the West End, and that his wife was a part-time secretary in a solicitor's office, also in that part of London.

'I take it you know about the murder of Alexandra Forbes,'

I said, as Madison showed us into his fussily furnished sitting room.

'Yes. What a dreadful thing to have happened. We knew them quite well of course. We've lived next door to each other for about three years now. As a matter of fact, they were already here when we moved in.'

I started with the mystery of Alex Forbes's car, but neither Madison nor his wife, who at that moment appeared with a tray of tea, was able to help much. They knew the car, but couldn't say, with any degree of accuracy, when it had been there and when it hadn't. But that was no more than I expected.

'Did you socialize with the Forbeses?' I asked.

'No,' said Stella Madison, pouring cups of tea and handing them round. 'They invited us in for a drink not long after we moved in, but there was very little contact after that.'

'Was there some friction, then?'

'Good heavens no,' said Stella. 'All four of us work and there's not much time for socializing. But, apart from that, they're a couple who keep very much to themselves. That suits us, too. We tend to prefer our own company. Of course, we've got our friends and so have they. Quite a lot, I think.'

'Have you met any of their friends?'

'No, we haven't,' said Stella and then glanced at her husband. 'Not exactly.'

'I've a feeling there's something you're not telling me,' I said.

'We wouldn't want to speak ill of the dead . . .' George Madison began.

'Mr Madison, someone murdered Alex Forbes and it's my job to find out who. You won't help by keeping things from me. Let me be the judge of whether what you know will be of any value in my investigation.'

Again there was an exchange of glances, guilty almost, before Stella Madison spoke.

'Over the last year or so George and I have noticed that there have been comings and goings.'

'What sort of comings and goings?'

'Young women. Most of them seemed to be about Alex's age, but some were older. Alex was much younger than Max, you know.'

'Yes, I did know,' I said. 'Did these women come in groups, or one at a time?' I was thinking of the occasions, a few years back, when Helga had held underwear parties at our house in Wimbledon.

'No, one at a time,' Stella continued, 'but please don't think we're nosey neighbours. It's just that we couldn't help noticing.'

'How often did you see these women calling?'

Stella hesitated. 'I suppose about twice a month. That we saw, that is.'

'What time of day would this have been?'

'Usually in the evenings, and sometimes at the weekend. Saturday and Sunday afternoons.'

'Have you any idea how long they stayed?'

'Oh no. We didn't make a point of looking. It's just that we noticed.' She sounded as though she regretted having mentioned it. 'More tea?'

'Thank you.' I handed Mrs Madison my cup and she busied herself refilling it. But then she paused and turned to face me. 'I did wonder . . .' She broke off, clearly embarrassed.

'Did wonder what?'

'Oh, what will you think of me?'

'I'll think that you're helping me, Mrs Madison.'

'I did wonder if Max was entertaining these women. You know, if he was . . .'

'Having affairs with them, you mean?'

'Oh, what an awful thing to think, but yes, it did cross my mind.'

'Did he ever mention that he and his wife went to nudist camps?'

Stella stifled a laugh. 'Good heavens, no,' she said. 'Just goes to show, doesn't it?'

I didn't know quite what it went to show, but I pressed on. 'Mr Forbes claimed to have been away for a fortnight recently. From the Wednesday following his wife's disappearance.'

Stella Madison shrugged. 'That may be so,' she said, 'but I couldn't say for certain. As I told you, we both work, although I'm only part-time.'

'There's something else you ought to know,' said George Madison, clearly prepared to be more forthcoming than his wife. 'There were times when we heard yells coming from next door. Quite loud, too, as though someone was in pain. These are good, solid Victorian houses, Mr Brock, and the walls are pretty thick. They knew how to build houses when they put these up. But we could still hear the yells.'

'What did you think caused them? I mean, did it sound as though someone was being attacked?'

Madison shrugged. 'Your guess is as good as mine. But it sometimes happened when we knew that one of their women callers was there.'

'And how long did this shouting go on for?'

Madison considered that for a moment. 'Only for a few seconds. Thirty at the most, I suppose.' He glanced at his wife and received a nod of confirmation. 'Then it would go quiet for perhaps half an hour. Then it would start again for another few seconds.'

'Did you ever ask Max or Alex what it was about?'

'Certainly not,' said Stella. 'I mean to say, it was none of our business to pry. It might just have been that the Forbeses were having an argument. Married couples do have arguments, you know.'

I did know. Oh yes, and how.

'Did Max Forbes tell you that his wife had gone missing?' asked Dave, coming to life for the first time in the interview.

'Yes, he did. He was quite agitated about it, naturally. It must have been, what, a few weeks ago?' Stella glanced at her husband. 'D'you remember when it was, George?'

'It was the middle of July sometime,' said Madison. 'I

can't remember the exact date other than to say it was a Tuesday – I remembered that because Stella doesn't work Mondays – but Max banged on the door just as we were setting off for work. He was in quite a state. He said something about having been to a livery dinner the previous night, and that when he'd got home Alex wasn't there. Apparently she hadn't left a note or anything like that, and he was obviously very worried. We had to rush off to work then, but I said that if there was anything we could do, to let us know. Anyway, when we got in that evening – I was in before Stella that night – I popped round to see him, to check if there was any news. But he said that she still hadn't shown up or been in touch. He said he'd rung the office where she worked, but nothing. I suggested that he told the police and he said he would. I even offered to drive him down to Lavender Hill, because I didn't think he was in a fit state to drive his own car.'

'What sort of car did he have?' asked Dave. I hoped he wouldn't tell Madison that Max Forbes had denied owning one. But I needn't have worried. Dave's a shrewd detective.

'It was a Toyota Corolla, I think. Certainly a Toyota, but quite an old model, probably about five or six years old. We had a joke about it some time ago. I asked him if it was a company car, and he said that, as the company was his, it probably was.'

'Does he still have it?' Dave looked up from his pocketbook.

'I suppose so, but I must admit I haven't seen it lately,' Madison said. 'But parking's damned difficult round here. Arriving home each evening's a nightmare, trying to find somewhere to park. Now that there's this damned congestion charge, we drive to Clapham Junction and park there, you see, then catch the train. Sometimes we have to leave our car streets away, just hoping that it'll be there in the morning. Crime round here is pretty awful, but then I suppose you'd know that, Mr Brock,' he added with an embarrassed smile. 'And that's why I can't help you about Alex's car. She could have parked it anywhere.'

'Did you happen to see Mrs Forbes leaving on the day she disappeared, Mrs Madison?' I asked. 'Your husband said that you don't work on Mondays.'

'No, I didn't, but I was out shopping for most of the day. At Arding and Hobbs,' said Stella Madison. 'It's at Clapham Junction,' she added unnecessarily.

'You mentioned earlier on that you occasionally heard yells coming from next door,' I said, including both the Madisons in my question. 'Did you happen to notice whether there was any such yelling around the time that Mrs Forbes disappeared?'

Again there was an exchange of glances between the couple. 'Not that I can recall,' said George Madison eventually.

Seven

As I was already in Battersea, and only minutes from where Sarah Dawson lived, I rang her on my mobile and suggested a quick bite to eat, even though it was quite late when Dave and I left the Madisons. I sent Dave home to Madeleine.

Sarah looked particularly stunning: black leather trousers and bomber jacket, and a white silk shirt relieved by a scarlet neckerchief, which she claimed were the first things she had laid her hands on 'as you've rushed me out, darling'. What a convincing liar the girl is. And, to complete the picture, her long black hair was worn loose. We grabbed a taxi and crossed the bridge to our favourite bistro in Chelsea.

'Busy?' Sarah asked, as we mulled over the menu to the accompaniment of a half bottle of Chablis.

I told her briefly about the Alex Forbes murder and she said she'd read about it in the paper.

'I'm really struggling with this one,' I said, 'but enough of work. How were your parents?' Sarah had been down to Cornwall to visit her ageing mother and father.

She gave an expressive shrug. 'As usual, complaining that they don't see enough of me.'

'Nor do I,' I said, trying to make light of a problem that obviously concerned her.

'They don't seem to realize how busy I am. And I can't just pop down for the day, not all that way. It's nearly six hundred miles to Helston and back.'

'What about your sister?'

'She's in an even worse position than me,' said Sarah. 'A working mother with two children, a new house to sort out and a husband on shift work.' Sarah's brother-in-law David was an air traffic controller at West Drayton and he and Margaret had recently moved from Raynes Park to Staines to be nearer the airport. 'But you know what parents are like. They never seem to understand.'

Fortunately my own parents had understood. My father had done shift work all his life, and my mother had worked in Woolworth's. But my mother-in-law had been a different ball game altogether. Constantly bitching because Helga wouldn't rush across to Cologne at the drop of a hat. Bit like Helga's attitude towards me, come to think of it.

Still, all that's behind me now. Helga's gone, my father's dead and my mother Sheila lives in a retirement flat at Streatham, quite close to where I live at Wimbledon. But she doesn't complain. I get in to see her whenever I can – as does my brother Geoff – but she understands the demands of the job, and always says it's enough for her to read of my exploits in the newspaper. I just hope there'll be a good one for her to read about soon.

'And how *were* your parents really?' I asked.

'Fit, and thoroughly enjoying their retirement, although I think Dad misses the office and messing about with deeds, wills and conveyances.' Sarah glanced up at me, briefly, and then added, 'They keep asking when I'm going to get married.'

It was the first time that Sarah had mentioned the subject of marriage since my divorce had been made absolute, but even so I knew that I shouldn't rush her into making a decision. Although Helga was out of the way now, there was still the question of the late Captain Peter Hunt. Hunt had been Sarah's fiancé, and had been killed in some damned silly war game on Salisbury Plain a few years back. I don't think she'd ever got over it, and was still a little bit in love with his memory.

'And what did you say to that?'

Sarah smiled. 'I said I was thinking about it.'

And that, for the moment, had to be a sufficient answer, both for Sarah's parents and for me.

I got to the office at Curtis Green at about ten on Saturday morning. Five days had now elapsed since the discovery of Alex Forbes's body, but as we had made little progress, I decided to play my full team, even though it was Saturday.

I had not, however, anticipated that it would include the commander. But the commander loved playing at detective, even though he hadn't much idea what criminal investigation was all about. Give him a complaint against police to get his teeth into and he's as happy as can be, but throw him a two-quid gas-meter break-in – yes, such things still happen – and he's gobsmacked.

'And how is the Forbes murder enquiry going, Mr Brock?' As befitted a weekend, the commander was wearing a sports jacket and a pair of grey flannels that would have been very fashionable fifty years ago.

I gave him a quick, but comprehensive, rundown on the progress of the enquiry so far, but even then he didn't seem to grasp the complexities of the case.

'Is there some significance in this man Forbes having gone to a nudist colony?' he asked, having read my brief note on the action pad.

'It's not unmeaningless, sir,' said Dave gravely. He knew how to irritate the boss.

'Mmm! Yes . . .' The commander spoke hesitantly, as he tried to untangle Dave's treble negative. He had been a bit wary of Dave ever since he had received a polite trouncing at Dave's hands when, none too subtly, he had tried to discover something of Dave's West Indian origins. Dave had told him that he'd been born in Bethnal Green. The commander glanced at his watch. 'I shall be at home should you need me, Mr Brock,' he said curtly.

'I'll try not to bother you, sir,' I said. I couldn't possibly imagine any contingency arising out of the death of Alex

Forbes that would require me to ring the commander at the weekend. Or at any other time.

'I've just passed the guv'nor on the stairs, Harry,' said Frank Mead as he ambled into the incident room. Despite being a very astute detective, Frank always gave the impression of being so laid back that I was surprised he didn't fall over. 'What was he doing here on a Saturday?'

I shrugged. 'Keeping up to date, just in case the assistant commissioner gives him a bell, I suppose,' I said. 'Got anything for me?'

'We've done a rundown on Parish, for what it's worth.'

'Good. Come into the office.'

'He seems to be what he says he is,' Frank said, settling into my only armchair. 'No visible means of support.' He laughed. 'Not what *we'd* call visible, anyhow. He does play the stock market and is quite successful at it, apparently. And there's no doubt he's giving Conchita a seeing-to. But so what? Good luck to him. After all, he's providing her with board and lodging, *and* paying her wages into the bargain.'

'How the hell did you find that out so quickly?'

'I picked Nicola Chance to make the enquiries; she speaks Spanish.'

'Good move, Frank.' DC Nicola Chance was one of the best detectives on the team. If there was anything to discover, she'd find it. But I hadn't known that she spoke Spanish.

'Nicola made a point of befriending the nubile Conchita on one of her outings to the shops. Seems she was delighted to meet someone who spoke her language.' Frank gave a sly grin. 'Apparently the girl's very happy with her lot, living in a decent house complete with swimming pool, and she's quite content being Parish's bed-mate. What's more, she's getting paid for it. Some people have all the luck. However, she wasn't too pleased when Alex Forbes turned up.'

'And did Alex Forbes visit Parish more than three times?'

'Yes, according to Conchita. She reckoned that Alex came to the house on at least six occasions and was in Parish's bed quicker than that. As I said, that did not please the Filipina girl one little bit. From what Nicola said, Conchita really got the hump.'

'I'll bet she did. And when was Alex last there? Did she tell Nicola that?'

'Yes, about four days before she disappeared, or at least when Max Forbes said she disappeared.'

So that was why Parish was so worried when I told him that Alex was married. The presence of a husband lurking somewhere in the background tends to disconcert philanderers.

'Looks as though a serious talk with Mr Parish is called for, Frank.'

'I've also spoken to the other three men whose names were in Alex Forbes's address book, Harry.' Frank glanced down at his 'things-to-do' book. 'Rory Simpson, Peter Morton and Jamie Ryan. They live in Putney, Streatham and Richmond respectively.'

'Richmond, eh? How very interesting,' I mused. 'And what did they have to say for themselves?'

'The mixture as before. They each had had, or were having, affairs with Alex Forbes. After a little persuasion each confirmed Alex's predilection for having her hide whipped, and admitted to having obliged her. Having compared what they said with the statements you took from Farrell and Griffin, it seems that these affairs all ran along very similar lines.'

'Is there any one of them you think I should talk to?'

Frank shrugged. 'Any one of them could have murdered her, I suppose, but you may attach some significance to the fact that Jamie Ryan lives in Richmond. Very close to where the body was found.'

'What sort of characters are these men?'

'Simpson's a surveyor and Morton is into computers, a programmer of some sort. Ryan's the odd one out. He's a tennis coach, so he says. In fact he goes in for sport in quite a big way, but he's as thick as two short planks. You might think it's worth having a chat with him. He was bobbing and weaving a bit, and I think he thought he was about to be nicked.'

'Why? Why should he think that?'

'It took a long time to get him to admit to the affair with Alex, and even longer for him to own up to whipping sessions with her. I think he was thinking GBH.'

'Yes, well, technically he's right. It was grievous bodily harm, after all, but I can't see the Crown Prosecution Service having a go at that.' I paused for a moment, thinking about Ryan. 'Could it be that he's playing thick? If he was loath to admit whipping Alex, it might just be that he knows what we know, about the marks being found on her, I mean. And, given where he lives, Richmond Park would probably be the first place he thought of to dispose of her body. OK, I'll have a word with him if you think he may be in the running.'

Frank shrugged. 'Just a feeling, Harry, that's all. By the way, are you free to see the Websters?'

'The Websters?'

'The Forbses' neighbours, on the other side from the Madisons. They said they'd be at home today, but I said you'd ring if you were going down there.'

The Websters at fourteen Crouch Road were no help at all. Naturally enough they acknowledged knowing the Forbses – as next-door neighbours they could hardly do anything else – but denied ever having heard any yells or screams coming from their house. They claimed that they had nothing to do with the Forbses beyond passing the time of day, and denied having seen any women callers. But I was not at all sure that they were telling the truth.

They also said that they had known nothing about Alex Forbes going missing, although they had seen reports of her murder in the press.

It seemed to me to be yet another case of not wanting to get involved. Suggest to the average punter that they may be called to give evidence at the Old Bailey and they'll run a mile.

I decided to push on to Richmond, to have a word with Jamie Ryan, tennis coach and sometime lover of Alex Forbes.

I was surprised to find him at home. I would have thought that summer Saturdays were ideally suited to teaching attractive young ladies how to play tennis, but he confessed to having spent most of the morning sitting in front of his television set watching cricket. Perhaps the bottom had dropped out of the tennis-coaching business.

'Detective Inspector Mead came to see you recently,' I began, 'in connection with the murder of Alex Forbes.'

'That's right.' Somewhat reluctantly, Ryan switched off the television and sat down again.

'How long had you known Mrs Forbes, Mr Ryan?'

The fact that I'd referred to her as *Mrs* Forbes elicited no reaction.

'I met her about two months ago, I suppose.'

'And how did you meet her?'

'Nightclub,' Ryan said tersely.

'Where?'

'Here, in Richmond.'

I could see that getting answers out of Ryan was not going to be easy. He certainly looked a bit dim, but that didn't mean he *was* dim. Maybe he was just being obstructive. With good reason, perhaps. Like he'd murdered Alex Forbes, for instance.

'DI Mead told me that you had a sexual relationship with her, and that you whipped her from time to time.'

Ryan ran his tongue round his lips. 'Yeah, that's right. But only because she told me to.'

'Did you always do what she told you?'

'No, but she said that's what she wanted.'

'How well d'you know Richmond Park, Mr Ryan?' Dave asked suddenly, looking up from his record-of-interview book.

'Richmond Park?'

'Yeah, big patch of greenery about a mile from here. All grass and trees and stuff, with gates at Kingston, Roehampton and Sheen. And Richmond.'

But Ryan didn't rise to Dave's sarcasm. 'Oh, yes, well, driven through it a few times,' he said. 'Going to a night-club in Kingston.'

'You do know, I suppose, that it was in Richmond Park that Alex Forbes's body was found,' I said, 'just inside the Richmond Gate?'

'Yes, that other policeman told me. The one who came the other day.'

Dave wrote down this exchange and glanced at me, a glance that said, *This guy's a bozo.*

'Do you have a freezer here, Mr Ryan?' I asked, deciding that he was too much of a dimbo to work out why I wanted to know.

'Yes.' Ryan was as puzzled by the question as I'd hoped he would be, which suited me fine.

'What sort of freezer is it?'

'Only a little one. It's the bottom half of the fridge. But I don't use it much. If I'm not out for meals, which is what I do most of the time, I usually put a pizza in the microwave. I do a lot of swimming and weightlifting, you see.'

I don't know why he should have mentioned swimming and weightlifting in connection with his microwave, but I was beginning to believe that this guy was on a different planet.

'Would you mind showing me your freezer, Mr Ryan?'

Ryan displayed not the slightest curiosity at what to any right-minded person must have seemed a strange request. 'Yeah, sure.' He stood up and led the way into the kitchen. He pointed at the refrigerator and opened both doors. 'There you are,' he said, standing back as if he were an electrical-appliance salesman about to clinch a deal.

'And this is the only freezer you have, is it?'

'Yeah.'

There was no way a human body could have been stored in the tiny compartment of Ryan's fridge–freezer. We returned to the sitting room.

'You're a tennis coach, I understand,' I said.

'Yeah, that's right.'

'Is that a full-time occupation?'

'No.'

'What else d'you do, then?'

'I'm an actor.'

Somehow that didn't surprise me. 'But that's not full-time either, is it?'

'No. I only do tennis coaching when I'm not acting. Sometimes I coach swimming.'

Sure as hell he wasn't doing any coaching right now, but he may have been acting.

'When did you last see Alex Forbes?'

I was getting increasingly impatient with Ryan, but I'd met suspects like him before. They play thick so that the police will go away believing them to be innocent. On the other hand it could be that they *are* thick. And *are* innocent. Like this guy? I didn't think so. Here was a man who clearly possessed the physical ability not only to overpower a woman like Alex Forbes, but to be able to lift her body effortlessly. And he lived much closer to Richmond Park than any of the other men we'd so far learned had been involved with her.

'About six weeks ago,' said Ryan with an expression on his face so innocent that it merely served to harden my suspicion of him.

'Six weeks ago was the last time you saw her?' I asked, wanting to make absolutely sure.

And he'd only met her two months previously.

According to Ryan, then, the relationship had lasted about a fortnight. But I found that difficult to believe. He had exactly the athletic build I imagined would have appealed to Alex Forbes. So, what went wrong? Based on what Mike Farrell had said about Alex being a nymphomaniac, I thought

I knew what it was. I decided it was time to shake Ryan up a bit.

'Mr Ryan,' I said, 'I believe that you murdered Alex Forbes and then dumped her body in Richmond Park. And I suggest you did it because you couldn't satisfy her sexual demands and she taunted you mercilessly about it. And you couldn't stomach that, could you?'

This approach is known as using 'copper's nose': following a deep-rooted suspicion in the usually vain hope that you'll get a 'cough' without a shred of evidence to support the allegation. It worked sometimes. Regrettably it did not work often.

But I'd met sportsmen like Ryan before. Vain, muscle-bound morons who were constantly checking their pulse rate against the sort of waterproof wristwatch that was guaranteed to be accurate to a depth of two hundred metres, and who talked drivel about their bodies being temples. But, when it came to the crunch, they were, to use Dave's favourite expression, all wind and piss. It was easy to imagine Alex's frustration at Ryan's failure to meet her exacting requirements and that was probably why she summarily dismissed him.

'I didn't murder her,' said Ryan calmly. There was no indignant outrage, no heightened tension, no demands that I prove it. Just a flat denial. Perhaps he was a better actor than I gave him credit for. Or even more stupid than I'd originally thought.

'Did you receive any postcards from Alex?' I asked.

Ryan frowned. 'No. Why should she have sent me a postcard?'

I struggled on. 'You say you're an actor. What sort of things do you act in?'

'Whatever my agent can find for me. I'm not one of those guys who wants to play Hamlet. In fact I hate Shakespeare. I just want to make enough money to live on comfortably. It's mostly as an extra, which pays quite well, and I've done one or two TV commercials. Sometimes I do modelling.'

That reckoned.

'How many times did you actually meet Alex Forbes?'

'Three times.'

'Here?'

'Yes.'

'And did you whip her on each of those occasions?'

'No. Only the last two. Then she said she didn't want to see me any more.' Ryan shook his head, apparently hurt that any woman could fail to find him irresistible.

'What sort of car d'you own?' asked Dave, deciding to take part again.

'I don't own a car.'

'You said just now that you occasionally drive through Richmond Park to get to a nightclub in Kingston. As there aren't any buses that go through the park, how d'you manage that? A bicycle perhaps?'

Again Ryan refused to be riled. 'No, a mate gives me a lift. We go clubbing together.' He paused. 'Only in the summer though.'

'What d'you mean, only in the summer?'

'The park shuts when it's dark, so then we have to go round by Ham Common.'

Reluctantly, I came to the conclusion that Jamie Ryan wasn't even bright enough to murder someone, let alone dispose of the body in such a way that would cause me so much hassle. I think the truth of the matter was that Alex Forbes had a brief dalliance with him and then moved on to someone who had got what it took to please her.

We got back to Curtis Green at about three o'clock, having missed lunch, much to Dave's annoyance, and I decided to call it a day. A mistake.

We had got no further than the top of the stairs when Colin Wilberforce shouted, 'Call for you, sir!'

'If it's the commander, I'm not here,' I said.

'No, sir, it's not,' said Colin.

I retraced my steps and picked up one of the battery of phones. 'Brock.'

And then it happened. Just when you think that an enquiry is chugging along smoothly, and that if you follow everything it says in the *How to Solve Murders* handbook you'll eventually come up with the murderer, someone chucks a bloody great boulder in the water. And the ripples start to spread.

'It's Bill Griffin here.'

'What can I do for you, Mr Griffin?'

'I've seen Alex Forbes, Mr Brock. This morning. In the West End.'

Eight

It was natural enough that I was highly doubtful about Griffin's claim to have seen Alex Forbes in the West End, but even the most unlikely snippets of information must be investigated, and Dave and I went down to his Chelsea houseboat immediately.

'Let me get this straight, Mr Griffin,' I said, sitting down on the bunk opposite him. 'What you're telling me is that you believe you saw Alex Forbes this morning. Is that right?'

Griffin half smiled, as if doubting my ability to grasp what he had said. 'There's no believe about it, Mr Brock. I most certainly did see her. It was just before lunch, and I was in a taxi on my way to Oxford Street. As we were cutting through Carfax Street, I happened to glance out of the window and there was Alex coming out of one of the shops. I stopped the cab and ran back, but she'd disappeared in the crowds.'

'Mr Griffin, Alex Forbes is dead,' I said patiently. 'Her body was found in Richmond Park last Monday and she was positively identified by her husband Max the same day. But now you say that you have seen her. You obviously saw someone who looked like her.'

'I do know what she looks like, Mr Brock,' Griffin said sharply.

'Look at it from my point of view, Mr Griffin. I've been to—'

'For Christ's sake, Mr Brock, I do know what she looks like,' Griffin repeated, cutting across what I was saying. 'I tell you, it was definitely her. God Almighty, I've screwed her often enough, and I've taken nude photographs of her.

75

D'you think I *wouldn't* recognize her?' He was beginning to lose his cool now.

'All right, all right,' I said, holding up a hand. 'Let's suppose for one moment that it was her. How d'you explain her husband identifying her?'

'He must have made a mistake.'

'But he was married to her and, if you'll forgive me for saying so, probably knew her even better than you.'

'OK, forget it. I was just trying to help, that's all. I knew it'd be a waste of time ringing you. But I do know what I saw.'

'All right, let's follow it through. Which shop did you think you saw her coming out of?'

'I didn't see the name of it, but I think it was one of those fashion boutiques.'

'Well, if we can find it, we'll make some enquiries there and see if they can recall seeing someone fitting her description.'

'There's just one thing,' said Griffin. 'Her hair is blonde now.'

'I see. It was a blonde who looked like Alex Forbes.' I found it difficult to avoid sounding sceptical.

'It *was* Alex, I tell you,' said Griffin, smoothing a hand over his bald head.

We went straight from Griffin's houseboat to Carfax Street and found the only fashion shop in the road, a small and select establishment full of overpriced garments, the justification for which presumably was that they were the current 'must have' items. There was a staff of three: a manageress and two assistants.

Dave was clearly taken with this trio of attractive young women and, knowing him as I did, I suspected that he was going to have a go at spinning out our enquiry the better to appreciate them. But not if I could help it. He started by showing the manageress, a curvaceous brunette, a photograph of Alex Forbes and explained that she was now a blonde.

'I don't recall having seen her,' said the manageress, having studied the print closely, 'but we do get very crowded in here on Saturday mornings. We've had scores of customers in here today. Not that they bought very much,' she added gloomily. Presumably it affected her commission.

The two assistants – who had clearly taken a shine to Dave – examined the photograph too, but neither of them could be certain that they had seen the woman Griffin thought was Alex Forbes. 'It's possible,' said one of them, 'but to be honest we've had quite a few women in here today who looked like her.'

'Thanks anyway,' said Dave, taking back the photograph.

'You should bring your wife in one day,' said the manageress to Dave. 'I'm sure we could manage a discount for her.'

Dave always suspected the motives of those who offered preferential rates for police. 'You don't sell tutus,' he said.

And with that enigmatic throwaway line, we left.

'Well, that was a blow-out, guv,' said Dave as we made our way back to Curtis Green. 'So, what d'you reckon? After all, Griffin does know the girl well.'

'So does Max Forbes,' I said. 'And we passed a dozen women in the space of ten minutes who could have been mistaken for Alex.'

'Of course,' Dave went on, 'Griffin could have been right about the woman, but wrong about the shop.'

'Don't you start, Dave. The woman's bloody well dead. Anyway, I'm not traipsing up and down Carfax Street on the off chance of someone having seen a woman we know to be dead. Perhaps you'd like to pop over to the mortuary and see if the body's still there,' I added sarcastically.

I tried to assess Griffin's 'sighting' logically. Max Forbes had identified the dead woman as his wife. Her car had been taken to France the day after she went missing, but was she in it? And she had apparently sent postcards from Belgium at about that time. But – and this was where it all went pear-shaped – according to Henry Mortlock, she was probably already dead and in a freezer cabinet when all that happened. Unless it was Griffin who had gone with her to France and later murdered her.

Initially, I was drawn to the possibility that Griffin's claim to have seen Alex could be an elaborate smokescreen, but if it was I failed to follow the logic of it. If he was the killer why should he invite further police attention with such a bizarre tale?

No, he really believed he'd seen her. But it was a classic case of mistaken identity.

'I think we'll get a search warrant for Max Forbes's place and turn it over, Dave,' I said.

'What, now?' Dave was clearly alarmed that his weekend was in danger of vanishing.

'No, Monday.' And that was not through any concern for Dave's welfare. I needed to think the whole thing through. Seriously, calmly and logically. It also occurred to me that we should have searched the Forbeses' house as soon as possible after the discovery of Alex's body. Better late than never though.

'We should have done that straight away,' said Dave, reading my thoughts.

'Yeah, I know,' I muttered.

As I couldn't conveniently get a warrant in time to execute it before Max Forbes went to work on the Monday, I decided that early on Tuesday would be the best time.

And that's when we hit him.

'I have a warrant to search these premises, Mr Forbes,' I said.

Max Forbes, unshaven and still in his dressing gown, was openly stunned. 'What the hell d'you want to search my house for?' he demanded. 'It's eight o'clock in the bloody morning, for God's sake.'

'Because your wife has been murdered, Mr Forbes,' I said, as Dave and I followed him into the hall, 'and there may be vital evidence here that will lead me to her killer.'

'Will it take long? I have an appointment at ten fifteen this morning.'

'I don't know. It's quite a big house.'

'But what d'you hope to find?'

'I don't know, Mr Forbes. But it is routine to search the house of someone who's been murdered. I'm sure you understand.'

'Well, I suppose you'd better carry on,' Forbes said, somewhat grudgingly.

Dave signalled to the crime-scene examiners, who were waiting in their vans. Moments later half a dozen of them, attired in their white boilersuits, trooped into the Forbeses' house.

'That should get the neighbours going,' Dave whispered.

'Is there anything in particular you're looking for, Mr Brock?' asked Linda Mitchell, the senior CSE.

'For a start, any correspondence written to Alex Forbes by a man, or anything written *by* her.' I still needed a good sample so that our tame graphologist could have another go at the postcards she'd supposedly sent from Belgium. 'And if there's a chest freezer, examine it closely. See if it could have contained a body.'

'OK.' Linda began to brief her team and I went into the sitting room to talk to Max Forbes again.

'Is it all right if I carry on and have a shower and get dressed?' asked Forbes, standing in front of the empty fireplace.

'I'd rather you didn't get in the way, Mr Forbes. It'll make my officers' task that much easier if you stay here, and it'll be quicker too, if they can move through the house methodically.'

'But I've got to get ready for work,' Forbes protested.

'I'm sure you want us to find whoever killed your wife, Mr Forbes, and, for all I know, we may find some evidence of that here.'

'I don't know what you expect to find,' Forbes said churlishly, as he seated himself in an armchair. He waved a hand at a sofa. 'You'd better sit down.' It wasn't a very graceful invitation.

'You told us that Mrs Forbes was having an extramarital affair,' I said. 'In which case it's possible that she had other lovers, apart from those listed in her address book, I mean' – Forbes shrugged his shoulders at that – 'and we may find details of them here somewhere.' I knew damned well there had been others, and I had interviewed four of them, but there could well have been more. Many more.

One of the CSEs appeared in the door and beckoned.

'Linda would like you to have a look in the cellar, Mr Brock,' he whispered when I joined him.

I followed the CSE down the open wooden staircase to the cellar. In a corner, illuminated by one of the team's flood-lights, was a chest freezer.

'What have you got, Linda?'

'It's just an ordinary chest freezer, Mr Brock, three hundred and ninety-six litres, but I thought you'd want to look at it.'

'How d'you know it's three hundred and ninety-six litres?'

'It's stamped on a metal plate on the side,' said Linda, smiling.

'Anything in it?' I didn't mean food; I meant evidence that would point towards Alex Forbes's killer.

'Very little actually. Just a few joints of meat, a couple of chickens and some frozen vegetables. I'll make sure it's examined thoroughly and I'll let you know if we find anything evidential. However, we also found this.' Linda twisted the floodlight round so that it lit up a whole array of chains, leather straps and whips neatly arranged on hooks on the opposite wall. Close by was a large, leather-padded, X-shaped framework with straps at each point of the X. 'Looks like fun,' she said with a wry smile.

The crime-scene team finished their search at ten minutes to twelve, long after an angry Max Forbes had spent at least half an hour on the telephone rearranging his day.

'Well?' he asked truculently, as we were on the point of leaving. 'Did you find anything?'

'I don't know, Mr Forbes.' I wasn't going to talk to him about the bondage equipment that Linda had discovered in the cellar until I had reports about anything else that had been found.

'What d'you mean, you don't know? You spend nearly four hours taking my house apart and then tell me you don't know if you've found anything.'

'I apologize for the disruption, both to your professional and domestic routine, Mr Forbes,' I said soothingly, 'but I have to wait for the scientific report.'

'He's not very happy, is he, guv?' said Dave as we left the complaining Max Forbes. 'Anyone would think he didn't want us to find out who killed his missus.'

After lunching frugally in a dubious Wandsworth pub, Dave and I drove to Hampstead.

The charming Conchita greeted us like old friends and conducted us to Clive Parish's study.

'Policemen come see you more,' she bellowed at Parish's back.

Parish swung round from the computer screen he'd been studying and stood up. 'Just keeping an eye on the market,' he said. 'Come through to the sitting room.'

It was a stark room. There was no carpet, just polished floorboards. A minimum of modern furniture had been placed with geometric symmetry and the white walls were adorned with large, abstract paintings. And they *were* paintings rather than prints.

'Have a seat, gentlemen,' Parish said as he sat down himself, 'and tell me what I can do for you.'

'Alex Forbes came to see you on more than three occasions, Mr Parish, didn't she?'

'How the hell did you find that out?' Parish had a smile on his face as he posed the question.

'I'm a detective,' I said, and smiled too. 'I'm paid to find things out.' But then I became serious. 'But it doesn't help me if people withhold information from me. In fact it just wastes my time.'

'Point taken,' said Parish, and had the good grace to look

contrite. 'OK, so we had an affair, but I broke it off. I didn't think it would matter to you chaps any more. It was at least six weeks ago that I saw her last.'

'And why did you break it off?'

'Two reasons really. Firstly, it turned out that she was keen on bondage and whipping, but I'm afraid I'm not into that sort of stuff. The first three or four times were great, but then she said she wanted me to tie her up and whip her. To be frank, I could foresee no end of complications.'

'Such as?'

'Oh come on. You must know what I mean, surely? If she'd cried rape, where would that have put me? If I'd told you chaps that she'd asked me to tie her up and make love to her, would you have believed me? Certainly a bunch of working-class wallies sitting on a jury wouldn't have done. Unless they actually indulged in it themselves, which is unlikely: the plebs are remarkably strait-laced about sex. Anyway, I told Alex that enough was enough. I was quite happy to carry on with straight sex, but I was having nothing to do with anything kinky.'

Supercilious bastard, I thought. 'And what did she say to that?'

'She flew off the handle, really threw a tantrum, and said that if I hadn't got the balls for it, she'd find someone who had. Then she flounced out and I never saw her again.'

Interesting. Very similar to the performance she put on at Bill Griffin's houseboat. And probably at Jamie Ryan's, too.

'You said there were two reasons,' Dave chipped in.

Parish crossed his legs at the ankles and looked down at his suede chukka boots. 'Conchita was the other reason,' he said.

'Your housekeeper objected, did she?'

'She's actually a bit more than my housekeeper.'

'That's why you've kept her on, then,' said Dave. 'She's no good at housekeeping, but is OK at the other, is that it?'

'That sums it up rather neatly,' said Parish. 'Hell, d'you blame me?'

'Not really, no,' said Dave.

'Look, I'm sorry I misled you before, but I really didn't want to get involved.'

'Well, you are involved, Mr Parish,' I said. 'As a matter of interest, did you get a postcard from Alex recently?'

Parish looked up in astonishment. 'Yes, I did. Whatever made you ask that?'

'Do you still have it?'

'Yes, I think so. Hang on a moment.' Parish left the room, to return only a minute or so later. 'There you are,' he said, handing me the sort of picture postcard with which we were rapidly becoming familiar. 'I must say that I found it a bit strange, considering the acrimonious way in which we parted.'

The card was a photograph of the beach at Ostend. I turned it over. The postmark was illegible and the message, as the others had been, was brief: *Having a great time. A.*

'When did you receive this?'

'The end of July sometime, I think. A few weeks ago, anyway. I just tossed it in a drawer. But I did wonder if she wanted to renew our affair and I was tempted to ring her and tell her to forget it.'

'You knew her phone number, then.'

'Of course. I told you, she gave me her business card.'

'So, you only ever rang her at work.'

'Yes, I didn't know where she lived.'

And that was as far as we could take it. For the time being. I was still unhappy about Parish. He was too confident, too glib, for my liking. That we had to drag the information out of him about his affair with Alex Forbes naturally made me suspicious. He was unmarried – so he said – and therefore a free agent. Nevertheless, I told Dave to arrange for someone to check if he really was divorced.

There was no justification at this stage for searching his house: instinct told me that we wouldn't find anything. And that had nothing to do with Conchita's cleaning skills. Or lack of them. He had admitted to an affair with the dead woman, and that she had visited his house. We also knew that he had a freezer – and probably a large one – but then so have a lot of people these days.

Somewhat disheartened at constantly going round in circles, Dave and I got back to the office at about four o'clock. Linda Mitchell, the senior CSE, was waiting to see me, and her report further depressed me.

'There wasn't much, Mr Brock,' she said, 'but I can give you a summary, if that'd be helpful.'

'Go ahead.' I waved her towards the armchair.

'We found quite a lot of corres, some written by Alex Forbes and some by her husband. I seized samples of both, and they're with the graphologist. But there weren't any that appeared to have been written by anyone else. We found some fairly long strands of hair in the chest freezer, possibly human, and they're being examined at the lab. Finally we found some black hair dye in the bathroom cabinet.'

'I wonder if Alex Forbes's hair was dyed,' I mused. 'I suppose you didn't find anything for dyeing hair blonde, did you?'

'No, just the black,' said Linda. 'And that's the sum total of the search,' she added apologetically, as though it was her fault that nothing incriminating had been found.

'Thanks, Linda. How long before we get any results?'

'I've told them to speed things up. Should be hours rather than days.'

Ten minutes later, Frank Mead turned up.

'Come in, Frank,' I said with a tired sigh. I never seem able to get down to the bloody paperwork without being interrupted.

'Couple of things, Harry,' Frank began. 'Firstly, all that the CSEs found in the boot of the Mercedes were some hairs that are a DNA match for Alex Forbes.'

'Proves nothing,' I said gloomily. 'Probably fell in there when she was getting her shopping out. At least, that's what Max Forbes will say. And the other thing, Frank?'

'I've been doing some checking on the Mercedes.'

'Don't tell me it was a ringer. That's all I need.'

A ringer is what coppers – and second-hand car dealers – call a vehicle that has been stolen and given a new identity before being sold on.

'No, it's kosher, but it's not a company car.'

'You surprise me. I'd've thought that was the very least that estate agents like the one she worked for would have given their staff. A Rolls-Royce even.'

'I had one of the skippers check with the dealer who sold the vehicle.'

'Who was this skipper?' It's always good to know who made the enquiry, then you know how reliable the information is. There are some detective sergeants who couldn't detect a bad smell.

'DS Challis, Harry. He's the new guy we got from the Stolen Car Squad.'

'Good choice. And what startling information did he come up with?'

'The car was bought for Alex Forbes on the twenty-fifth of May this year.'

'Bought *for* her, did you say?'

'That's right. And it was bought for her by one Clive Parish of nine Drovers Lane, London NW3.'

'Christ!' I said. 'If only I'd known that a couple of hours ago.'

Nine

On Wednesday morning – nine days into the enquiry – I got the results of the search of the Forbeses' house.

This time the graphologist was more positive than he had been the last time. Given better examples of handwriting to work on, he had come up with the firm opinion that the post-cards had *not* been written by Alex. That was all very well, of course, but it would have been even more helpful if he could have said who *had* written them.

The strands of hair found in the chest freezer proved to be human, and a DNA analysis of them matched the sample taken from Alex Forbes's body. The obvious deduction was that some of Alex's hair had dropped into the freezer when she leaned over it. Much as I'd surmised that the hairs found in the boot of Alex's car fell in there when she was removing something.

There was no evidence, however, that a body had been stored in the freezer, the report said. But, it continued, that didn't mean it hadn't.

Bloody marvellous!

A fingerprint examination of the house had yielded little. Max and Alex's prints had been found, of course, along with a few others, none of which could be identified in the national fingerprint collection. And that meant that whoever had left them in the house did not have a criminal conviction.

Well, there were no surprises there, but neither did it take me any further forward.

There was, however, one other matter that was niggling me. Frank Mead had discovered that Parish had bought a

Mercedes for Alex Forbes, but did she have another car, a company car perhaps? And, if so, had she used that car when she left home on the fifteenth of July? Maybe Max Forbes had used the Merc and driven it to France with someone other than his wife. Although he claimed to have gone to the Black Forest via Karlsruhe – by boat and train – we had been unable to verify his story.

I telephoned Skinner, the manager of the estate agents where Alex had worked. 'Mr Skinner, did Alex Forbes have a company car?'

'No, none of the staff does. But she had a car of her own, a Mercedes, and she charged mileage whenever she used it on company business.'

'Has she always had a Mercedes?'

'No. She used to have a Ford Focus, but she changed it for the Merc quite recently.'

'Can you say how recently?'

'Just a moment,' said Skinner. And it *was* just a moment; he was obviously a man who took a close personal interest in his employees' claims for expenses. 'The twenty-seventh of May was the first time she put in a claim at the enhanced rate, Chief Inspector.'

'One other question, Mr Skinner. What were the exact dates that Mrs Forbes visited Clive Parish's house?'

'I'll have to call you back on that.'

Five minutes later, he did. 'Alex Forbes first called on Parish on Friday the third of May, Mr Brock. And she visited him again on the seventh and the tenth.'

At last I had some firm information on which to base my further questioning of Clive Parish.

But first I needed to have another word with Max Forbes. I rang his office but was told that he was working at home today. Good.

'Oh, not again.' It was evident that Max Forbes was not at all pleased to see Dave and me. 'I am trying to do some work, you know. Yesterday was a write-off, thanks to you.

But you'd better come in, I suppose,' he said, leading us into the front room.

'Mr Forbes, we are trying to discover who murdered your wife, and I'm afraid that requires the police to undertake all sorts of enquiries. I'm sorry, but there it is.'

'If you say so. I'll just go and turn off my computer. Shan't be a minute.'

'Happy soul, isn't he?' said Dave, casting an envious eye around the elegant sitting room as we waited. 'I don't think he gives a toss.'

'Now, what is it you want this time?' asked Forbes, as he came back into the room. 'Did you find what you were looking for yesterday?'

'Not really. We discovered some hairs in your chest freezer that matched those of Mrs Forbes—'

'What the hell did you expect?' Forbes protested. 'She used it on a regular basis, putting food in and taking it out. It's what freezers are for. Everyone has one these days.'

'Similar hairs were found in the boot of your wife's car,' I said. 'Have you any idea how they might have got there?' I knew it was a stupid question, but I posed it deliberately. It doesn't hurt to let suspects think that policemen are a bit slow in grasping things.

'Oh, for Christ's sake!' said Forbes, clearly exasperated. 'She tended to put things in there . . . and take them out,' he added sarcastically.

'We also discovered some rather strange equipment in your cellar: leather straps and chains and a large frame.' I waited to see what his reaction to that would be.

'So what?' Forbes didn't seem at all disturbed by our discovery of his kinky gear or my allusion to it.

'Am I to understand that you and your late wife indulged in that sort of thing.'

'Well, it wasn't there to be looked at. But what the hell's it got to do with you? That sort of thing's not illegal.'

'And you actually used it in the cellar, did you?' I asked,

mindful of what the Madisons next door had said about hearing yells and screams.

'Too cold down there. We used to bring it up here, to the sitting room.'

'Including that X-shaped frame?'

'Yes, it's only padded aluminium tubing. It's very light. It has claw feet that grip the carpet and we lean it against the wall.' Forbes was quite frank – proud almost – about what he and Alex had got up to, as though it was the most natural thing in the world to tie each other up and beat hell out of each other. There really are some strange people around.

'And it was just you and your wife who used this equipment, was it?'

'Well of course it was. We didn't hold parties.'

'You never entertained other like-minded people?' I asked, recalling what Stella Madison had said about seeing frequent female callers.

'Of course not. What the hell is all this, anyway? I don't see what any of this has to do with the murder of my wife.'

'As I said at the outset, Mr Forbes, the police are duty-bound to make exhaustive enquiries in a case of murder.'

'Perhaps you should consider making them in places where you might get some answers, then.' It was obvious that Forbes was rapidly tiring of our intrusive questioning. But if he *was* guilty of his wife's death, he might just make a mistake. That's how criminal investigation works.

'How long had your wife owned her Mercedes, Mr Forbes?' asked Dave.

The sudden change in the line of questioning momentarily threw Forbes and he didn't answer immediately. 'About two months, I think it was,' he said eventually. 'Why?'

'And did she own it?' Dave persisted.

'It was a company car,' said Forbes.

Dave, among whose many skills was shorthand, was writing down question and answer as quickly as they were being posed and responded to. 'It wasn't,' he said, glancing up. 'We've checked.'

'Why ask me then, if you know?' snapped Forbes. 'She must've bought it herself.' He was floundering now, and it was obvious that he was either lying or he really had no idea where the car had come from.

'It's a top-of-the-range Mercedes,' said Dave. 'I doubt she could have afforded it on the salary she was getting as an estate agent's negotiator.' He could be extremely persistent when he got going. 'Or did she have a private income?'

'I don't know what she earned,' said Forbes irritably. 'We each had our own money. I never asked her where the damned car came from. Anyway, what's it got to do with her death?'

'Did she have another car before the Mercedes?'

'Yes, a Ford Focus, but she sold it when she got the Mercedes,' retorted Forbes, his irritation at these seemingly pointless questions now only thinly veiled.

'The Mercedes travelled to the continent, from Dover to Calais, on Tuesday the sixteenth of July,' I said, picking up the questioning again. 'The day after she left home. There were seen to be two people in it, one of whom could well have been your wife. I'm interested to know who the other person was. Was it you, Mr Forbes?'

Max Forbes gave a loud, exasperated sigh. 'I thought we'd been through all this,' he said. 'I told you before, Chief Inspector, that I went on holiday on the Wednesday after Alex went missing. I went from Dover to Calais and then down to Karlsruhe, to a nudist camp. And I stayed there for a fortnight. Now, if you've no more stupid questions, I'd appreciate it if you'd leave me to get on with some work.'

But I wasn't going to give up just yet. 'Were you having an affair at the same time as your wife, Mr Forbes?'

'No, I wasn't. And it'd be none of your damned business if I was.'

'So far, four men have been interviewed who admit to having had affairs with Mrs Forbes,' I said. 'Are you aware of any others?'

'I told you before' – Forbes was speaking wearily now – 'that my wife and I did not have a sexual relationship. I told

90

you that the first time you came here, the day you found her. I agreed that she should find satisfaction elsewhere. I told you about Farrell, but as far as I know there was no one else. And even if there was, I don't bloody well care. Now, for God's sake will you leave me alone?'

We walked back to Lavender Hill police station, where Dave had parked the car, preferring, when possible, not to leave it in the street in Battersea. The locals have a habit of vandalizing cars, and a police car – even a nondescript one – is an attractive target.

'We'll go back to the office,' I said, 'and then grab a bite of lunch.'

'Oh good,' said Dave.

'Then we'll go back up to Hampstead and sort out Parish. That bugger's playing fast and loose with us. It's time we got a bit nasty.'

'Well past time, guv.'

'And we'll take Nicola Chance with us, see if she can get Conchita on one side and have a few more words with her.'

'Yeah, good idea,' said Dave, and then changed tack. 'Interesting, what Forbes said about his nasty little toys.'

'What about them?'

'He said that he and Alex didn't have a sexual relationship, and he repeated it just now. So, what's the point of all this sado-masochism kick if it's not sexual? He said they both used it.'

'But maybe they didn't use it on each other, Dave, despite what Forbes claimed. Don't forget what the Madisons said about female callers. Anyway, we only have Forbes's word for it that he and his wife didn't have sex together. Somehow, I don't think our Mr Forbes is being quite straight with us.'

'I don't think there's anything straight about Mr Forbes at all,' commented Dave. 'In fact, I reckon he's as bent as a corkscrew.'

'Misser Parish in water,' said Conchita, showing no surprise at our reappearance at the Drovers Lane house.

'In the pool as opposed to the bath?' queried Dave.

'What?'

Nicola Chance rapidly translated Dave's question, and Conchita's reply. 'He's in the pool, Skip.'

'Tell her that Sergeant Poole and I can find our own way. In the meantime, Nicola, you stay here with Conchita and have a chat with her. You know what to ask.'

We left Nicola talking to Conchita, who didn't seem at all surprised that the woman she had befriended in the supermarket turned out to be a police officer.

We crossed the baroque hall and down the passageway that led to the swimming pool.

'Good afternoon, Mr Parish.'

'Ah, the police again.' Parish, attired in swimming trunks, was reclining on a wheeled lounger, reading the *Financial Times*. 'Come in and take a seat. Have a swim if you feel like it,' he added with a sarcastic laugh.

'I don't greatly appreciate coming up to Hampstead every five minutes,' I said, deliberately sitting on one of the aluminium chairs, so that I was higher than Parish.

'Oh, so what's the problem now?' Parish put down his newspaper, sat up and turned, putting his feet on the ground.

'I understand that you bought a top-of-the-range Mercedes as a gift for Mrs Forbes,' I began. *Let's see what you make of that, sport.*

'Oh, you found out about that.'

'Yes. Why didn't you tell me that when I was here the last time?'

'Didn't think it was relevant. After all, men do buy presents for their lady-friends, don't they?'

'Not usually presents that are that expensive.'

'It's all relative. After all, a few thousand pounds is nothing to me.'

'Where were you between the sixteenth of July and the sixth of August, Mr Parish?' asked Dave, his record-of-interview book at the ready.

'My God! Are you suggesting that I had something to do

with Alex's death?' Parish ran both hands through his hair and then sat forward, elbows on knees and hands loosely linked.

Dave said nothing, just waited patiently, pen poised and his gaze fixed firmly on Parish. Even I felt threatened.

'I don't know offhand. I'd need to have a look at my diary. But why? What's so special about those dates?'

'The sixteenth of July was when Alex Forbes's car left Dover for Calais, and the sixth of August was when her body was found. When her car left Dover it contained two people. Her husband denies that one of them was him. Was it you?'

'Jesus Christ! Look, I told you before, the last time I saw the girl was when she stormed out of here about six weeks ago.'

'Did you ask for your car back?' Dave asked.

'No. It wasn't important.'

'How long had you known Alex Forbes when you gave her this expensive present?'

Parish pondered the question for only a moment or two. 'About three weeks, I suppose.'

'Why?'

'Why what?'

'Why did you give her a car? Wouldn't a bottle of perfume have been enough to be going on with?'

'What I do with my money is my business,' said Parish sharply. But he was beginning to be a little less blasé than he had been before.

I let Dave carry on. He was doing very well, but I wasn't going to tell him. It doesn't do to let detective sergeants think they're too good.

'According to our enquiries, Mr Parish,' Dave continued, 'you first met Alex Forbes on the third of May, when she came here to value your house. And she came again on the seventh and the tenth. And yet on the twenty-fifth you buy her a very expensive car. That seems overly generous to me.'

'You *have* done your homework, haven't you?' said Parish

sarcastically. 'Well, in actual fact, I met Alex Forbes long before she came here to do a valuation.'

Time for me to have a go, I thought. 'And when would that have been?' I asked.

'Last year sometime. About June, I think.'

'So, why didn't you tell me this before?' Now for a little squeeze. 'I'm beginning to wonder if you're deliberately obstructing a murder investigation, Mr Parish, and if so, why. Obstructing police in the execution of their duty is an offence, you know,' I added. Not that I imagined the lily-livered lot at the Crown Prosecution Service being prepared to have a go at that.

'Now hang on. Why should I do that?'

'You tell me.'

'To be perfectly honest, it was all a bit sordid. You see, I met Alex through a contact magazine, one of those SM publications.'

'I thought you said you weren't interested in sado-masochism. In fact, you talked at some length about the possibility of being charged with rape if it all went wrong.'

'Yeah, I know, but it's not something one discusses in polite company, is it?'

'I don't fall into the category of polite company, Mr Parish, I'm a policeman. Who made the contact, you or her?'

'She did. I put an advert in one of those magazines and she replied. I invited her up here to the house and we took it from there.'

'So, in fact, you were into this whipping business from the start.'

'Yes.' Parish half whispered his reply.

'When she came to value your house – this house – was that a coincidence?'

'Not exactly. I didn't want to sell the place, still don't, but I did it so that she could come here during the day a few times.'

'Lucky it was Mrs Forbes who turned up,' I said, wondering what Mr Skinner would have thought about the deception if he'd known. And what Parish would have thought if, instead, Skinner had sent the callow youth we'd encountered in his front office. On the other hand he might not have minded. 'But to get back to Sergeant Poole's question, Mr Parish, where were you between the dates he mentioned?'

'I said I'd have to look at my diary.'

'Perhaps you'd do so, then.'

Shoving his feet into a pair of leather mules, and slipping on a towelling robe, Parish left us.

But when he returned he was even less happy than when he'd left. 'Who the hell's that talking to Conchita?' he demanded.

'That,' I said, 'is Detective Constable Chance.'

'Why's she talking to my housekeeper? You didn't ask my permission.'

Good, you're getting rattled at last. I was beginning to tire of this well-heeled layabout.

'Because you've been less than frank with us, Mr Parish.' I decided it was time to get tough, and Dave shot me an about-time-too glance. 'I'm investigating a murder and this is my third visit here. Two of those visits would have been unnecessary if you'd been open and honest with me. But, as you've not been, I'm entitled to get the information I require from whatever source I think may be forthcoming.'

'Well, if you think I killed her, you're barking up the wrong tree.'

'The dates, Mr Parish,' Dave reminded him.

Parish opened the leather-bound A4 Filofax diary he had brought back with him. 'I was here for the whole of that period,' he said. 'By here, I mean not out of the country. I had one engagement in London, but apart from that I didn't leave the house.' He snapped the book shut.

'Who was that engagement with?' I asked.

Parish smiled; it was almost a sneer. 'My solicitor.' He opened his diary again and turned to a plastic wallet at the back that was designed to hold business cards. Taking one out, he handed it to me. 'That's him. Feel free to check.'

Nicola Chance was waiting in the car when we left.

'Anything?' I asked.

'I had a long chat with Conchita, sir, and she's not a happy bunny. It seems that Madam Forbes supplanted her in Parish's bed for a couple of months. There were naked frolics in the pool, as well, and on one occasion she walked in and found a nude Alex tied to the diving board.'

'Did she say what Parish's reaction had been?'

'Yes, sir, he asked her if she wanted to join in. I don't think it's a good idea to upset that young Filipina lady,' she added.

'Why, what was her response?'

Nicola chuckled. 'She told him to perform an impossible biological act, sir. But she said it in Spanish and he didn't understand a word of it. Well, I imagine he didn't, because Conchita said he just laughed.'

'And was Parish here during the dates that Alex was allegedly in France?'

'No, sir, he wasn't, but Conchita doesn't know where he'd gone.'

'Did she get the impression that he'd gone on holiday?'

'More or less, sir. She said he took a suitcase with him and drove off.'

'On those precise dates?'

'No. She said that Parish left here on the nineteenth of July and got back on the twenty-fifth.'

'So, he could have been in France at the same time as Alex,' I mused. 'Not that it proves a bloody thing. France is a big place.'

Ten

'This Parish guy is jerking us around, Dave. When we first saw him, he said he couldn't recall meeting Alex at all, and then, oh yes, of course, she was the girl who came to value his house. Albeit three times. Then he tells us, reluctantly, that they did have an affair, but only straight sex. And, when we front him with his purchase of the car, he finally admits that he's known her for over a year and that they went in for mutual flagellation. And, apart from anything else, he was adrift for some of the time that Alex was allegedly in France or wherever. In my book there can only be one reason for all of that bobbing and weaving.'

'That he topped her, guv?'

Despite my professed dislike of oranges, Dave was peeling one. But, as the gorgeous Madeleine had said they were good for him, who was I – a mere DCI – to object?

'Well, look at it this way, Dave. Alex fancies Parish rotten because he's stinking rich, he's got a bloody great house with a swimming pool, and he comes across with exactly the sex she loves. All of this she wants. For good. But Parish doesn't want a wife, just a playmate. And one he can ditch as soon as he tires of her and goes on to the next one. But Alex won't give up and he tops her. Can you come up with a better reason? Or a more likely candidate?'

'Nope!' Dave dropped peel into the wastepaper basket. 'But how do we prove that Parish had anything to do with it? All right, so he knew her. But then so did Farrell and Griffin and Ryan.'

'And God knows how many others who we haven't yet traced,' I said gloomily.

'So, what do we do? Hit him again?'

'I think we'll have to, Dave, but somehow we've got to have more proof of his involvement.'

'Could take him down the nick and put the frighteners on him.' Dave put the last segment of orange in his mouth and wiped his fingers on his handkerchief.

I considered that option, but only for a moment. With all the money that Parish had, there'd be an army of lawyers, all screaming wrongful arrest and false imprisonment, beating a path to the door of the nick within minutes of us knocking him off. Anyway, knowing what a smug, self-opinionated, overconfident bastard he was, I was certain that he'd exercise his legal right to stay silent.

'No, Dave. When and if we nick him for Alex's murder, I want to make sure that it sticks.'

'What about Griffin's claim to have seen Alex?' Dave asked. 'Anything else we can do about that?'

'Pie in the sky. We've still got her body in the mortuary, and Max Forbes is in no doubt that it's her. No, Dave, Griffin *thought* he saw her, but he actually saw someone who looked like her. Case closed.'

'I wish it was,' mumbled Dave. 'I'm supposed to be going on leave in a fortnight's time. With Madeleine,' he added, knowing that I would be disinclined to upset any plans involving his wife.

'There is something you can do.'

'I was afraid there might be. What?'

'Give Skinner a ring and find out the index mark of the Ford Focus that Alex owned before Parish gave her the Merc. Then check with the DVLA and find out who owns it now. Might be worth getting the crime-scene examiners to give it the once over.'

Dave looked doubtful. 'Think they'll find anything, after all this time, guv?'

'Why not?' I said. 'They're miracle-workers at the lab.'

And I meant it. Our forensic scientists had frequently pulled our chestnuts out of the fire for us.

Dave made the calls. Skinner had a record of the car's number – which didn't surprise me – and the Driver and Vehicle Licensing Agency at Swansea came up with the name and address of the new owner: Sidney Gill of sixty-five Campbell Road, Wandsworth. Not very far from Crouch Road, Battersea, although there wasn't really anything to be read into that.

'We shall pay Mr Gill a visit, Dave.'

'Very good, sir.'

It was obvious that Dave didn't think much of the idea: he was calling me 'sir' again.

Assuming that everyone went out to work these days, we left it until the evening.

The woman who answered the door was a shapely blonde in her late twenties or early thirties. She was clad in jeans and had boobs that stretched the white tee-shirt she was wearing almost to bursting point. That should interest Dave, I thought. Dave is a committed boobs man.

She looked at us suspiciously and, from what we learned about her later, she might well have been assessing our suitability as potential clients.

Having put her mind at rest by telling her we were police officers – well, I suppose it put her mind at rest – I said that we wished to speak to Mr Sidney Gill.

'There is no Mr Gill,' said the woman. 'I'm Sydney Gill. That's Sydney with a Y. Two Ys actually,' she added with a smile.

'The DVLA spelt it with an "I", guv,' muttered Dave, rightly assuming that he was about to get the blame for this embarrassing example of apparent police incompetence.

Dave knew the police officer's first rule: if it all goes pear-shaped, thrash around for someone else to blame.

'We'd like to talk to you about a car you bought recently,' I said.

'Oh Lord! You'd better come in.' The woman led us through to a back room, tastefully if austerely furnished. The television was switched on and, in front of the fireplace, there was an ironing board on which was a pile of un-ironed clothing. 'Just catching up,' she said, turning off the TV. 'The evenings and the weekends are the only chance I get at the moment. I've been working quite a lot lately.' She shooed a cat off one of the two armchairs and invited us to sit down. 'Am I in trouble, then?' she asked. 'I didn't get caught by one of those nasty speed camera things that you've put up all over the place, did I?'

'No, it's nothing like that,' I assured her. 'My colleague and I are investigating a murder.'

'A murder!' Sydney Gill looked suitably impressed. 'Was it round here somewhere?'

'Nearly. It was the murder of the woman from whom you bought your car,' I said.

'Good Lord! D'you mean Alex Forbes?' There was no sharp intake of breath, no sudden dramatic shock at hearing such awful news. 'I didn't know about that. But then I'm out of the country quite a bit.'

And perhaps Sydney Gill didn't read newspapers when she *was* here. Anyway, murders are so commonplace these days that anyone could be forgiven for missing a single column-inch at the bottom of page seven. They don't even qualify for the front page any more, unless they're someone famous. And Alex Forbes didn't fall into that category.

'Did you know her? Socially, I mean, rather than just being the person you bought the car from.'

'Er, not exactly.'

'How well *did* you know her, then, Miss Gill? It is *Miss* Gill, is it?'

'Yes, I'm not married.' There was a slight hesitation before she replied. 'It was Max I knew.'

I sensed that there was more to this business than the mere purchase of a second-hand car from Max Forbes's late wife. 'As I said, Miss Gill, I'm investigating a murder. It would be helpful if you were completely open with me. Anything you say will be treated in the strictest confidence,' I said, without meaning a word of it.

She pulled a chair from beneath the table and sat down. For a moment or two she concentrated on twisting the ring she wore on the little finger of her left hand. 'Max and I had an arrangement,' she said at last, and looked up.

I supposed that to be a euphemism for an affair. 'Am I to take it that it's now at an end?'

'No, I don't think so. Well, I hope not.'

'What d'you mean, you don't think so?'

'Max hasn't rung me for about four or five weeks. And that's a bit unusual.'

'Have you tried ringing him?'

'No, he always rang me. He told me never to phone him at home. Ever.'

'Well, he has been coping with the death of his wife.' But, I thought, if he'd been having an affair with this gorgeous girl – who must have been at least thirty years his junior – I don't suppose he was all that cut up about the murder of his wife. 'And this was a sexual relationship, was it?'

'I suppose it was, in a manner of speaking.' Sydney gave a sly smile. 'But I know what you're thinking.'

She was right about that. I was wondering how in hell's name an ageing Lothario like Max Forbes could pull a girl young enough to be his daughter, particularly when Alex had told Griffin that Max was gay.

'The answer's simple: he paid me for my services,' Sydney continued. 'Incidentally, he was a very clever artist. Did you know that? He once did a very tasteful sketch of me. I'll show it to you.' She opened a drawer in the table and took out a charcoal sketch of herself in the nude. 'There, don't you think that's good?'

'Wonderful,' said Dave, looking over my shoulder and spending a little longer than was officially necessary in examining the depiction of a naked Sydney. 'How did you meet him?' he asked.

'Through a contact magazine. I get a lot of work through contact magazines.'

Dave nodded. 'Thought you might have done.'

'What actually happened to Alex?' Sydney turned to face me again.

'She was found strangled in Richmond Park about ten days ago.'

'What on earth was she doing there?' The question was delivered in matter-of-fact tones. Again, there was no element of shock, just curiosity.

'That's one of the things I'm trying to find out, Miss Gill. Incidentally, did Alex Forbes know about your affair with her husband?'

'It wasn't an affair. It was a business arrangement.'

'Oh, I'm sorry.' The sketch of Sydney suddenly took on a meaning. 'You were his artist's model, were you?'

Sydney Gill threw back her head and laughed. 'No. All right, I posed for him once or twice, like there.' She pointed at the sketch on the table. 'But what he paid me for was to tie him up and whip him.'

'And did Alex know about this?'

'Max said that she didn't care. Mind you, I'm not sure that she knew about it, not that I gave a toss. Anyway, Max said that she was having an affair. Theirs was a very open marriage, according to him.'

'Sounds like it,' I said. 'Did he tell you who Alex was seeing?'

'I think he said it was a Mike someone.' She paused, pondering the question. 'Yes, it was a man called Mike Farrell.'

'Did Max ever mention any other men who Alex might have been involved with?'

'No. In fact he hardly mentioned her at all.'

'Did you always go to Crouch Road, rather than Max coming here?'

'Of course. That's where all the kinky gear was. You know, the chains and the whips and all that.' Sydney chuckled as she mentioned the equipment. There was no sign of embarrassment.

'And who did what and with which and to whom?' Dave smiled disarmingly at the girl.

'Well . . .' Sydney leaned back and gazed thoughtfully at a Vetriano print over the fireplace. 'He used to like me strapping him naked to a frame he'd had specially made, and then whipping him as hard as I could. I suppose it gave him some sort of kick. I don't understand it, but it definitely turned him on. So what? Personally I think it's a bit sick. But he paid me well, so what the hell.'

'And did you have sexual intercourse with him after you'd beaten him?'

'God Almighty, no. I didn't fancy him at all. He was much too old for me. I like them young and beefy.' She shot a quick glance at Dave, and smiled. Dave smiled back.

'And when was the last time you saw Alex Forbes, Miss Gill?' I asked.

'I only met her the once, and that was the day I bought the car from her.'

'How did you hear that the car was for sale? Not a contact magazine, surely?' I added, smiling.

'No. Max told me that his wife had got a new car and wanted to sell her old one. I got it for a very good price.'

'And that was the only time you met her, was it? When you bought the car.' I wanted to get that absolutely clear.

'Yes. Max made sure she was out of the way on every other occasion that I went round there.'

'And how often was that?'

'Once or twice a month, but it depended largely on when I was free.'

'And when was it that you bought the car?' I knew what the DVLA had told Dave, which accorded with what Skinner had said about Alex charging a higher rate of mileage for the Mercedes, but we'd been given so many bum steers since the start of this enquiry that it would be useful to have it confirmed.

Sydney Gill thought for a moment or two. 'It was about the end of May, I think. Shall I get the log book?'

'No, that's fine.' According to Swansea, the car had changed hands on the thirty-first of May. 'Miss Gill, I should like to have your car examined by forensic scientists.'

'But why? Surely you don't think I had anything to do with Alex's murder.'

I was keeping an open mind about that. Maybe Sydney Gill *did* fancy Max – perhaps for his money, rather than sex – and that the murder of Alex was the removal of an inconvenient impediment to achieving her goal. Had Sydney Gill, with Max's connivance, strapped Alex to the frame before beating her to death?

'It's possible that she shared the car with someone who may prove to be her killer,' I said. 'All manner of evidence can be discovered these days, even after this length of time.'

We may even find evidence of a body being conveyed in the boot.

'Does that mean that you'll have to keep the car?'

'Only for a day.'

'But I use it to get to and from work, and to the airport when I'm working abroad.'

'Murder is a serious crime, Miss Gill,' I said. 'I can obtain a warrant to seize it, but I'd rather have your co-operation.'

'When will this be, then?' she asked.

'Tomorrow? Or I can make it Saturday if that's easier for you.'

'Saturday would be better.'

'As a matter of interest, Miss Gill, what do you do for a living? You mentioned the airport. Is that where you work?'

'Heavens no. I'm a film actress. I work in London mostly, but we do occasional shoots in Amsterdam.'

'And what sort of films d'you make?' asked Dave, but suddenly we both knew what her answer would be.

'The sort that policemen would regard as rather risqué, I think.' Sydney smiled sweetly at Dave and then ran her tongue round her lips.

Well, well, one gets surprises every day. But today was not one of those days.

We went straight from Sydney Gill's place to Crouch Road.

'Mr Forbes, I'm afraid I need to speak to you again.'

'Oh, come in then.' There was an attitude of weary resignation about Max Forbes now, as though he was wondering if this nightmare would ever end. 'What is it now?'

'You told us that you were not having an affair.'

'So?'

'But you were, weren't you?'

'What makes you think that?'

'Sydney Gill makes me think that,' I said.

'Oh, so you've been talking to her, have you?' I think Forbes was beginning to realize that few secrets could be kept from nasty, nosey policemen like me. 'Yes, Sydney and I did have an affair. Well, a sort of affair.'

'And is it over now?'

'Yes, definitely.'

I imagined that to have been an instant decision, a direct result of Sydney Gill having told me about it. Oh well, bad luck, Sydney.

'Earlier you told me that you and Mrs Forbes did not share a sexual relationship.'

'That's so, but I didn't say I was impotent. What I said was that I could no longer satisfy her. There, does that answer your question, Mr Brock?' Forbes raised his head and peered down his nose at me as he spoke.

'Not quite. Miss Gill said that although you paid her to perform certain acts on you, you didn't have sexual intercourse. Is that correct?'

'That is correct, yes. Although I don't know what that has to do with the death of my wife.'

'Were there any other women with whom you had a similar relationship?'

'No.' I thought that Forbes was going to confine himself to monosyllabic answers from now on, but I was wrong. 'I don't think you appreciate, Mr Brock, that I adored Alex. Oh sure, I was that much older than she was, and I didn't come up to her expectations in bed. But we resolved that. I let her do what she wanted – which was to sleep with other men – but she always came back. And she knew what I needed, but I had to buy it.' He shrugged, possibly at the unfairness of his wife having the pick of bed-mates while he was obliged to make sordid arrangements with an actress who probably charged him the earth. 'But Alex didn't mind, and I think that, in her own way, she loved me as much as I loved her. And God, I'm going to miss her.' For a brief moment he looked incredibly sad, but then he collected himself again.

Well, that was the first sign of any emotion he'd displayed. Being uncharacteristically charitable – for me, anyway – I imagined it to be a delayed reaction to the death of his wife.

'Did you and your wife have a wide circle of friends, Mr Forbes?' asked Dave.

'Why?' Forbes stared distastefully at Dave. I think he'd taken a dislike to him. Probably because he was black. But Dave knew how to deal with people like that. After all, if he could sort out the commander, the Max Forbeses of this world would be no problem.

'Because we wish to eliminate the fingerprints that we found here when we searched your house the day before yesterday.'

'I lived here with my wife,' Forbes said, slowly and patiently, as though explaining the obvious to a pair of idiots. That suited me fine: let him think we're idiots. 'The only other person who came here was Sydney Gill. Unless, of course, Alex entertained when I wasn't here, which she may well have done. But if you're talking about parties, or dinner parties – that sort of thing – then the answer's no.'

Liar! The Madisons saw a succession of women calling at the house. They couldn't all have been collecting for Christian Aid, surely.

'How long had you and Mrs Forbes been married?' Dave

was slowly extracting all the details of Max Forbes's personal life.

'Four years.'

'How did you meet?'

'What is all this? How will that sort of information help you to find out who killed her?'

'I don't know, neither does my chief inspector,' said Dave. 'That's why I'm asking.'

'We met through a magazine,' said Forbes, after apparently agonizing over whether he was going to answer at all.

'And that would have been an SM magazine, would it?' Dave's pen waggled threateningly again.

'Yes, but there's nothing wrong with that. We were married six months later. And we've been idyllically happy.'

'Did you ever travel in Mrs Forbes's Ford Focus car?' This time the pen pointed straight at Forbes.

'Why d'you want to know that?'

'Because we're having it examined scientifically.'

'Good God, whatever for?'

'Any evidence that may lead us to finding Mrs Forbes's killer,' I said. 'If we know that your fingerprints are in it, it'll save time when it comes to comparison for elimination.' Forbes was bright enough to know what rubbish that was, but let him think that we're dim plods. It sometimes helps.

'Yes, I did travel in it occasionally.'

'Did anyone else that you know of?'

'I should think there were hundreds,' said Forbes triumphantly. 'She used it for work and conveyed potential clients in it to view properties.'

Thanks a lot. I should have thought of that myself.

'Thank you, Mr Forbes,' I said. 'I think that'll be all for the moment, but we may have to see you again.'

'I don't doubt it,' said Forbes.

Eleven

Friday morning and another weekend looming. Should I bring the team in on Saturday and possibly even Sunday? And, if I bring them in, what the hell will they do, given that this enquiry is getting bogged down? Colin Wilberforce, the incident-room manager, had already arranged with the forensic science lab to give Sydney Gill's car the once over tomorrow, but apart from that, zilch.

Anyway, the commander would only fret about the overtime bill I'm running up. He seems to think it's possible to budget for a murder in advance of it happening. *I wish!* But then, as I've mentioned before, the commander was never a detective during his long and undistinguished career, at least not until some genius at the Yard, working her fingers to the bone in 'human resources', decided to turn him into one at the stroke of a pen. The bloody job's hard enough without that sort of impediment.

All we'd achieved yesterday was to learn that Max Forbes – despite 'adoring' his late wife – had enjoyed a regular scourging at the hands of a ravishing actress.

But then, as is wont to happen, the kaleidoscope got shaken again and the whole picture changed.

'There's a Detective Superintendent Ferguson for you on line two, sir,' said Colin.

'Ferguson? Where's he from, Internal Investigations? I'll bet Forbes has complained of being harassed.'

'Hampshire Constabulary, sir.'

'Good God! *That* Ferguson.'

Jock Ferguson and I had been inspectors on some futile

course at the police college in Hampshire a few years ago. Being a local officer, Jock knew all the best pubs – which did my liver no good at all – but, on the plus side, enabled both of us to pass three fruitless months in a blissful, drunken haze.

And that was a good thing as far as I was concerned. The police college is where the intelligentsia in our ranks – of which I'm not one – believe the Holy Grail of coppering is to be found. It is there that one is encouraged to sit around discussing the finer points of such subjects as 'person management', the intellectual aspects of law enforcement and the cerebral approach to criminal investigation. All of which was far removed from my first knock-off, of a drunk on Victoria Embankment, only yards away from my office. But I sometimes question if the wunderkinder who run these courses have ever arrested anyone in their lives.

I grabbed the phone and flicked down the switch. 'Jock, I thought you were dead.'

'And bollocks to you, Harry, you old bastard,' said Ferguson, bellowing down the phone in his tortured Scots accent. 'How are you?'

'Struggling. But I suppose you're sitting there doing the bloody crossword.'

'I need some help with a missing-person enquiry, Harry,' said Ferguson.

'Oh, come on, Jock,' I said. 'I'm tucked up with a God-awful murder, and much as I'd like to help you—'

'Aye, I know fine you Met blokes are flogging yourselves to death up there, Harry, but there's a possible tie-up with your job.'

'Flogging is not exactly the word I'd've used in the circum-stances, Jock,' I said. 'So, what've you got?'

'I spoke to some guy in your Missing Persons Branch at the Yard who told me you were doing the Alex Forbes murder.'

'That's right, but what's it got to do with your job?'

'Got a minute while I tell you the tale?'

I glanced at the clock. 'Yeah, go on then.'

'Three months ago a Corporal Dan Hockley was sent with his unit from Aldershot to Belize on a six-month tour. He and his wife – she's called Karen, by the way – corresponded regularly, and spoke once a week on the phone. The army get concessionary calls apparently. But he's heard nothing from her since about the end of June, and his telephone calls weren't answered. He eventually told his commanding officer of his concern and the upshot was that he was sent home on compassionate leave last week to try and sort it out.'

'What are you doing, Jock, running a welfare organization for the army?'

There was a chuckle from the other end of the phone. 'Aye, I sometimes wonder, laddie. But the truth of the matter is that Hockley thinks his wife's run off with another man, and when I spoke to him he eventually admitted that it wouldn't be the first time. She's had affairs before and they've rowed about it in the past. On one occasion he came home early from an exercise on Salisbury Plain and found her in bed with a sergeant-major.'

'There's nothing new in that,' I said.

'True. I spoke to the military police and they told me that Hockley was a sergeant at the time and apparently he knocked hell out of this other guy. The result of that little to-do was that Hockley got busted down to corporal for striking a superior rank. Bit unfair, I thought, but that's the army for you. It's a hell of a problem with soldiers. They go off on some junket and their wives are left at home in Aldershot, where there are also a lot of single squaddies. Well, you can guess the rest, Harry.'

'Only too well, Jock,' I said, with feeling. 'Happens to coppers as well. But what's this got to do with my enquiry?'

'With Hockley's consent, we searched his married quarters. They're in Gort Road in Aldershot. It was all neat and tidy and looked as though his missus had decided to do a runner with someone else after all, although there was no note or anything like that.'

'Sounds like a straightforward domestic, Jock.'

'Aye, maybe, but knowing what we know about her, it may be a bit more sinister than that. We came across a secret address book belonging to her, carefully hidden away behind some storage jars on the top shelf of a kitchen cupboard. We've been checking through the addresses and telephone numbers, most of them local to Aldershot, and it looks as though it was her personal list of fancy men. We've made enquiries and some of these guys admitted to having had it off with her. But there was also a London phone number that went out to sixteen Crouch Road, Battersea. The subscriber to that number is a guy called—'

'Max Forbes,' I said.

'Aye, that's the fellow,' said Jock. 'I wonder, Harry, if you can have a word, see how well he knew Karen Hockley, and when was the last time he saw her. Or if he knew of a friendship between his wife and Karen Hockley. And, of course, if Forbes has any idea where she might have gone.'

'It'll be a pleasure, Jock. As a matter of interest, d'you know if this Hockley woman was into kinky sex?'

'Not as far as I know. Why, does this Forbes man go in for it?'

'Yes, him and his late wife. We found a load of gear in their cellar – restraints and whips, that sort of stuff – and Forbes has admitted that he and his wife used it. We also discovered that a rather gorgeous actress pops round to Max Forbes's place from time to time and whips him half to death. Funny old world, ain't it?'

'What does he do for a living, this guy?'

'He's an artist and runs an advertising agency.'

'Funny lot, artists,' said Jock mysteriously.

'Was there any evidence that Karen Hockley was bisexual?' I asked. 'Because I wouldn't put it past Alex to have been a two-way player.'

'Yes, according to her husband, she was. Mind you, Corporal Hockley's not entirely lily-white himself. I gave

111

him a sharp talking-to about wasting police time and he eventually admitted that he and Karen had sometimes done the old three-in-a-bed routine with another girl. But that's not all. After the last three-in-a-bed session there was a tremendous cat-fight. Karen broke the other woman's nose and knocked a couple of her teeth out. We've spoken to she of the broken nose, but she hadn't a clue where Karen had gone. Didn't care, either.'

'They sound a charming couple,' I said. 'Did you lift any fingerprints from Hockley's pad when you did your search?'

'Yes, but we don't know who most of them belong to, apart from Dan Hockley's of course. We're working our way through the address book and a few of the names in it had left their dabs at Gort Road. But we've still got some unaccounted for. There were a few identicals about the place that are most likely Karen's.'

'I've got a set of elimination prints from Max Forbes, Jock. I'll have them sent down. Oh, and I'll send down the other prints we lifted from Crouch Road and haven't been able to ID. Might be a tie-up.'

'Good, that might knock a few more off my list, and possibly yours. She certainly seemed to put herself about, this lassie.'

'I'm thinking on my feet here, Jock,' I said slowly, 'but if Alex Forbes had it off with your Karen Hockley, it might just be that Karen murdered her after some sort of lesbian spat and then did a runner.'

'Could be, Harry. We know Karen Hockley was a violent woman and I'm ruling nothing out. If you find her it might solve your job and mine.'

'OK, Jock, leave it with me. I was wondering what to do with my weekend.'

'Thanks, pal. Give my love to Helga.'

'Helga and I are divorced, Jock.'

'Oh, sorry to hear that.' And Jock ended the call without another word. Coppers know better than to pry. As some smart sergeant once said: *divorce in the force is a matter of course.*

Jock Ferguson was as good as his word. A couple of hours later a despatch rider from Aldershot arrived in my office with copies of the fingerprints lifted from the Hockley house, together with a recent photograph of Karen Hockley, a long-haired blonde. In return, I sent Jock copies of the prints taken from the Forbes house.

'She doesn't look unlike Alex Forbes, does she?' said Dave, after examining the photograph. 'I wonder if this is who Bill Griffin saw in Carfax Street.'

'We should be so lucky, Dave,' I said. But then I paused. 'Even so, it might not be a bad idea to show it to him. See if you can track him down, either at his houseboat or his studio. See what he says.'

By four o'clock that afternoon it was beginning to come together. Dave returned from seeing Griffin, who, predictably, had said it was possible that he'd mistaken Karen Hockley for Alex Forbes, but he was by no means sure. The woman he'd seen was certainly a blonde, but now with short hair. Dave's impression was that Griffin was even beginning to doubt that he'd seen an Alex Forbes lookalike at all. My own view was that both Alex Forbes and Karen Hockley looked like dozens of other women and that Griffin's 'sighting' was possibly wishful thinking.

For good measure, Dave had revisited the boutique in Carfax Street. But that got us no further forward. The staff said that the woman in the photograph might have been in their shop on the day Griffin thought he'd seen Alex, but they couldn't be sure.

Far more helpful, however, both from my point of view and Jock Ferguson's, was the positive ID that Fingerprint Branch had made. The prints Jock believed to be Karen Hockley's had been found at sixteen Crouch Road.

I rang Jock Ferguson at Aldershot and told him what we'd found. His glad news was that Alex Forbes's prints from Crouch

Road matched some of those found in the Hockley house.

So there we had it. Karen Hockley had visited sixteen Crouch Road, and Alex Forbes had been to the Hockleys' house in Gort Road, Aldershot. So what?

Karen Hockley's details had already been put on the Police National Computer and, with Jock's agreement, I now got Colin Wilberforce to add my name to the entry as a party interested in her whereabouts.

'And now, Dave,' I said, 'we'll have a heart-to-heart with Max Forbes.'

'Mr Forbes, I'd like you to take a look at this photograph,' I said, handing him the print of Karen Hockley.

For some moments, Forbes studied it. 'Beyond saying that she's a good-looking girl, Mr Brock, I can't say that I've ever seen her before. Why d'you ask? Is she connected in some way with the death of my wife?'

'I was hoping you could tell me. When we searched this house, her fingerprints were found here.' I was pretty sure they were her prints, but until we found her we couldn't be certain. 'She's called Karen Hockley, *Mrs* Karen Hockley. Does that name mean anything to you?'

'No, it doesn't, and I have to say I'm mystified. It's obvious from what you say that she's been here, but it must have been when I was out, because I've never seen her.'

'So, she must have been a friend of your wife.'

'That's the only possible answer, I suppose.' Forbes shook his head. 'Alex did have her own circle of friends, some of whom I never met.'

I realized that my next question was going to be a delicate one, and that it might well offend the late Alex Forbes's husband, but it had to be asked nevertheless. 'Was your wife bisexual?'

Max Forbes spent a few moments staring blankly at the empty fireplace and there was a long pause, a very long pause, before he answered. 'Yes, she was,' he said quietly. But then he hit back. 'But there's nothing wrong with that,' he added defensively.

114

'D'you think it's likely that she and this Karen Hockley had a sexual relationship?'

'It's possible, I suppose. I really couldn't say.'

'To your knowledge, did your wife ever go to Aldershot?'

Forbes raised his eyebrows in surprise. 'Aldershot? What on earth would she have wanted to go to Aldershot for?'

'Her fingerprints were found in a house there.'

'I suppose she may have gone there to value a property. The estate agents she worked for took in a fairly wide area when it came to expensive properties.'

'I don't think that's likely,' I said with a smile. 'The house your wife visited is an army married quarters.'

'Good God! I wasn't aware that she knew any army officers.'

'It was occupied by a Corporal Hockley and his wife Karen, the woman whose photograph I just showed you.'

You're not going to like that, Maxie, my old son, are you? And he didn't.

'A *corporal*!' Forbes was clearly outraged that his wife's prints had been found in the house of a corporal, and it seemed to shock him even more than having to admit that his wife had been bisexual. 'I can't believe that Alex would ever have consorted with a corporal,' he said.

I was tempted to point out to Max that he had consorted with an actress who beat hell out of him. Regularly. But now was not the time for smart remarks of that sort.

'There is no evidence that she had anything to do with Corporal Hockley,' I said. 'I think it more likely that the relationship was with Karen Hockley.'

'Maybe,' said Forbes, but he appeared unconvinced. 'Anyway, why all this interest in this corporal's wife?'

'She's been missing since about the end of June, Mr Forbes. It is possible that she and your wife went somewhere together – the day your wife left home – and that Karen Hockley was the person who murdered her.'

'I see. And you've no idea where this woman's gone?'

'None, I'm afraid. But we shall find her. Eventually.'

'I hope you do,' said Forbes. 'I want to see this terrible business cleared up so that I can get on with my life.'

The more I thought about it, the more I became convinced that there had been a relationship between Alex Forbes and Karen Hockley, and that there had been some sort of disagreement resulting in Alex's murder. We knew, from what Jock said, that Karen Hockley was not above using violence. And, if she had been the murderess, that would have been a very good reason for her to disappear.

There were a couple of things I needed to ask Jock Ferguson, things I should really have asked him at the outset.

I rang Aldershot police station. Jock was still at his desk.

I told him what we had learned so far, which, in all honesty, was precious little, but it was early days. At least as far as his enquiry was concerned.

'Jock, a couple of things. Did Karen Hockley have a car?'

'Yes, she did, Harry, but it went missing about the same time she did. Well, I imagine it did. The local lads have checked the streets in and around Aldershot and there's no sign of it. I've circulated it via the PNC but heard nothing. It's bound to turn up somewhere, I suppose. Trouble is that young coppers seem to walk around with their eyes shut these days. If they walk about at all. What was the other thing? You said there were a couple of things.'

'When you searched the Hockleys' house, did you come across any sado-masochism contact magazines?'

'I'm not sure. Give me a few minutes and I'll get one of my guys to check. Is it important?'

'I don't know, Jock, but I'm interested to know how a sophisticated London estate agent met up with a corporal's wife who lived in Aldershot.'

Jock Ferguson called back ten minutes later. 'Yes, Harry, there were some of those magazines, tucked away in Karen's wardrobe.'

'Well, Jock, I reckon that if we find Karen Hockley, we'll have solved your missing-person enquiry and my murder.'

Twelve

'What about putting that picture of Karen Hockley out, guv?' suggested Dave. 'You know, may be able to assist police in their enquiries.'

'Dave,' I began patiently, 'when you've been in the job as long as I have, you'll have discovered that that's one sure way of guaranteeing that the subject of such an appeal is going to run for cover, probably abroad.'

'Yeah, but there are passport controls, guv. Might catch her going out. Or coming in.'

'Enough of your jokes, Dave. When did you ever see an immigration officer paying any attention to British passports? Last time we came in from Paris, you may recall, we waved ours at the guy and he didn't even open them.'

'But he did say "Have a nice day",' said Dave. 'So what d'you suggest we do?'

'I think we'll have to leave it the way it is. Right now, I reckon Karen Hockley's roaming about somewhere without the faintest idea that we're desperately keen to have a chat with her. But if we put posters up outside every nick in the country, she'll take fright and do a runner.'

'It was only a suggestion,' said a somewhat disappointed Dave.

But, despite what I'd said to Dave, I knew that there might yet come a time when we had no alternative but to publish Karen Hockley's photograph. After all, looking for a thirty-year-old good-looking blonde who had chosen to lose herself was a needle-in-a-haystack job. Let's face it, there are hundreds of good-looking blondes about, although few seem to come my way.

'The postcards, guv.' Dave was occasionally given to making enigmatic statements like that.

'What about the postcards?'

'If Mr Ferguson can lay hands on a sample of Karen Hockley's handwriting, our tame graphologist just might come up with a positive comparison.'

Dave, you're an absolute bloody genius.

'Mmm! Not a bad idea, Dave. I'll give him a ring.'

'How's that going to help, Harry?' Jock asked when I'd explained what I wanted.

I told him about the postcards that had been sent from Belgium – ostensibly from Alex – to Max Forbes, Farrell, Griffin, Parish and the estate agent, Skinner, and maybe others we'd yet to trace. I also told him that the graphologist had ruled out the possibility that they had been written by Alex Forbes.

'And if they'd been written by Karen Hockley,' I continued, 'it might prove that she was in Belgium, and what's more, she may still be there. Not that I can think of a reason *why* she should have written them.'

'Take it as done, Harry,' said Jock. 'I'll speak to Karen's husband right now and see if I can get enough for your chap to work on. Her little black book might be sufficient,' he added with a chuckle. 'There's plenty of writing in that.'

Thanks to the *diktat* of that dream factory they call the Home Office, the police forces of this country are now 100 per cent budget-conscious. These days police officers are constantly punching calculators instead of catching criminals – when they're not filling out reams of useless and oft-duplicated forms – and to keep expenses down is far more important than suppressing crime. These unrealistic financial gymnastics affect not only the Metropolitan Police, but every other force as well. It is no wonder, therefore, that everyone from inspector up to our own dear commissioner – to say nothing of numerous chief constables – is in the running for an ulcer.

Being a Saturday, police officers are thinner on the ground than on weekdays, if you can believe that, and there were none to spare in Hampshire – without incurring overtime, that is – to do unimportant things like ferrying possibly crucial pieces of evidence in a murder case. As a result, the sample of Karen Hockley's handwriting came by a somewhat tortuous route: a traffic-division car from Aldershot handed it over to a Surrey traffic car at the border between the two constabularies, which in turn handed it on to a Metropolitan car at Kingston. Which gave it to another car at Wandsworth, which gave it to another car at Chelsea, which gave it . . .

But it got to me eventually. Hurrah!

You wouldn't think it was the twenty-first century, would you?

But Ferguson might just as well have sent it by post; graphologists don't work on Saturday afternoons. Well, they would, given the chance, but as it would cost an arm and a leg, it's definitely taboo even to suggest it.

I plucked a lengthy document – marked for my attention – out of Colin Wilberforce's in-tray and stared at it with a mixture of astonishment and disbelief. It was a discussion paper that had been floated by a team of brains at the Yard – masquerading as policemen – and sought opinions about the merits of recreating the Metropolitan Police Band.

I tossed it into the wastepaper basket. I really hadn't the time to consider whether such a proposal would be good for morale – it certainly wouldn't do anything for mine – or if a quick blast of 'A Policeman's Lot is not a Happy One' at football matches would make the yobs on the terraces start a love affair with the Old Bill.

'Dr Dawson on line three, sir,' said Colin Wilberforce.

'I'll take it in my office,' I said, wondering what Sarah could possibly want on a Saturday morning. She wasn't working today either. In fact, it seemed that only coppers turned out at the weekend in the great crusade against crime. And only those at the cutting edge: there was no sign of the commander. Thank God!

'What are you doing tomorrow, darling?' asked Sarah guardedly.

'What, setting aside any demands of the commissioner, unsolved murders and a mountain of paperwork, you mean?'

'Yes.' Sarah had long ago become accustomed to my cynicism. 'Setting all that aside.'

'In that case, nothing. Why d'you ask?'

Usually Sarah would suggest a visit to the theatre, dinner at our favourite bistro, or a take-away at her flat, straight out, without any pussyfooting about. I had an uneasy feeling that she had something not too attractive lined up.

'Er, David and Margaret have invited us to lunch,' Sarah said hesitantly. 'What d'you say?'

'Yeah, fine.' She'd got me. I couldn't come up with an excuse that fast, even though Staines was a place I wouldn't wish to go to on any day of the week, whatever the reason. I'd met Margaret, Sarah's sister, and her husband David, when they lived at Raynes Park, albeit briefly. I'd taken Sarah there one night after her flat in Battersea had been burgled. 'Subject to the usual caveat, of course.'

'Yes, I know. You might get called out,' Sarah said with a sigh of resignation. She had got used to our dates being cancelled at the last minute, but that's a risk a girl takes when she goes out with a CID officer.

'It happens,' I said. 'What time shall I pick you up?'

'How long will it take us to get to Staines?'

'It's about eighteen or twenty miles, I suppose. Better allow an hour, even though it's a Sunday. Half past eleven suit you?'

'See you then,' said Sarah.

It was an incredibly boring day. We arrived at just after half past twelve, and lunch was nowhere near ready.

Margaret was a plain, pleasant-enough girl, but she was neither a good cook nor a capable housekeeper: the house was a tip. And she was nothing like her sister in looks, character or efficiency. We eventually got lunch at gone three in the afternoon. Conversation was impossible: the Gibsons' two children, aged six and four, were constantly interrupting and generally running riot.

Margaret's husband, David, an air-traffic controller at West Drayton, was a humourless, carping little man. He spent most of the time we were there breathing on his spectacles and polishing them, and complaining about his job: the stress, the unsocial hours and the poor pay.

I refused to sympathize; this guy didn't know when he'd got it good. But then he threw in one or two barbed comments about the generosity of police pensions, a subject guaranteed to get me going. I pointed out that the police contributed 11 per cent of their salary towards their pensions, and suggested that if he wanted to improve his, he should do the same. That shut him up and we parted the best of enemies.

It was at Sarah's instigation that we left as soon as was politely possible, but even then it was almost seven o'clock. Most of the way back to Battersea she was apologizing for having inflicted such an awful day on me.

'Don't worry, darling,' I said, placing a hand on her knee. 'To quote a well-known phrase, one can pick one's friends but not one's relatives.'

'I'm so sorry, Harry. I shouldn't have asked you to come with me,' Sarah said, continuing with her sackcloth-and-ashes routine. 'It was an awful thing to do to you on your day off.'

I laughed. 'It's all right.'

'I really don't know why she married him. I can't stand him, and our parents don't like him either. She met him at some tennis-club dance, and, to be honest, I think it was the first time a man had paid any attention to her. So, when he asked her to marry him, that was that.' As we approached her Battersea flat, Sarah shot a sideways glance at me. 'Would you like to stay the night?' she asked.

I imagined it was her idea of making it up to me for inflicting her family on me, but I didn't think it was a good idea. Not for that reason anyway.

'Much as I'd love to,' I said, 'I've got an early start in the morning.' I hadn't, of course.

On Monday morning the support services of the Metropolitan Police awoke from their weekend reverie, and I sent the sample of handwriting across to the graphologist with a request for an urgent analysis.

Two hours later I got the answer. The handwriting on the postcards was definitely not that of Karen Hockley. And that meant we still didn't know whose it was.

Back to square one.

It was after lunch that I made a decision, a rarity for me, but then I am a senior officer, and senior officers are, by nature, disinclined to make decisions. Wait long enough and the need for a decision will be overtaken by events. But not this time. 'I think we'll go to Aldershot, Dave,' I said.

'That'll be nice, sir,' said Dave, as he pointedly glanced at the clock. He obviously visualized another late night. 'What for?'

'I think it's time that we had a chat, face to face, with this Corporal Hockley. If Mr Ferguson can arrange it.'

I picked up the phone. I think Dave was hoping he wouldn't be there.

Jock Ferguson promised to ring me back within minutes. And did so.

'That's it,' I said, as I replaced the receiver. 'Hockley's at home and Mr Ferguson will meet us at Aldershot nick and take us out there.'

The drab house in Gort Road was, Jock Ferguson assured me, a typical army quarters. It was furnished adequately if unimaginatively and the only variation from all the other quarters in the road was, I imagined, the few personal ornaments and knick-knacks, and the make of television and hi-fi. There again, perhaps not.

Dan Hockley was a squat, muscular individual, about

five-ten with closely cropped hair. He also had a broken nose, but that might have been the result of a fight he'd had with one of his wife's paramours, rather than an engagement with one of Her Majesty's enemies.

'I know that Mr Ferguson has spoken to you about the disappearance of your wife, Mr Hockley—'

'It's *Corporal* Hockley, sir.'

'As you wish, and you don't have to call me "sir". I'm not in the army, I'm a policeman. However, as I was saying, I know that Mr Ferguson's spoken to you, but I'd like to hear it from you.' I knew that Jock wouldn't be offended by my asking for a repetition. It's the way detectives work: get the story first-hand.

Nevertheless the corporal's account accorded exactly with what Jock had told me, including the fight that had lost Hockley his third stripe, and he even admitted that his wife was bisexual. And added the gratuitous information that, in his opinion, she was a slag. I wondered why he was so worried about her disappearance; it struck me that he'd be better off without her.

'How often did you have sexual intercourse with Alex Forbes?' I asked confidently, as though I knew this to be the case. Which I didn't.

Hockley's mouth opened and closed, and then a sort of stunned how-the-hell-did-you-know-that expression crossed his face. But he didn't answer.

'Corporal Hockley, I should make it clear to you that my interest in the disappearance of your wife is confined to any connection it may have with my investigation into the murder of Alex Forbes. In the circumstances, I advise you to tell me the truth.'

'You're not saying that you think Karen—'

'I'm not saying anything yet,' I said. 'Just answer the question, please.'

'Only once,' said Hockley eventually.

'And when was that?'

After some thought, Hockley said, 'About the beginning of May, I think. It was just before I was posted to Belize.'

'And it was just the once that you had sex with her, was it?' I wanted to get that perfectly clear.

'Yes, just the once.'

'Why was that? Didn't you fancy her too much?'

There was a long pause before Hockley answered. 'She said she didn't want to do it with me again.' There was a further pause, but eventually he made an admission that must have been very difficult for a macho soldier of his type. 'She said I was no good at it.'

Oh dear! So poor old Hockley had also joined the swelling ranks of Alex Forbes's inadequate lovers.

'Was your wife here at the time?'

'Yes.'

Interesting, but not surprising.

'And what did she think about you banging Mrs Forbes, Corporal Hockley? Cause another fight, did it?'

'No.'

'She didn't mind then, is that it?'

'She bloody well joined in,' retorted Hockley savagely, giving me an unforgiving look. 'And Alex said that Karen satisfied her more than I did. The bloody cow.'

I wasn't sure whether he meant Alex or Karen. Not that it mattered. 'And how often did Alex's husband Max come here?' I asked, making yet another assumption.

'Never, as far as I know. Anyway, I never met the guy,' said Hockley. 'In fact, until you called her *Mrs* Forbes just now I didn't know she was married. Well, I thought she might have been divorced.'

'Did the three of you – you, your wife and Alex – ever engage in any sort of deviant sex? You know the sort of thing: whips and bondage. Anything like that.'

'Not while I was here.'

I didn't believe him, but he probably thought it was illegal, which technically it was. For what it was worth, he was later proved to have been lying.

'Did Alex Forbes come here while you were away?'

Hockley shrugged. 'Possibly. I don't know. We was posted

to Belize on the fifteenth of May. What happened after that is anyone's guess.'

'Did you ever go to Battersea?' Dave asked.

Hockley glanced at Dave, as if noticing him for the first time. 'Battersea? Why should I want to go there, Sarge?'

'To see Alex Forbes?' Dave tapped his teeth with his pen.

'I told you, she said she didn't want nothing more to do with me.'

'Did your wife ever go there, then?' We both knew from the fingerprint evidence that Karen had visited the Forbeses' home, but Dave was obviously doing a bit of cross-checking.

'Haven't the faintest,' said Hockley. 'I don't know what she got up to after I went.'

And there we left it. Corporal Hockley was a bit of a thicko, but I thought he'd been telling us the truth. More or less. Certainly he wasn't in the frame for the murder of Alex Forbes. She'd been sighted after he went abroad. But then a thought crossed my mind as we drove back to Aldershot police station.

'Jock,' I said, 'do we know for certain that Hockley left for Belize on the fifteenth of May?'

'I've not confirmed it, Harry, but we can soon check.' Jock changed direction and five minutes later drew up at the headquarters of the Royal Military Police detachment in Queen's Avenue. 'We'll get the RMP to find out for us,' he said. 'They'll know exactly who to ask, and it'll save us running around in circles.'

Jock introduced us to a military police captain and explained the problem. One phone call later, the captain told us that Hockley's unit had gone abroad on the fifteenth of May. And Hockley was with them.

'Captain,' said Dave. 'When we entered the army's bit of Aldershot, we were stopped by some of your chaps.'

'Of course,' said the MP captain. 'We're on a high state of alert at the moment because of the terrorist threat.'

'And they also noted our car number on a clipboard. At least, I presume that's what they were doing.'

'Correct. My NCOs take details of all vehicles entering Aldershot Military Town. Why d'you ask?'

It was then that Dave posed a question that was to have quite an effect on the course of our enquiry.

He leaned across the military police officer's desk and wrote a couple of car numbers on his pad. 'Can you tell me if either of those cars recently came through one of your checkpoints?'

'Shouldn't be too difficult. We've got all this information on computer and we keep it for ages.' The captain made another phone call and moments later gave us the answer. 'Yes. The first vehicle entered Queen's Avenue on two occasions: on Sunday the fifth of May at fourteen twenty hours, and again on Monday the twentieth of May at nineteen fifteen hours, each time it contained a female driver, but no passengers. The second vehicle was noted going through on Friday the twelfth of July at eleven hundred hours. There were two people in it: a female driver and a male passenger. But we don't have details of the identities of any of them, I'm afraid. We don't record that information unless there's something suspicious about the vehicle.'

Dave glanced at me with a triumphant expression. 'The first two sightings were of Alex Forbes's Ford Focus, guv,' he said, 'and the second one was her Mercedes.' And, putting away his pocketbook, he added, 'I reckon that Alex Forbes was a bloody sex maniac.'

'Took you a long time to work that out, Dave,' I said.

Thirteen

On Tuesday morning, I sat at my desk and wondered which way the enquiry into Alex Forbes's death was going to turn next. The information that her car had been through the Aldershot checkpoint on three occasions – once with a male passenger – wasn't necessarily proof that she'd been to the Hockleys' quarters in Gort Road, or even that she had been the woman driving it.

Assuming that it was her, however, and given the number of men who had, so far, admitted to an affair with her, the man in the car could have been just about anyone. But I decided to start with the usual suspects, as we say in the constabulary business.

And, as if that wasn't enough, Jock telephoned me that morning to say that Corporal Hockley had gone absent without leave.

'How can he have done?' I asked. 'He was on compassionate leave. I know the army's a strange organization, but you can't go absent without leave when you're already on leave, surely to God.'

'His leave expired yesterday, Harry. Apparently the army made an arbitrary decision that his wife had left him and he didn't qualify for any more compassionate leave. He was ordered to report back at first parade this morning, but he never showed up. They went round to his quarters and he'd gone.'

'Perhaps he went out for cigarettes, or a newspaper,' I suggested.

'No, he didn't,' said Jock with a chuckle. 'They got the

quartermaster to open up his house, just in case he'd topped himself, I suppose. There was a note on the kitchen table, addressed to his commanding officer, saying that he'd gone to look for his wife and would be back when he'd found her. At the bottom of the note he'd written "Don't wait up". Cheeky bugger. Apparently the colonel's going ballistic. Hockley's car was gone, too, so I've circulated it on the PNC. You never know, some copper might be wide awake enough to spot it.'

'Terrific!' I said, and wondered whether Hockley's desertion was in some tenuous way connected with the murder of Alex Forbes. I was not convinced that he'd gone looking for his wife, not after the way in which he'd bad-mouthed her.

'Well, you've got to laugh, haven't you?' said Jock, his policeman's black humour kicking in.

I put the phone down and turned to Dave. 'Hockley's bloody well deserted, would you believe. Left a note saying he'd gone to look for his wife.'

Dave slowly dissected an orange. 'Perhaps he knows where she is, guv,' he said thoughtfully. 'She could have telephoned Belize in a panic and told him she'd done Alex in. So, he spins his colonel some fanny about her going adrift and gets sent home on compassionate. On the other hand, he might just have got fed up with Belize and fancied a few home comforts.'

'Thanks a bundle, Dave. But, setting aside that unlikely reason, why would Karen Hockley want to top Alex anyway? That's the one thing for which there doesn't really seem to be a motive.'

'Whole load of reasons, guv.' Dave put a segment of orange in his mouth and spat a pip into the wastepaper basket.

I decided that a conversation with Madeleine about Dave's orange fetish was well overdue.

'Such as?'

'Hockley told us his missus was a two-way operator and, according to Max Forbes, so was Alex. So, let's take a for-instance. Suppose Karen didn't fancy Alex any longer – assuming she did in the first place – but that Alex was threatening her in some way to carry on with their lesbian affair. Maybe she only liked it when it was part of a three-in-a-bed caper, and we know that happened, because her licentious soldier husband told us so. Maybe she only had it off with Alex the once, to rile the bold corporal. Don't forget that Alex told Hockley he was a bloody useless performer and that she preferred his wife. Supposing that Karen doesn't want to go solo with Alex, but Alex won't take no for an answer, there's a fight and Karen tops her.'

'Possible, I suppose,' I said, but I had reservations.

'On the other hand,' Dave continued, casting his orange peel into the wastepaper basket, 'Karen might have topped her because she didn't like being tied up and whipped.'

'If that actually happened, Dave.'

'We don't know it didn't, guv, and, let's face it, Alex had form for it, a lot of form. But we also know that Karen Hockley was a violent woman. Don't forget what Mr Ferguson told us about her, that she had a fight with another woman, broke her nose and knocked a few of her teeth out. So, she may have enjoyed getting her own back by laying into Alex. One day it goes too far and, oh dear, Alex has snuffed it.'

'But why take the body all the way to Richmond Park to dump it?'

'Why not?' said Dave laconically.

I don't know why I listened to Dave. I usually finished up being more depressed than when he started. But I had to admit that, as far as motives went, the one he'd just propounded wasn't a bad one.

However, I suppose I'm rapidly becoming a staid old copper, disinclined to go off on some wild goose chase. *Stay with what you've got, Brock.*

'Be that as it may, Dave, we'll start by talking to Parish once more, see if he can account for the days he was away, and then we'll talk to Max Forbes again, because he could have been the bloke who travelled to Aldershot with Alex on the twelfth of July.'

'Or it could have been Farrell or Griffin or Morton or Ryan or Simpson,' commented Dave drily.

We rang Parish's doorbell three times before a breathless Conchita opened the door. She was wearing a bikini and her long Titian hair was dripping wet.

'Hello,' she said brightly. 'Misser Parish in water. Come.'

Conchita displayed no sign of embarrassment at being so scantily attired, and she turned and walked confidently across the hall towards the passageway that led to the pool.

'Cor!' said Dave quietly.

'Policemen come some more,' Conchita yelled at Parish. He might have been in the water when she left him, but now he was lying on one of the recliners that were ranged along the side of the pool.

Her immediate duties at an end, Conchita stretched out on a wheeled lounger some feet away from Parish, closed her eyes and appeared to take no further interest in us.

'Good God!' said Parish. 'Don't you chaps ever give up?'

'Not when we're investigating a murder, Mr Parish,' I said.

'You mean you haven't caught him yet?'

'Who says it was a "him"?'

'Ah! A woman, perhaps?'

'Have you ever been to Aldershot?' I asked.

'Certainly not. It sounds an awful place. Why d'you ask?'

'Just something that came up in the course of our enquiries.'

'What, something that suggested *I'd* been there?'

'Not necessarily, but we know that a man accompanied Alex Forbes to Aldershot on the twelfth of July in the Mercedes that you bought for her.'

'The saucy little bitch. Well, it wasn't me, old boy.'

'Where were you on that date, Mr Parish?'

'God knows. Want me to check my diary again?' Without waiting for a reply, Parish swung himself off his recliner and strode out. Minutes later he returned, holding his large desk diary. 'Here all day. Ask Conchita.'

Apart from the fact that neither Dave nor I spoke Spanish, I was fairly certain that Parish's live-in lover-cum-house-keeper would corroborate his claim not to have ventured forth from Hampstead. I gave up on that one.

'I think you have some questions to ask Mr Parish, Sergeant,' I said, glancing at Dave.

'Yes, sir,' said Dave. 'Mr Parish, when we spoke to you last, you said that you were here between the sixteenth of July and the sixth of August, apart from one day when you went to London to see your solicitor.'

'What of it?'

'But you weren't, were you? In fact, you were away from home between the nineteenth and the twenty-fifth of July.'

'Who the hell told you that?' For some seconds Parish stared at Dave.

Dave just stared back.

'Is there some significance in those dates?' Parish asked.

'Depends where you were,' said Dave, adroitly avoiding Parish's question.

'In Paris.'

'On business?'

Parish glanced across at Conchita. 'How about some tea?'

Conchita opened her eyes and looked at Parish. '*Qué?*'

I glanced at Dave, who was doing his best to suppress a laugh. 'I never believed that Spanish-speakers really said that,' he muttered.

'Tea,' said Parish loudly, and then made a dumb charade out of drinking from an invisible cup.

'Ah, tea, *si.*' Comprehension dawning at last, Conchita stood up and, doubtless aware that she was being watched by three pairs of lecherous male eyes, walked provocatively towards where I imagined the kitchen to be.

'Was it on business?' Dave repeated his question.

'No, as a matter of fact I spent a long weekend there with a girlfriend. But Conchita thinks I went on business. No sense in upsetting the girl. She might give notice. As I said before, she's no bloody good at housework, but there are other duties she performs exquisitely.' Parish shot us a lascivious grin.

'I presume you can substantiate that claim,' persisted Dave. 'About being in Paris, I mean.'

'If I have to, but so far you've given me no reason why I should. If you care to disprove it, then we'll talk again, eh?'

And there we left it. Once again the tea arrived too late.

I was rapidly tiring of Max Forbes. In fact, I was inclining more and more to the theory that it was he who had murdered Alex. But although gut instinct may sway a jury, it would take more than that to convince the Crown Prosecution Service, and even more to persuade a judge that there was a case to answer.

Nevertheless, it was a fact that every piece of information we'd obtained from him had had to be forced out, and some of that – the trip to the Black Forest nudist camp, for instance – had not been substantiated.

'What is it this time?' There was a tired resignation in Forbes's greeting, but an air of nervousness about him too. He walked into his sitting room leaving Dave to shut the front door.

Just for a change, I decided to let Dave question him. 'When were you last in Aldershot, Mr Forbes?' he asked without any preamble.

'Aldershot? I've never been to Aldershot. What a curious question. Why d'you ask?' Forbes sat up, a little straighter than he had been before. 'Ah!' he said, suddenly making the connection. 'It's to do with that girl you asked me about. What was her name? Hoskins, was it?'

'Hockley, Karen Hockley,' said Dave.

'Yes. The woman you say murdered my wife.'

'We didn't say that she'd murdered your wife, Mr Forbes,' said Dave. 'We said that it was one of the possibilities we were considering.'

'So you did, but is this to do with her?'

Dave never answered a witness's questions, and didn't do so now. 'On Friday the twelfth of July, at eleven a.m., Mrs Forbes's car was seen in Aldershot. There was a man in the passenger seat. Was that man you, Mr Forbes?'

'No, it most certainly was not. It was probably one of her fancy men. Why don't you ask Farrell? I believe she slept with him more often than with anyone else.' Forbes was beginning to get ratty now. Or was it rattled? It was useful having Dave ask the questions: it gave me a chance to study the man's reactions.

'Were there others, then, apart from Mr Farrell?' Dave raised his eyebrows and looked all innocent, despite our having previously told Forbes that we knew of others. But he'd obviously forgotten, or was now choosing not to remember.

'Probably. I told you, my wife and I didn't have a sexual relationship.' Forbes glanced pointedly at his watch. 'Is this going to take much longer?' he asked.

'Supposing I was to tell you that we have proof that you had a sexual relationship with Karen Hockley, Mr Forbes,' I said, 'both here and in Aldershot. What would you say to that?' There was absolutely no foundation in the allegation – even though it was, in my mind, a strong possibility – but I was interested to see what his response would be.

Forbes laughed. 'I'd ask you to produce that proof, Chief Inspector. At the risk of repeating myself, I've never met the woman. I didn't even know of her existence until you mentioned her name last time you were here.' Then he decided to go on the offensive. 'Look, I appreciate that you have a job to do, but I'm getting a little weary of these constant questions. It's almost as if you suspect me of murdering my wife.'

'Why should you think that?' I asked.

'Because you keep on asking questions about me, and *my* personal life, rather than Alex's.'

'The investigation of a murder is a complex matter, Mr

Forbes,' I said, 'and if we are to find the killer we have to ask questions of all manner of people. Including the bereaved. I'm sorry, but there it is.'

'Well, it strikes me that you're not getting very far. It's a fortnight since Alex's body was found, but you seem no nearer catching her murderer than when you started.'

You're dead right there, sport. We're floundering.

'That's how it may appear to you, Mr Forbes, but I assure you, we are making progress.'

'It doesn't seem like it,' said Forbes. 'All you've done so far is to ask me about my sex life.'

'You went to the Black Forest on the seventeenth of July and returned a fortnight later, I believe you said.' Although Dave had referred to his pocketbook, I knew it was a ploy. He was sufficiently conversant with the details of the case not to have to refresh his memory.

'That's correct. But why are we going over all this again?'

'Is there anyone who can verify that?'

'I doubt it. There was a woman—' Max Forbes suddenly stopped what he was saying, obviously regretting having mentioned her.

'Yes, Mr Forbes? A woman?'

'I met a Frenchwoman in the second week I was there and we got to know each other, that's all.' It was a reluctant admission.

'And her name?'

Forbes chuckled. 'She said her name was Françoise Garnier, but I don't think it was. People tend to use a *nom d'emprunt* at nudist colonies.'

'A what?' asked Dave, raising his eyebrows and slipping into his stupid-policeman mode.

'An assumed name.' Forbes smiled condescendingly as he translated the French.

Well done, Dave. Let him think you're a bit of a dimbo.

'This sighting of Mrs Forbes's car.' Dave did not intend to let the matter drop. 'Were you aware that your wife went to Aldershot on that day?'

'What was the date again?'

'The twelfth of July.'

Forbes shrugged. 'I really have no idea. As I've said many times, my wife and I tended to lead separate lives. She did her own thing and I did mine.' He glanced at his watch again. 'Now, unless there's anything else . . .'

'No, not for the moment, Mr Forbes,' I said, as Dave and I stood up.

As we drove away from Max Forbes's house towards Lavender Hill, Dave said, 'Well, we didn't get much out of him, guv. Not that I expected to.'

We stopped at the junction as a Ford Focus turned into Crouch Road.

'Hello,' said Dave. 'That's Alex's old car, and Sydney Gill's driving it. It looks as though Max's business arrangement with her isn't over. No wonder he kept looking at his watch.'

'I've just thought of another question I want to ask him,' I said, more out of devilment than the need to garner further evidence, which I knew we wouldn't get anyway. 'Give it quarter of an hour and we'll go back.'

We parked in the yard of Lavender Hill nick for fifteen minutes and then returned to Crouch Road.

The door of number sixteen was eventually opened by Sydney Gill wearing an all-embracing, scarlet satin robe.

'Oh my God, it's you!' As her hands flew to her face in a gesture combining embarrassment with surprise, the robe fell open to reveal a tightly fitting, black latex swimsuit. I presumed it was her working gear; it was certainly more attractive than the power-dressing of your average businesswoman.

'Yes, Miss Gill, it's us,' I said. 'Is Mr Forbes available?'

There was a brief moment of restraint before Sydney Gill dissolved into a fit of the giggles. 'I'm afraid he's tied up at the moment, Chief Inspector,' she said.

Dave turned rapidly and retreated to the car, his shoulders shaking.

'Perhaps we'll come back another time,' I said, keeping my face as straight as possible, 'but do tell him we called.'

Who said that policemen don't have a sense of humour?

But, joking apart, I had just thought of something. 'Are you likely to be at home tomorrow, Miss Gill?'

'Yes. Why?'

'I've a few questions with which you may be able to assist me.'

'OK. Drop in any time you like,' she said, and smiled. 'I've nothing on tomorrow.'

With some regret, I came to the conclusion that she wasn't speaking literally.

Fourteen

Sydney Gill was more formally dressed when we called at her Wandsworth house on Wednesday morning, and made no reference to our meeting the previous evening.

'Come in,' she said. 'I'm just making some tea if you'd like some.'

We settled in Miss Gill's sitting room and waited while she busied herself in her small kitchenette.

'Now, what can I do to help?' she asked, dispensing tea and eventually seating herself opposite us.

'This is a serious question,' I began, so that there would be no misunderstanding, 'but can you tell me exactly how you restrain Max Forbes on that apparatus of his?'

As far as Sydney was concerned, this was obviously a commercial matter and there was no trace of levity as she described how she undertook her 'business arrangement' with Forbes.

'Sure. I think I told you that he'd got an X-shaped frame thing at his house,' she said.

I nodded in agreement. 'Yes, I've seen it.'

'Well, he sets that up in the sitting room and I secure him to it by his wrists and ankles, with straps. He's naked, of course, except for the leather mask he insists on wearing.'

'Go on.'

'Actually, it's a hood. It goes right over his head with just holes for his eyes and mouth. The hood is held in place by a leather strap that is buckled round his neck and is then linked by chains to the uprights so that the head can't be moved. There are some crazy people about, aren't there?'

'And how wide is this strap?'

Sydney thought about that for a moment. 'About two inches wide, I should think.'

For the next five minutes, we made desultory conversation while we finished our tea, and then I stood up. 'Thank you, Miss Gill,' I said, shaking hands with her. 'You've been very helpful. And thank you for the tea.'

'Is that all?' She seemed surprised that we'd come all this way just to ask one question.

'Yes, that's all.'

'What was that all about, guv?' Dave asked, on the way back to Curtis Green. He appeared as puzzled as Sydney Gill had been.

'It sounds to me very much as though the restraining strap on the hood that Sydney mentioned could have been the ligature – as Henry Mortlock insists on calling it – that strangled Alex Forbes. Now, I don't know whether the laboratory can retrieve any evidence from Forbes's load of sick apparatus, but I'm going to have a go. We'll get a warrant and seize it. Or rather, you'll get a warrant.'

'Thanks, guv,' said Dave.

When we arrived back at Curtis Green there was a message waiting for me.

'Would you ring Superintendent Ferguson at Aldershot, sir,' said Colin Wilberforce.

'What's on your mind, Jock?' I asked, once I'd been put through to his office.

'Hockley's been arrested, Harry,' Jock said. 'He got as far as Guildford, jumped a red light and was nicked by Surrey traffic officers.'

'Have you spoken to him yet?'

'No, I've only just heard about it from Surrey. I think I told you that I'd put him on the PNC. They rang me direct.'

'Where is Hockley now?'

There was a chuckle from the other end of the phone.

'Banged up in a guardroom here in Aldershot. By the way, just on the off chance, I got the military to give me the note that Hockley left for his commanding officer. It's on its way to you now, in case the handwriting means anything in connection with your postcards.'

When it arrived, I had the note sent straight across to the lab with a request for an urgent comparison. But the graphologist's initial report merely served to confuse things further. He was of the opinion that the postcards from Ostend – that we originally thought Alex Forbes had written – could *possibly* have been written by Dan Hockley. Experts never commit themselves further than to say 'possibly'.

I rang Jock back and told him the result, and then floated the idea that somehow or another this leery soldier had managed to send postcards from Belgium at the same time that he was supposedly in Belize. Or had got someone to do it for him. But who? And why?

'I suppose there was no way he could have gone AWOL from Belize and finished up in Belgium, is there, Jock?'

'I'll check, Harry, although I very much doubt it. But, even if he did, how the hell would he have got from Belize to Belgium? It's thousands of miles away and it'd cost an arm and a leg. Certainly more than a corporal could afford. Anyway, I think the army would've noticed if he wasn't there.'

Jock didn't waste any time. An hour later he came back with the answer. Hockley had definitely been in Belize for the whole period from the fifteenth of May until his return on compassionate leave on the eighth of August. Two days after we'd found Alex Forbes's body in Richmond Park.

'The postcards must have been forged, then,' said Dave, as he peeled yet another orange.

'Thanks for that profound assessment, Dave,' I said.

But Dave was right, which left me in somewhat of a quandary, but only a slight one.

Should we rush off to Aldershot and interview Hockley again, or get a warrant and seize Forbes's sado-masochism equipment?

I decided that as Hockley was in custody – and probably wouldn't have anything to tell us anyway – he could wait. On the other hand, as Dave had pointed out, and Jock Ferguson had more or less confirmed, the postcards must be forgeries, and right now the only person I could think of with the necessary skills was the artist Max Forbes. But I wasn't going to put that to him yet. One step at a time.

Dave went to South-Western Court and obtained a search warrant for Max Forbes's house at Crouch Road.

We waited until six o'clock that evening to execute the warrant, because I wanted Max Forbes to be present when we seized his property. It's very easy for a suspect to deny ownership subsequent to a search if he wasn't there at the time, and I intended to make sure that no allegations of planting evidence were going to foul up my investigation. We'd been messing about for long enough, but now I was beginning to see daylight. *Or was I just fooling myself?*

It was immediately apparent that Sydney Gill had mentioned to Forbes that we'd returned the previous day, and he looked distinctly embarrassed when we turned up again.

'Yes?'

'I'd like to have another look at the equipment you use, Mr Forbes,' I said.

'So, Sydney Gill's been shooting her mouth off again, has she?' Forbes snapped angrily. 'Well, I'm afraid that's not possible. What I do in my spare time and in my own home is a personal matter, and I'm fed up with your prurient interest in my private life.'

'I have a search warrant and I shall seize anything I perceive to be evidential,' I said, handing him an official document. 'That's your copy.'

Without a word, Forbes snatched it and turned on his heel.

'It would save time, yours as well as mine, if you produced the leather hood you wear when you're indulging your fantasies, Mr Forbes,' I said, catching up with him in the hall.

140

Still saying nothing, Forbes led us down to the cellar and, opening a suitcase, took out a leather hood. 'There, satisfied?' he demanded, handing it over.

'Is this the only one you possess?'

'Yes. What d'you want it for, anyway?'

'Scientific tests, Mr Forbes.' But I wasn't going to tell him the reason that lay behind those proposed tests. I gave the hood to Dave. 'Bag it up, Sergeant,' I said.

On Thursday morning, Dave and I took the hood to the laboratory at Lambeth to make sure that the scientists there got their skates on. We'd wasted enough time on this enquiry and, now that I had the germ of an idea, I didn't want to waste any more. I also rang Henry Mortlock, the pathologist, and pleaded with him to join us so that he could be present when the hood was examined.

Even so, I had to wait until after lunch for the report.

A preliminary examination, the report said – forensic scientists always talk of the *preliminary* examination, just in case they're later proved to be wrong – showed that the leather strap with which the hood was secured *might* have been the strap that suffocated Alex Forbes. Regrettably there was nothing identifiable on it that would connect it with Alex, apart from the scientist's grudging admission that the dimensions were about the same as the marks found on her neck.

But the crucial piece of evidence, a piece that gave me a glimmer of hope, was that they had also found that a DNA analysis of a human hair caught up in the interior stitching of the hood matched a sample taken from Alex Forbes's head.

I leaned back in my chair with a self-satisfied expression on my face. 'Well, how about that, Dave?' I said, having given him time to read the report.

'So what, guv?' Dave slung me a Silk Cut. He'd obviously given up trying to give up smoking. I'd have a word with Madeleine, but I was in no position to criticize: I couldn't seem to summon the willpower to give up either.

'What d'you mean, so what?'

'What does it prove? We know that Alex Forbes was into this flogging lark, so she probably wore the hood when it was her turn. That would account for the hair. As for the post-mortem marks on Alex's throat, the report only says they *may* be a match with the strap on the hood.'

'Yeah, well, it's good enough for me, Dave. I think we'll have him in and see what he's got to say for himself in more formal surroundings, like Lavender Hill nick. For one thing, he said that he and his wife went their separate ways – and he said it several times – but he later admitted that he and Alex both used the equipment. But did they use it on each other? We know that he employs Sydney Gill to give him a thrashing. But he said that he had to "buy it", by which I presume he meant that he had to pay for the services that his wife refused to provide. And maybe his wife got someone else to give her a hiding when Max wasn't there. I tell you, Dave, Forbes's story is full of inconsistencies.'

'So, when do we do this?' asked Dave, glancing at the clock. It was five past six.

'No time like the present.'

'We won't get a warrant at this time of night, not without finding a beak at his home.'

'Don't need one, Dave. We'll nick him on suspicion of murder.'

'*Vox clamantis in deserto,*' said Dave.

'And what the hell does that mean?' I asked.

'The voice of one crying in the wilderness,' said Dave smugly.

'I thought it was English you studied at university,' I rejoined, somewhat testily.

'Yeah, but you've got to know a bit of Latin. It's one of the root languages of English . . . sir.'

'Smart-arse,' I said.

It didn't work out that easily though. But in my experience of sixteen years in the CID, things rarely work out easily.

Oh, if only I was a television cop. All done and dusted in fifty minutes. Two hours at best.

For once we were able to park right outside Max Forbes's house. We hammered on the door but, as coppers are prone to say, there was no answer to repeated knockings.

We went next door, to the Madisons' house at number eighteen. George Madison answered the door.

'I'm looking for Max Forbes,' I said. 'I don't suppose you happen to know where he is?'

'No, I don't,' said Madison. 'Well, not exactly.'

'Not exactly?'

'About an hour ago, Stella saw him putting a suitcase into his car, and then he drove off. Is there anything I can help with?'

'No, there's not, Mr Madison, and thank you.'

'What d'you reckon, guv?' asked Dave, when we were back in the car.

'The bastard's done a runner,' I said.

'Guilty knowledge,' said Dave. It was another of his profundities. 'But didn't he say that he didn't own a car?'

'Yes, he did. But Madison told us he owned a Toyota.'

'Forbes is a congenital liar,' said Dave.

'Where did you learn a word like that, Dave?' I asked. It was a joke question. I knew that he had a degree in English.

'From Madeleine, guv. She's very well educated is Madeleine.' Dave could make jokes too.

I had grown tired of the whole bloody business. I rang Sarah on my mobile and she told me to come round. And bring a take-away. I sent Dave away with the car, dropped into a Chinese and walked round to Sarah's flat bearing succulent goodies.

I don't know if Chinese food possesses any aphrodisiac qualities, but I stayed the night.

I was a little late in arriving at the office on Friday morning. And it was just my luck that the commander was already in the incident room, parading about like a tin Jesus on wheels, peering at photographs and thumbing through messages as though he understood what they all meant. To the restrained annoyance of Colin Wilberforce, who hated anyone – me included – messing about with the ordered routine of his office.

'Ah, Mr Brock, good morning,' said the commander, looking pointedly at the clock. 'I just popped in to see how the Forbes enquiry was going.'

I signed the duty book – with the correct time – and gave the commander a thumbnail sketch of the progress of the enquiry so far. It didn't need more than a thumbnail.

'So, you think that this Max Forbes may be a suspect, do you?'

'That's the way I'm thinking at the moment, sir, yes. The fact that he took off in a car he denied owning shortly after we'd seized the leather hood is enough for me to wonder why.'

'I'm sorry, I don't follow the significance of this hood you're talking about.'

I repeated the details of the lab report.

'But if he and his wife practised this, er, sexual deviance' – the commander sniffed – 'it makes sense that a hair of her head would be found in a hood that they used, surely.'

I really hadn't the time to explain the finer details of the investigation – to say nothing of the twists and turns – to this pseudo-detective. 'Trust me, sir. I hope to have a result very shortly.'

God Almighty, did I just say that?

'Good, good. Well, keep me posted, Mr Brock.'

And with that the commander left us in peace, doubtless to seek solace in his pile of paperwork. The commander was very good at paperwork.

'First of all, we put Max Forbes on the PNC,' I said to Dave.

'What, to be nicked?'

'No, to locate but not to question. I don't want him to think he's in the frame.'

144

'Or even strapped to it,' observed Dave drily. 'But I think he thinks that already. Otherwise, why's he done a runner?'

'Perhaps to get away from us.'

'I just said that, sir,' said Dave.

'Well,' I continued, 'being charitable' – Dave scoffed – 'it may just be that the strain of our constant enquiries is getting him down. After all, his wife has been murdered.'

'Yes, that's much too charitable,' said Dave. There were times when his cynicism matched my own.

'And, secondly, I think we'll arrange a press release ...' I paused in thought for a moment. 'If we say that we think Forbes may be ill – undergoing a traumatic reaction to the death of his wife, say – and that we're worried that something may have happened to him, that may flush him out. And I think it's time we published a photograph of the missing Karen Hockley.'

'That was my idea originally, guv,' said Dave. I suspected that he was a bit put out, but he'll learn, in the fullness of time, that senior officers always pinch their subordinates' ideas and then claim them as their own.

I rang the head of news at the Yard. 'Bob,' I said, 'I need your help.'

The upshot was that all editions of that night's *Evening Standard* carried a photograph of Karen Hockley and a cleverly juxtaposed paragraph about the missing Max Forbes, but not otherwise suggesting that there was a connection between the two.

It failed to find either Karen or Forbes, but it did bring forth an unexpected and very helpful result.

At ten o'clock that evening, Gavin Creasey, the night-duty incident-room sergeant, rang me at home.

'I've just had a couple of weird calls, sir,' he said. 'One came in at ten past nine and the second one about five minutes ago.'

'Yes, go on.'

'They were both from the same woman. She was very nervous and it sounded as though she regretted having called

145

at all. But she said that she knew Max Forbes and had something to tell us.'

'Did she give a name, Gavin?'

'Not the first time, sir. When I asked her who she was, she rang off. I did a check and the call came from a mobile which goes out to a Melissa Watson of fifty-four Willerby Road, Tulse Hill, SW4. But then she rang again, five minutes ago. This time she sounded more confident. She repeated that she'd met Forbes and wanted to give us information. And this time she confirmed her name as Melissa Watson. I asked how we could contact her and she was adamant that we should ring her on her mobile at precisely ten to nine on Monday morning. She said she works in a building society in central London, but she didn't say which one.'

Fifteen

At ten minutes to nine on Monday morning, I rang the number that Gavin Creasey had given me.

A nervous female voice said, 'Hello?'

'Melissa Watson?'

'Yes.'

'This is Detective Chief Inspector Brock of New Scotland Yard, Miss Watson. Or is it *Mrs* Watson?'

'It's Mrs Watson.'

'I understand that you have something to tell me.'

'Yes, I think so.'

'Where and when can I meet you, then?'

There was a lengthy pause and then I heard Melissa Watson say, 'Just coming.'

'I'm sorry, what did you say?'

'I was talking to the manager. She's just opening up. I've got to go.'

'Yes, but when can I meet you?'

There was another pause and then Mrs Watson said, 'Can I come to a police station?'

'Yes, any one you like. Where are you?'

'Victoria Street.'

'Are you anywhere near Belgravia police station? It's not far from Victoria Coach Station.'

'Yes, I know it. My lunch break is from half twelve to half one. I'll come straight round then.'

At twelve thirty, I was waiting in the front office of Belgravia police station. Sensing that Melissa Watson's information

147

could well be of a delicate and embarrassing nature, I'd brought DC Nicola Chance with me as well as Dave Poole, with the intention of substituting her for Dave at the interview. But if, as I'd often found in the past, Melissa Watson was one of those women who preferred not to discuss sexually explicit matters in the presence of a female officer, Dave would be on hand to take over. And I had a feeling that Melissa Watson's information *would* be of a sexual nature.

As the woman was giving up her lunch break to see me, I'd sent Nicola out to buy a low-calorie snack and a soft drink for her. We detectives can be quite cunning at times.

At twenty minutes to one, a woman entered the police station. She looked to be in her late twenties and had short, blonde hair, almost mannish in cut. She glanced nervously around the foyer before approaching the counter.

'I've come to see Inspector Brock,' she said to the clerk.

'And your name, madam?' enquired the clerk.

'It's all right,' I said, stepping forward. 'I'm Detective Chief Inspector Brock. If you'd like to come with me, we can talk in private.'

I took her into an interview room and introduced her to Nicola Chance.

'I've got some sandwiches here for you, Mrs Watson,' I said, 'just in case you don't have time to get any lunch.'

'Thank you, that's very kind.' Melissa Watson looked apprehensively at Nicola, and I concluded that, as I'd anticipated, she would be uncomfortable talking to me in her presence.

'Would you rather that Miss Chance wasn't here?' I asked.

'Would you mind awfully?' Mrs Watson smiled apologetically at Nicola.

'Not at all, but there'll have to be another officer here, a man.'

'That's all right.'

Having got Dave Poole into the interview room, and waiting until Melissa Watson had taken a bite of her sandwich, I said, 'I gather from the conversation you had with

148

one of my sergeants on Friday evening that you have something to tell me.'

'This is all terribly embarrassing for me,' said Melissa, blushing, 'because I'm married and my husband doesn't know anything about it.'

'I give you my word that anything you tell me will remain strictly confidential,' I said, and this time I meant it. It had obviously taken a lot of courage for this woman to come forward.

'I don't know whether it will help,' Melissa began, 'but there was a piece about Max Forbes in Friday night's paper. I know him, you see. And his wife.'

'Would you like to tell me how you met?'

There was a longish pause and then, hesitantly, Melissa said, 'I answered an advert in a contact magazine.' She glanced nervously at Dave before returning her gaze to me. 'My husband doesn't know,' she said again, and looked down at her half-eaten sandwich. 'I'm bisexual, you see,' she mumbled, almost inaudibly.

'I'm not a judge of morals, Mrs Watson,' I said. 'I'm investigating a crime. That's my only interest in what you may have to tell me.' I paused. 'This was a magazine that puts such like-minded women in touch with each other, was it?'

'Yes. I left a message on something the magazine calls voicemail, and a couple of days later I got a return voicemail giving Alex Forbes's phone number. So, I rang her.'

'And what happened next?'

'We talked for a bit, and described ourselves to each other, and then made an arrangement to meet.'

'Where?'

'It was at her house in Battersea. That suited me fine because I live at Tulse Hill and it's not very far from Battersea.'

'And so you went there, did you?'

'Yes.'

Foolish woman, going to the house of someone you've

never met, particularly for an assignation of the sort Melissa Watson had described.

'When was this?'

'It was a Saturday afternoon. The fourth of May as a matter of fact. I remember particularly because it's my brother's birthday.'

'Did you tell your husband where you were going?'

'No, of course not. He was at Craven Cottage watching Fulham. He's football mad is Darren.'

'And Alex Forbes was at the house when you got there?'

'Yes.'

'And Max Forbes?' I could see it was going to be hard work extracting information from Melissa Watson.

But then she glanced at her watch and obviously realized that, if she didn't get on with her story, she'd be late getting back to work. 'No, he wasn't there to start with. At least, if he was, I didn't see him. Anyway, Alex and I had a cup of tea and chatted for a while. Then we went into a back room, got undressed and started to make love on a divan. It was all tastefully arranged. There was just a black fur coverlet on the divan – actually it was nylon, not fur – the curtains were drawn and there were lighted candles dotted about. But it was what happened next that was so awful.'

'And what did happen next, Mrs Watson?'

'After about twenty minutes, Alex stood up and said that she wouldn't be a moment, but she was going to get a glass of water. But when she came back, Max was with her. I was terribly embarrassed, still being naked, with this strange man leering at me. There weren't any bedclothes to hide under – the wretched coverlet was tied down – and my clothes were on a chair on the other side of the room. At first I thought he wanted to watch us. Some men enjoy that. But they took me completely by surprise: they pulled me off the bed, twisted my arms up my back and dragged me into the next room. They were both quite strong and I just couldn't resist them.' Describing her ordeal was starting to be too much for the woman and her eyes reddened with the first onset of tears.

'Take your time, Mrs Watson,' I said. 'Go on when you're ready.'

The tears were flowing quite freely now and Melissa searched her handbag for a tissue. She dabbed carefully at her eyes before continuing. 'There was this X-shaped frame leaning against the wall and they tied me to it. Then they put this hood over my head and did it up round my neck so that I could hardly breathe. I thought I was going to die.' There was a pause and she gave a convulsive sob. 'And then they started whipping me.'

'I'm sorry, Mrs Watson, but I have to ask if, at any time, you agreed to this?'

She looked straight at me. 'No, never.' The answer was firm but anguished. 'I'm not into that sort of thing.'

'How did they tie you to the frame, Mrs Watson?' asked Dave.

'With leather straps round the wrists and ankles. It was horrible.'

'And did they both assault you?' I asked.

'I think so. I couldn't see, but, after a few minutes, I heard Max say to his wife, "Your turn now, darling." Then I was whipped again, for another two or three minutes.'

'And then they let you go?'

'Yes. After about ten minutes they undid the straps and let me get dressed. Then Alex asked me if I'd like to come back again another day. To play more games, she said. She had the cheek to say that she knew deep down I'd enjoyed it.'

'And what did you say?'

'I agreed because I thought that if I refused they would kill me, or keep me prisoner. You read about these things in the papers, but I never thought it would happen to me. I was really scared, and I had no intention of ever going back there.'

'While you were there, Mrs Watson, did you see Alex Forbes whipping her husband or, more importantly, him whipping her?'

'No, I didn't.'

'You're quite sure?'

'Absolutely.'

'And did Max Forbes have sexual intercourse with you, by force or otherwise?'

'No. He didn't rape me, if that's what you mean. And I certainly wouldn't have gone with him willingly. It seems that what they did to me was enough to give them their pleasure. I think they were really sick people.'

I now asked a question to which I knew I'd get a negative answer, but I had to ask it anyway. 'Do you wish to prefer charges against Max Forbes, Mrs Watson?' Regrettably, Alex was beyond our reach.

'I couldn't possibly,' said Melissa. 'My husband would find out if I had to go to court. I had enough trouble hiding the marks of the whip from him.'

I knew it was no good trying to persuade her that her identity would be protected, and I didn't try. Apart from anything else, unfair though it would undoubtedly be, I knew that defence counsel would destroy her simply for having gone willingly to another woman's house for sexual pleasure.

'Would you be prepared to make a written statement about all this, Mrs Watson?' It was a formal question and got the answer I expected.

'Good heavens, no,' she said.

'What a bastard, Dave,' I said, when we were back at Curtis Green. 'There we have prima facie evidence that Max Forbes committed acts of indecent assault and grievous bodily harm, if not malicious wounding, and there's not a bloody thing we can do about it.'

'Not unless he admits it and cops a plea, guv,' said Dave.

'Fat chance of that,' I said. 'You've met the guy. He's not going to admit anything.'

'He might not need to,' Dave said.

'Meaning?'

'The chafe marks on Alex's body were round the neck,

the ankles and the wrists. That was how Melissa Watson described the way the Forbeses strapped her to the frame. It's beginning to look as though that's where Alex died. And if it wasn't Max who killed her, it must have been someone else who called at the house.'

'You could be right, Dave,' I said. 'How many unidentified prints did the crime-scene examiners lift when we spun Max's drum?'

'Dunno, guv. Maybe half a dozen.'

I rang through to Frank Mead's office and asked him to come in.

'Frank, can you arrange for elimination fingerprints to be taken from Farrell, Griffin, Morton, Parish, Ryan and Simpson? I want to know if any of them tally with those found at sixteen Crouch Road.'

'Sure,' said Frank. 'I'll get on to it straight away.'

'Supposing they refuse?' put in Dave.

'No problem,' said Frank, casting a critical glance at Dave. 'If they refuse we nick 'em on suspicion of murder and get a superintendent to authorize it.' And, as he left the office, he added a parting shot. 'You need to bone up on your Police and Criminal Evidence Act, Dave.'

'I still fancy Max Forbes for it,' Dave said, somewhat churlishly. He didn't like getting caught out in matters of criminal law.

'So do I,' I said. 'But we still don't know where he is.'

'He'll come, guv,' Dave said, with more confidence than I felt right now. 'I wouldn't mind betting he's beetled off to his nudist camp again. If he was ever there in the first place.'

'That's a possibility, I suppose,' I said thoughtfully. 'Another word with *Hauptkommissarin* Heidi Stolpe of the Karlsruhe Police might prove to be useful. And, while I'm at it, I'll see if anything is known of this Françoise Garnier who Forbes says he got to know while he was there.'

'Yeah, but we don't want to get into extradition, guv. It'd take forever and a day.'

Dave was right about that: extradition was a nightmare.

'Don't worry. I'll just ask the Germans to see if he's there. Then I'll think about how we can tempt him back.'

Dave shrugged. 'I reckon the whole thing's a scam, guv. Personally I don't think he went anywhere near the Black Forest. And I don't believe all this fanny about going from Dover to Calais as a foot passenger and then catching a couple of trains. And we now know he's got a car, something he denied in the first place. But I'd love to know exactly what he was up to during that fortnight. He's definitely dodgy.'

'You do catch on fast, Dave,' I said.

I telephoned Heidi Stolpe, explained the problem and gave her a description of Max Forbes.

'What is your particular interest in this man, *Herr* Chief Inspector?' she asked.

'I suspect him of having murdered his wife, *Frau* Stolpe.' I took a chance. 'Or is it *Fräulein?*' After all, I may finish up having to go to Karlsruhe, and a few days with this lady could be quite enjoyable. If she was as young as she sounded.

'It's *Hauptkommissarin*, and I'll let you know as soon as I can.' And with that rebuke Heidi Stolpe replaced the receiver more firmly than I thought necessary. I suppose that, having been married to Helga for sixteen years, I should have learned about German women by now.

However, *Frau* or *Fräulein* Stolpe did not allow that little exchange to get in the way of her professional duty. An hour and a half later, she called back.

'There is no one fitting the description of Max Forbes staying at the camp at present,' she said, 'although that's not conclusive, of course: there are a lot of people there. But I made some enquiries about this Françoise Garnier. It is her real name, and it seems that she did in fact stay there for two weeks from the twenty-fourth of July.'

'Do you have an address for her?' I asked, and was careful to add, '*Frau Hauptkommissarin.*'

There was a chuckle from the other end and she said, 'Why don't you just call me Heidi, Harry?'

Like I said, German women are an enigma.

'OK . . . Heidi, but do you have an address for this Françoise Garnier?'

'Yes, I do. She is *Madame* Garnier and she lives in Paris.' And Heidi gave me the full details.

I mulled over this information and wondered what I could do with it. Or about it. A word with *Madame* Françoise Garnier could be extremely valuable. But there again, it might turn out to be another bum steer. The big problem was going to be persuading the commander of the need for such expense. But I decided to try anyway.

'But why d'you think this woman's evidence might be of use, Mr Brock?' The commander shuffled a few bits of paper around his desk. He was always much happier when he was playing with paper.

'It may serve to prove where Max Forbes was during this vital fortnight, sir,' I said. 'I'm more and more inclining to the possibility that he murdered his wife.'

'Hmm! Yes, well . . .' The commander had reached a crisis of indecision. I knew the signs. 'Well, I suppose . . .' He dithered and then reached for the telephone. I knew instinctively that he was going to ring the deputy assistant commissioner. There was a brief conversation during which, I have to say to the commander's credit, he was quite persuasive. But then the responsibility wouldn't be his. He replaced the receiver. 'All right, Mr Brock,' he said. 'The DAC says you can go.'

I called Dave into my office. 'We're going to Paris to talk to *Madame* Garnier,' I said.

'But neither of us speaks French, and she won't speak English. The French never do,' said Dave.

'In that case,' I said, 'we'll have to enlist the aid of Henri Deshayes. He *does* speak English.' Henri Deshayes was an *inspecteur* in the *Police Nationale* in Paris who had helped us on a previous occasion. We had struck up a relationship very quickly, but then detectives are like that, regardless of nationality. Investigators of crime don't have too much time to spend on developing contacts. It has to be instant rapport or nothing will get done.

Colin Wilberforce 'surfed the net' – whatever the hell that means – and found the flight times from Heathrow to Charles de Gaulle airport. Much as I dislike flying, we didn't have time for the luxury of the far more pleasant Eurostar. Once I'd established that *Madame* Garnier was in Paris, I wanted to go there the following morning, see her and return the same day. But first I had to get Deshayes to set it up for me.

'*Bonjour*, 'Arry. 'Ow are you? Wanting the 'elp of the finest police force in the world, once again?' There was a Gallic chuckle.

Henri Deshayes, in common with all Frenchmen, had this problem with aspirates and always called me 'Arry. Just to even the balance, I always called him Henry. With an emphasis on the H. But we got on well; this sort of badinage among policemen of all nationalities is commonplace.

I explained the purpose of our visit to Paris. 'But obviously I need to know that *Madame* Garnier's there, Henry. Could you find out if she's in Paris at the moment, and if she'd be willing to see us?'

'I will do it at once, 'Arry,' said Deshayes. 'We 'ave these marvellous things in Paris called the telephone. She will be in the book for sure. I'll ring you back pronto.'

Ten minutes later Deshayes called back. 'Yes, she is at 'ome, 'Arry, and is willing to talk to you. She is wondering what it is about, but I pretended I didn't know. I don't want to be queering your pitcher, eh?'

'I think you mean queering my *pitch*, Henry.'

'That's what I said,' Henri replied. 'So, what time will you be arriving at Charles de Gaulle?'

'Eleven ten your time.'

'Good. I'll be there to meet you. I've arranged for you to see *Madame* Garnier at 'alf-past two, so there will be time for the Paris police to treat you to lunch, eh?'

'I can see that things are getting better all the time, Henry.'

Sixteen

Although Henri Deshayes had told me that the chic *Madame* Françoise Garnier was fifty-two, she had the appearance of a woman in her early forties, and lived in a richly furnished apartment on the Île St-Louis, one of the most fashionable parts of Paris. And she spoke perfect English.

'You and your colleagues would like coffee?' she enquired, once we were settled in comfortable armchairs. 'It is prepared already.'

She indicated a small table on which were a coffee pot, bone-china cups and saucers, a creamer and sugar bowl, all set out on a silver tray.

'Thank you, that would be most welcome.'

I glanced around her elegant sitting room. It was a maze of chintzes and valuable paintings, and there were dozens of little china ornaments of the sort that my mother used to call dust traps. But doubtless *Madame* Garnier had a cleaning woman to worry about that. In a glass-fronted cabinet there was a collection of Limoges porcelain.

'Is that a Monet?' asked Dave, indicating one of the smaller paintings.

'Yes, it is. How clever of you.' *Madame* Garnier smiled sweetly at Dave before addressing me. 'You are from London, Inspector Deshayes tells me,' she said, as she poured the coffee.

'Yes, we are,' I said.

'Ah, I spent many happy days there as a student, learning your language. In Tooting. You know Tooting?'

'Yes, of course.' I found it difficult to visualize anyone spending happy days in Tooting, but each to her own.

'I was studying to become a language teacher, you see, at London University. I also speak German. But now I no longer work. Apart from the occasional private lesson.'

'I went to London as well,' said Dave. 'Goldsmiths.'

Madame Garnier smiled once more at Dave. 'I could tell you were well educated, young man,' she said.

I glanced at the gallery of silver-framed photographs on a table set against the wall opposite the window. They were of a boy and a girl taken through various stages of their upbringing from infancy to adulthood, on to wedding pictures and finally to proud parenthood.

'They can't possibly be your grandchildren,' I said. Detectives are very free with compliments when getting a witness in the right mood to co-operate. Will do anything, in fact. I've even gone so far as to eat seedcake, which I detest.

'Ah, but you are a flatterer, Mr Brock.' *Madame* Garnier laughed. 'I like your English friend, *m'sieur*,' she said, glancing at Deshayes. Turning back to me, she said, 'I understand that you wish to ask me some questions. I don't really know how a little old French lady can help officers from the famous Scotland Yard, but if I can I shall.'

Far from being what her description of herself implied, Françoise Garnier was a good-looking woman and her short, blonde hair was coifed to perfection in a style that was uniquely French. She had an attractively rounded figure, set off to advantage by the exquisite silks in which she was dressed. I imagined that her wardrobe must cost her husband a fortune. If there was a husband, but that question was answered for me later.

'I believe you were in the Black Forest in July, *madame*,' I began. I didn't mention exactly where; people are sometimes reticent about revealing that they are practising nudists.

But *Madame* Garnier was not one of them. 'Yes, my husband Maurice and I were at the nudist colony there. We go quite often. It's pure escapism, a wonderful feeling of abandonment, to leave all your clothes in your cabin along with your worries. But why does that interest you?'

'I'm investigating the murder of a woman whose husband told me that he met you there.'

'I see. A murder, eh?' Françoise Garnier nodded her head slowly, as though this sort of enquiry was run-of-the-mill. 'My husband and I met many people there,' she continued. 'Who was this man?'

'His name is Max Forbes.'

Madame Garnier shook her head. 'It is not a name I know,' she said. 'I do not recall meeting such a person.'

Dave handed me the folio of photographs that we had brought with us, and I took out one of Max Forbes. 'This man, *madame*,' I said, handing it to her.

'Ah! But that is Victor. Victor Smith, the artist. Yes, I knew him. In fact he did a sketch of me. I will show you.' *Madame* Garnier rose from her chair and left the room. Returning a few moments later, she handed me a well-executed Conté-pencil drawing of her unclothed self. Given that she was now fully dressed, I could only wonder whether it was a true depiction, or if Max Forbes had exercised a measure of artistic licence. But, if it was accurate, the fifty-two-year-old *Madame* Garnier was in good shape. Literally.

'Looks like a Botticelli,' murmured Dave, leaning across to examine the picture.

I never ceased to be amazed at Dave's occasional flashes of erudition. But, that said, no matter what subject is raised, it is always possible to find a CID officer somewhere who knows something about it.

'I think your colleague is something of an art expert,' said *Madame* Garnier. And, turning to Dave, she asked, 'You studied art at university?'

'No,' said Dave. 'English.'

Mischievously, she answered him in French. *'C'est bon!'* she said.

'You say his name was Victor Smith, *madame*?' I said, ignoring the compliment she had paid Dave. It doesn't do to let one's sergeant get too conceited.

Madame Garnier chuckled. 'That is what he called himself, but I think it was a pseudonym. The English are often a little coy about letting people know that they are nudists. But it is not necessary to hide one's identity from other nudists, is it?' She shrugged, apparently mystified by Forbes's deception. 'What is wrong with taking one's clothes off?'

'Can you remember the exact dates you were at this camp?' I asked.

Madame Garnier took a small diary from her handbag and thumbed through it. 'Yes,' she said, 'Maurice and I were there for two weeks exactly, from the twenty-fourth of July.'

That certainly tallied with what *Hauptkommissarin* Heidi Stolpe had discovered, and confirmed Max Forbes's claim that the second week of his holiday there had coincided with Françoise Garnier's first week. So, he had been there after all.

'How well did you get to know this man you knew as Victor Smith?' I asked.

The Frenchwoman smiled. 'Not as well as he would have liked,' she said. 'To be quite frank with you, I think he was wanting to make love to me.'

'Really?'

'You're shocked, Mr Brock.'

'No, just surprised.' But it was surprise at her candour.

'Ah, well, you see, Englishmen seem to have this romantic illusion that French women spend all their time making love, *n'est-ce pas*?'

'If you say so.'

'And it's true, I think. Well, I love doing it anyway. But I like to choose who I do it with. And Victor was not one of those men that I would have enjoyed. Do not look so shocked, *m'sieur*. Maurice has his lovers and so do I.'

I was amazed at the turn in the conversation. Suddenly this voluptuous grandmother was talking quite freely about sex.

'So, you turned him down.'

'Of course I did. I prefer young men who have good, firm bodies with muscles, and stamina, and the ardour to make passionate love. Not old men like Victor. *Mon Dieu*, he was the same age as my Maurice. He could not have satisfied me. Anyway, his wife was there.'

'*His wife?*' This was a revelation. 'Did you meet her?'

'Of course.'

'And did she appear to be making advances to other men while, er, Victor was making them to you?'

'Oh, very much so, yes, she . . . How is the best way of saying it? She paraded herself. Teasing, yes? But I think she was one of those women who was also interested in other women. You understand what I mean?'

'Yes, I do.'

'But I am not, not while there are still men about.' Françoise Garnier gave a little laugh and her eyes twinkled provocatively.

'And what was Victor's wife calling herself, *madame*?' I asked in an attempt to get the conversation back on course.

'Gail, I think it was. Yes, Gail Smith.'

I plucked another photograph from the folder, one of the late Alex Forbes. 'Would that be her?'

Madame Garnier examined the photograph for only a few seconds. 'Yes, that is her, without a doubt. She had a beautiful body, that girl. I envied her.'

Suddenly, in a luxurious Paris apartment overlooking the Seine, the kaleidoscope had been shaken once again. Shaken in such a way that the whole of my enquiry seemed to have been based on a false premise.

If what *Madame* Garnier had said was true – and I had no reason to disbelieve her – Alex Forbes had been in the Black Forest as late as the thirty-first of July. *A whole fortnight after Max Forbes had reported her missing.*

I produced the photograph of Karen Hockley. 'Did you by any chance see this woman there, *madame*?'

Françoise Garnier studied the print for some time before handing it back. 'No, *m'sieur*, I have never seen this woman before.'

Oh well, you can't win 'em all.

*   *   *

161

We arrived back in London just after seven o'clock and went straight to Curtis Green.

'Well, I don't know, Dave. What the hell do we do now?'

It was a rhetorical question. I didn't expect Dave to know the answer any more than I did.

'Find Forbes for a start, I suppose.'

'Yes . . .' I mused. 'But where the hell is he?'

'One thing's for sure, guv, he'll have to come up with some pretty convincing answers when we do find him.'

'Well, we'll let it sweat until the morning.'

I rang Sarah Dawson and suggested supper somewhere.

'I've been trying to get hold of you all day, darling. Where have you been?' Sarah asked when I arrived at her flat.

'In Paris talking to the sexiest grandmother I've ever met in my life.'

Sarah gave me a playful punch. 'No, where have you really been?'

'It's true,' I said, and described the interview I'd had with Françoise Garnier. I don't think that Sarah believed a word of it, but the exciting recollection of that seductive Frenchwoman had had its effect. After dinner, I took Sarah back to her flat, and stayed the night. Again.

'This is becoming a habit,' said Sarah later, as she nestled closer.

'Are you complaining?'

'Did I say that?'

Things looked a bit clearer next morning, just a little.

'I think there's only one thing left, Dave. We'll have to circulate a photograph of Max Forbes as someone who may be able to assist us with our enquiries.'

'Sure as hell we need someone to assist us,' said Dave phlegmatically.

I sighed, more with frustration than anything else. I knew that we would be inundated with phone calls from people who'd seen Max Forbes everywhere from Land's End to

John O'Groats, but it was a chance we had to take. There was no alternative.

And then I had another idea.

'It's Harry Brock,' I said, when I got through to Jock Ferguson at Aldershot.

'How are you getting on with your murder enquiry, Harry?'

I gave Jock a quick rundown on what Dave and I had learned in Paris before turning to the reason for my call. 'Where's Corporal Hockley now, Jock?'

'*Private* Hockley's done a runner again, Harry.'

'*Private* Hockley?'

'Aye, Harry, he appeared before his colonel the day before yesterday. He declined a court martial, went up before the brigade commander and got busted down to private. No sooner had they cut off his stripes than he went over the wall.'

'What wall?' I was beginning to get totally confused by the military.

'Well, actually, there aren't any walls, Harry, not any more, but it's an army expression for going absent. I think the next move, when they catch him again, is a few weeks in chokey and then they'll kick him out.'

'So, you've no idea where he's gone.'

'I think that's more or less what I just said, Harry.'

'Would you have any objection to my circulating his details, Jock? I think this guy knows more than he's telling.'

'I never mind other people doing a bit of work for me, Harry, but I've done it already. I tried ringing you yesterday, but your guy told me you were in Paris.' He sighed. 'You Met blokes have all the luck. Incidentally, I took the liberty of adding your name to the circulation about Hockley.'

'Thanks. You're a pal,' I said.

We gave the press a photograph of Max Forbes and, just for good measure, asked them to publish one of Karen Hockley again.

As I'd predicted, circulating details of the principals in Alex Forbes's murder not only resulted in hundreds of phone calls to police stations all over the country, but probably made me the most unpopular detective in England. Or Scotland, Wales and Northern Ireland for that matter. To say nothing of the Channel Islands and the Isle of Man. The telephones in the incident room never stopped ringing and I had to have extra lines installed, and bring in additional staff to man them.

I thought the commander was likely to have a nervous breakdown when he saw the cost involved. These arrangements do not come cheap.

But the next day there was a glimmer of light.

A phone call from a PC at King's Cross informed us that the previous evening he had happened upon a fight between a man fitting Hockley's description and a prostitute working in the area. I told the PC to get his little blue-serge body up to Curtis Green as soon as possible.

'Tell me all about it,' I said, when PC Farmer appeared in my office.

'I was on toms patrol last night, sir, three to eleven,' began Farmer, an officer of about forty-five or so. 'About half-past ten I did my final walk round, near the station.'

'That's the railway station, is it?'

'Yes, sir. Well, as I rounded the corner, there was a bit of a tussle going on, quite a way down the street. This guy was having a go at one of the girls. He'd grabbed hold of her and it looked as though he was trying to tear her blouse off. It's a bit dark round there, but that was the way it looked. Anyway, by the time I got to them, the other girls had weighed in and chummy was definitely getting the worst of it. But the minute he spotted me he took off. I had a go at chasing him but, although I work out at the gym, he still got the better of me. I couldn't get anywhere near him. He was bloody fit, that guy.'

'Fit like a soldier in his prime, perhaps?'

'Could be, sir, but that's the point. I spoke to the girl he'd been having a go at and, from her description, and from what I saw of him, I reckon it could've been this Hockley that

164

you're looking for. Anyway, I went back and had a chat with the ladies.'

'What was the fight about, did the girl say?'

'The usual. She said that she'd named a price that he reckoned was too much. Must have been a skinflint, that bastard. The girls round King's Cross don't charge all that much, that's why they're there. It's the bottom end of the market, to coin a phrase. Anyhow, she'd said she wasn't going to budge from her quote and told him, in no uncertain terms, to try the other girls, but that he'd get the same tariff. It's a bit of a closed shop, the old toms' trade.'

'Yes, I did know that, Farmer. I walked a beat myself, many years ago.'

Funny that, the way street coppers forget that we all started out by pounding the pavement.

'Ah, yes, I suppose so, sir. Anyway, apparently this guy took the hump, probably because the other girls started taking the piss, the way they do. So matey cuts up rough, grabs hold of the girl and rips her blouse open. Well, that's as good as a red rag to a bull to that lot. All for one and one for all, that's them. Like I said, they all started having a go at him then and just before he legs it I noticed he had quite a cut down his left cheek. Bleeding a lot, it was. I reckon one of the girls probably chivved him with her ring. Most of the girls wear a sharp ring, just in case.'

It was a pitifully small contribution to our tiny pile of evidence, but I made sure that all officers in the King's Cross area were issued with photographs of Hockley and were told that he probably had a cut on his left cheek. And, for good measure, I circulated the same information to West End Central police station in case Hockley decided to try his luck in Soho.

But even if we caught him, the best he could be charged with was being an absentee from military service, and indecent assault. Not that I thought a prostitute would be eager to give evidence against him: street women have an inherent dislike of courtrooms. They have their own methods, and she probably thought that giving him a facial scar was retribution enough.

But, more to the point, if he was trying to have it off with a tom, it was unlikely that he'd found his wife Karen. Maybe.

But, shortly after PC Farmer had left Curtis Green, one of the incident-room telephonists took another call, and that seemed far more promising.

DS Colin Wilberforce came into my office clutching the message flimsy.

'Call just come in, sir, from a Dominic Kelly. He said that he met a girl last night in a club . . .' Colin glanced briefly at the message. 'In Fulham, he said, and he reckons she told him her name was Karen Hockley.'

'Did this guy give an address, Colin?'

'Yes, sir.' Colin glanced at the message again. 'He lives in Worthy Lane, Putney. Number fifteen, sir.'

'Is he there now?'

'No, sir. He's at work apparently, so the girl who took the call said. But he'll be in at about seven this evening.'

'Got a phone number?'

Colin handed me the flimsy. 'All in the message, sir.'

Seventeen

'Yes, I'm Dominic Kelly.'

'I telephoned you earlier, Mr Kelly,' I said, once Dave and I had introduced ourselves. I was rather surprised that so young a man – I reckoned he was about twenty-five – should be living in a house that was probably worth upwards of three-quarters of a million.

'Yeah, sure, come in.' The young man escorted us into a spacious front room and invited us to take a seat.

'D'you live here alone, Mr Kelly?' It was not necessary for me to know. It was just interest, and the thought that I must have gone wrong somewhere in my youth. When I was about his age, Helga and I, and our baby son, were living in a cramped, rented flat in Earlsfield.

'Good lord, no. Not permanently, I mean. I couldn't afford this sort of place, not on a bank clerk's pay. This is my parents' home, but they're away at the moment. On holiday in the Caribbean. Been there a month already and they've got another two weeks to go.' Kelly gave a sigh of envy. 'I've actually got a bedsit in Elephant and Castle, but I'm house-sitting while Mum and Dad are away.'

'You met a woman called Karen Hockley last night, I believe.'

'Yeah. It was in a nightclub in Fulham and I got chatting to this girl at the bar. She told me her name was Karen Hockley. We had a few drinks and then we danced for a while, and then we had a few more drinks. You know how it goes.'

In fact I didn't know – I've never been to one of these

167

places, not socially anyway – but I let it pass. 'Can you describe her, Mr Kelly?'

Kelly thought for a moment. 'She was just a few inches shorter than me, and I'm six feet. About five-nine, I guess she was. Very good figure and a good-looker too. Oh, and she had blonde hair. But I didn't think any more about it until I saw her picture in this morning's papers with her name under it.'

'How old d'you think she was?' I asked.

'About thirty, maybe thirty-two, somewhere around there, anyway.'

'How was she dressed?' asked Dave, pocketbook at the ready.

'Clingy black dress, just above the knee, and cut low.' Kelly smiled, presumably at the recollection. 'Very low,' he added.

'Show Mr Kelly the photograph, Dave.'

Dave produced the print. It was the same one that had been published in the newspapers, but, being the original, was of a better quality.

'Yeah, I'm sure that's her, but, as I said, she's got blonde hair now, not black, and it was in a different style.'

'Different in what way?'

'Well, it's quite long in this picture,' Kelly said, tapping the photograph, 'but now it's short, to about here.' He indicated the bottom of his ears. 'Oh, and she had a tattoo on her shoulder, just there.' He reached over and pointed to a place well down on his left shoulder. 'A butterfly, I think it was.'

'And how did you manage to see that?' I asked, but I'd guessed already. *Of course I had.*

Kelly gave the sort of broad grin that indicates a conquest. 'I brought her back here. We had a few more drinks and we spent the night together. That's how I know about the butterfly, *and* that she had a good figure. She was something else, that girl, I can tell you.'

'Don't take offence at this, Mr Kelly,' I said, 'but it is rather important. Did you and Karen just have straight sex?'

Kelly appeared puzzled by the question. 'Yeah, sure. What other sort is there?'

Oh, the naïvety of youth.

'She didn't want to play games, like getting you to tie her up, or use a whip on her? Anything like that?'

'Oh, what, bondage, that sort of thing? No, nothing like that. Except . . .'

'Except what?'

'Yeah, she did get me to tie her wrists to the top of the bed, but that's not unusual, is it? I've met girls before who like having it that way. Ruined a couple of my old man's ties, that did, but he's got so many I don't suppose he'll notice. I hope.'

'May I see those ties, Mr Kelly?' I asked, thinking that there might just be some evidence from which the lab could obtain a DNA sample. I was not wholly convinced that Kelly had met the Karen Hockley we were interested in. There must be other women of that name, but, having seen the photo in the paper, he might just have convinced himself that the girl he'd met was the one we wanted to talk to. Unbelievable though it may be, it was the sort of coincidence that sometimes occurs and completely fouls up an enquiry.

'Sorry, but I bunged them in the washing machine this morning, together with the towel she was lying on. Like I said, it's my parents' house, and I don't want any tricky questions when they get home.'

Unfortunately, I knew that washing would have corrupted any positive test, apart from ruining his old man's ties. Oh well, you can't win every time. 'Did you make any arrangement to see Mrs Hockley again?'

'*Mrs* Hockley?' For the first time since we'd arrived, Kelly showed some alarm, probably at the implications of having slept with a married woman.

'Yes, she's married to a soldier who's stationed in Aldershot.'

'Oh God! He's not a paratrooper or anything like that, is

he?' Young Mr Kelly was clearly visualizing an unpleasant interview involving physical violence.

'I don't know. I think he's an infantryman of some sort. But I take it you arranged to see her again.'

'Not exactly. She gave me her phone number and said she'd like to do it again. If she wasn't there, she said to leave a message on her answering machine.'

And sure as hell she won't be there.

'What was the number she gave you?'

'It was an oh-one-two-five-two number . . .' Kelly searched his pockets and eventually pulled out an old receipt. 'I wrote it on that,' he said, giving it to me.

I glanced at it and handed it to Dave.

'That's Karen Hockley's home phone number all right, sir,' Dave said.

'Did she give you her address?' I asked Kelly.

'No, just her phone number.'

'And have you tried ringing that number, Mr Kelly?'

'Blimey, not yet. I only said goodbye to her this morning. But I didn't know she was married, so I shan't be ringing her at all now.'

'Did she say where she was going when she left you this morning?'

'No. We walked to East Putney tube station together, but my train came in first, so I don't know where she went. I presume she went back to wherever that number is.' Kelly pointed at the receipt that Dave was still holding.

'East Putney's on the District Line, isn't it?'

'Yeah, that's right.'

'And where did you travel to, Mr Kelly?'

'Bayswater. It's where I work.'

'And Mrs Hockley gave you no idea where she was heading this morning?'

'No. As I said, my train came in, she kissed me and said goodbye and that's the last I saw of her.'

'She could have gone south as far as Wimbledon, sir,' said Dave, studying the underground map in the back of his diary. 'Or north and changed at Earls Court. After that anywhere. If she went at all, that is, and didn't just leave the station after Mr Kelly caught his train. For all we know, she might still be here in Putney.'

'Did you give Mrs Hockley your phone number, Mr Kelly?' I asked.

'Not directly, no, but it's written on the phone in the hall, and on the one in the bedroom, so I suppose she could have made a note of it.'

I gave Kelly one of my cards. 'If she should contact you again, will you ring me immediately? Any time of the day or night.'

'Of course.' Kelly took the card and studied it. 'What should I do, agree to see her?' He was starting to sound quite worried now.

'That's up to you, but it would help us if you were to arrange to meet her again. It's entirely your own decision, of course. But, if you do, make sure you give us sufficient time to meet up with you before you meet her. We earnestly need to find this woman.'

'You haven't told me why you want to talk to her.'

I hesitated, but only for a moment. 'We think she may be able to assist us in a murder enquiry,' I said.

'Christ!' said Kelly. 'D'you mean she might have killed someone?'

'That, Mr Kelly, is something we have yet to discover,' I said.

And we left behind us one very worried young man.

'Well, that gets us precisely nowhere, Dave,' I said, once we were back at Curtis Green. 'What puzzles me is why she took the risk. If she's responsible for the murder of Alex Forbes, why go to a nightclub when she must have known that her picture's been in all the papers? And, on top of that, to use her own name.'

'There are three answers to that, guv,' said Dave. Today was a banana day, and he was carefully peeling one. 'Firstly, she doesn't read the papers and therefore didn't see her photograph. Secondly, because she didn't kill Alex Forbes, and therefore has nothing to worry about, and thirdly . . .' He paused. 'Thirdly, because she's a bloody nympho and can't do without sex.'

'Then why doesn't she team up with her husband again?'

'Perhaps she has,' said Dave. 'Either that or she doesn't know where the bastard is. And for that matter, neither do we.'

'Which is a pity, because he could tell us if she had a butterfly tattooed on her left shoulder.'

'What you might call an Aldershot tattoo,' said Dave.

Although it was now half-past seven, I telephoned Jock Ferguson. Being a CID officer, he was still in his office. In the Department, to get away by nine in the evening is regarded as an early night.

'We've had a possible sighting of Karen Hockley,' I told him. 'But it's a bit iffy.' And I went on to tell him what we'd learned from Dominic Kelly, including the young man's horror at discovering he'd spent the night with a woman who was not only married, but married to a soldier. Jock laughed at that.

'So, what are you doing about it, Harry? Put an obo on this club?'

'You must be joking, Jock,' I said. 'We haven't got the manpower for that. No, I'm relying on Kelly to let us know if she gets in touch again.'

'I think you might wait quite a long time for that,' said Jock, and I had to agree with him.

'Incidentally, d'you know if Karen Hockley had a tattoo of a butterfly on her left shoulder?'

Jock's throaty guffaw came through the phone. 'Now how the hell d'you expect me to know the answer to that, Harry?'

'I wondered if Hockley might have mentioned it when you were doing the missing-person report on his wife.'

'No, he said nothing about it. But we can ask him . . . when we find him.'

'Yeah, thanks a lot.'

But things started to move a bit faster after that. I was on the point of calling it a day, when my phone went.

'There's a call for you from a Dominic Kelly, sir,' said Gavin Creasey, who had taken over from Colin Wilberforce at six o'clock. 'Line two.'

I flicked down the switch. 'Brock.'

'Oh, it's Dominic here. Dominic Kelly. You came to see me earlier this evening, remember?'

'Yes, I remember, Mr Kelly. What's on your mind?'

'I'm at this club in Fulham again, and she's here.'

'Who, Karen Hockley?'

'Yes. But she's with another guy tonight.'

'Is she still there?'

'Yes, she's dancing with him now.'

'What does he look like? Can you give me a description?'

'I'm outside the club at the moment, on my mobile, but he's about the same height as her, as far as I can remember . . .' And Kelly went on to describe a man who could have been one of hundreds, if not thousands. I wondered if it was Dan Hockley, Karen's husband.

'Thanks, Mr Kelly.'

'D'you want me to follow her if she leaves?'

'No, don't do that,' I said hurriedly. 'I'll get the local police to meet you outside the club and you can point her out to them.' The thought of Dominic Kelly playing amateur detective horrified me. Assaults outside nightclubs are commonplace occurrences, and the last thing I wanted was Karen Hockley's latest boyfriend getting the wrong idea and giving Kelly a hiding. And if the 'boyfriend' turned out to be Karen's husband, the result could be even more serious.

I rang Fulham police station and got hold of the late-turn detective sergeant. Explaining the situation, I asked him to get round to this club and detain her. I just hoped that she'd still be there.

Thirty minutes later, the DS rang back. 'We have her in custody here at Fulham, sir,' he said. 'Are you coming down?'

'You bet your life I am,' I said.

It's about four miles from Curtis Green to Fulham police station. Fortunately the traffic was light and by virtue of what Dave calls 'positive driving', we made it in twenty minutes.

The detective sergeant who had called us was hovering in the front office, looking decidedly agitated. 'I've got her in the interview room, sir,' he said, 'but she's kicking up merry hell.'

'Probably doesn't like the idea of having been nicked,' I said. 'Is Mr Kelly here?'

'Yes, sir, we brought him here separately. He's in another interview room. If there's to be an identification parade, we don't want any allegations of him having seen her again in the nick. Know what I mean?'

'Yes, I do, Sergeant,' I said curtly. 'I've been a CID officer for quite a long time. Well, let's have a look at her, then.'

The woman in the interview room leaped to her feet as soon as I entered. She was not happy.

'What the hell is all this?' she demanded. 'I'm dancing with my fellah and suddenly the fuzz turn up and cart me down here.' She was about five feet nine inches tall, and had shortish blonde hair. And she was certainly about thirty. She was not, however, wearing the black dress that Kelly had drooled over; instead she was attired in jeans and a crop top. She did not, though, look anything like the photograph of Karen Hockley, but women are capable of changing their appearance quite dramatically.

'Mrs Hockley, is it?'

'No, it's not,' said the woman angrily.

'What is your name, then?' I was beginning to get disturbing vibes about all this.

'Piss off, copper. I've done nothing wrong and I don't have to tell you anything. What the hell is all this, anyway?' she demanded again. 'I've not been doing ecstasy or pot, or anything like that.'

I turned to the late-turn detective sergeant. 'Get Mr Kelly in here,' I said.

'But, sir, if we—'

'Just do it, Skip,' I said, with a measure of calmness that surprised even me. And certainly surprised Dave.

Dominic Kelly was brought along to the interview room.

'Mr Kelly, is this the Karen Hockley you met last night?' I asked.

Now, in the harsh light of the barren room, Kelly stared at the woman and his face drained of colour. 'No, that's not her,' he said.

'Big deal,' said the woman caustically.

'But this is the woman you pointed out to police in the nightclub earlier this evening, is it not?' I asked.

'Well, yes, but it was dark – it always is in those places – and I was quite a long way away from her. I really thought it was her.'

'Brilliant,' I said. 'Bloody brilliant. All right, Mr Kelly, you can go.'

'Thank you for your assistance, Mr Kelly,' said Dave, as the crestfallen Kelly left the room, doubtless lamenting that his first attempt to involve himself in a murder case had met with dismal failure. But it was only me who knew that Dave was being sarcastic.

I turned to the woman, now seated once again, her legs crossed, and drawing heavily on a cigarette. I was about to speak when the late-turn sergeant chimed in.

'This is a no-smoking area, madam.'

'Shut up, you clown,' said Dave.

'I'm extremely sorry for the inconvenience you've been caused, madam,' I began, 'but I can assure you that the police acted in good faith. The truth of the matter is that a member of the public believed you to be someone who could assist us in the investigation into a case of murder.'

'Oh, I see. You mean you thought I'd killed someone?' Judging by her cutting response, this woman was not going to give up. Perhaps she was thinking of adding slander to wrongful arrest and false imprisonment. Such are the hazards of a detective's life.

175

'Not at all. It's possible that the woman we are seeking may have vital evidence. There's no suggestion that she – and even less you – had anything to do with the death we are looking into.'

'Tough!'

'Yes, I realize that—'

'Doesn't stop me from suing you though, does it?'

'That is your right, madam,' I said, regretting that we now lived in a litigious society. 'If you wish to make a complaint, this officer' – I indicated the unhappy detective sergeant – 'will take you to an inspector who will record all the details.' Then I played my trump card. 'It will, of course, be necessary for you to make a full statement and later appear in court to give evidence in pursuance of your claim. Then there will be a disciplinary tribunal . . .'

'Well, you can stuff that,' said the exasperated woman. 'I'm not going through all that sodding rigmarole.'

I turned to the sergeant. 'Arrange for this lady to be taken back to the club, will you?'

'But there are rules about the use of police transport, sir, and I'm not sure—'

'Well, I suggest you just break the rules for once, Sergeant,' I said sharply. 'On my authority.'

There are some coppers who just don't know how to avoid complaints against the police.

Eighteen

It was late the next evening – the one following the fiasco of the woman whom Dominic Kelly thought was Karen Hockley – that things really started to go my way. In fact, I'd go further than that: it signalled the beginning of the end of the enquiry. Or, as Winston Churchill once famously said in connection with another fairly important matter, the end of the beginning.

I had just taken Sarah Dawson back to her flat and was contemplating . . . Well, let's not say what I was contemplating. Anyway, it was at that point that my mobile rang. I was in two minds whether to ignore it, but my sworn duty to uphold the Queen's peace prevented me from doing so. And if you believe that . . .

'It's DS Creasey in the incident room, sir.'

'Yes, what is it, Gavin?'

'Hockley's been arrested, sir.'

'Which Hockley?'

'Dan Hockley, sir.'

'Aha! Where?'

'You're going to like this, guv'nor,' said Creasey. 'Breaking into Max Forbes's house.'

'You're right, Gavin, I do like it. Where's he being held?'

'Lavender Hill nick, sir.'

I kissed Sarah a hasty goodnight, grabbed a flounder – *that is to say a taxi, as in flounder and dab: cab* – and within ten minutes was talking to the crew of the immediate-response car which had obligingly lifted Private Dan Hockley, renegade soldier.

'What's the story, then?' I asked the driver.

'We got a call at' – the PC glanced down at his log – 'twenty-three-ten, sir, originating from a Mr George Madison of eighteen Crouch Road. He said that he'd heard a crash from next door – number sixteen – and knew that his neighbour, Max Forbes, was away. We arrived to find the front door slightly ajar, and this nutter Hockley rampaging around inside, generally trashing the place.'

'Has anyone talked to the guy yet?'

'No, sir. We did a check on the PNC and found that he was flagged up for you to be informed, but that he was not to be questioned.'

'How did he get in?' I asked.

'He had a key, sir.'

'A key? Where the hell did he get a key from?'

'Don't know, sir. Like I said, we didn't question him, but when we searched him we found it in his possession. We tried it in the door of number sixteen and, bingo, it fitted.'

'Did he have anything else on him?'

We both knew I wasn't talking about a lottery ticket, loose change or a credit card. We were thinking about the offence of going equipped to steal.

'A balaclava helmet, sir, a torch and a pair of rubber gloves.'

'Right. Good knock-off. Well done.'

The PC preened himself slightly. 'All in a night's work, sir,' he said, and went off for a quick cup of tea in the canteen.

Hockley was looking extremely sorry for himself when I entered the interview room. But he jumped up and snapped to attention. He promptly reeled off his number, rank and name – he claimed he was still a corporal – and announced that he was not going to say anything further.

I laughed. 'The Geneva Convention doesn't apply to British soldiers banged up in Lavender Hill nick, lad,' I said mildly. 'Just sit down, and smoke if you want to.' I told Dave to switch on the tape recorder and give it the requisite information about who was present and all that nonsense.

'I don't smoke,' said Hockley.

Maybe he didn't smoke. I should worry. On the other hand, he might have thought that it was some sort of softening-up process on the part of the devious police.

I told Dave to caution Hockley. I could never remember the words myself, and I'd yet to acquire another little card with it all on. It was an unfortunate but necessary preamble to an interview with a suspect, and often had the effect of ensuring that he clammed up without saying another word. But I suppose that's what our fearless legislators intended, their primary concern always being the care of the accused's interests and to hell with those of the victim.

'Now then, Mr Hockley—'

'It's Corporal Hockley.'

'Not what I heard. I understand that you're now a private.'

'Oh, you know about that, do you?'

'Yes, I do, and I also know that the cut on your face was the result of an altercation with a prostitute in King's Cross.' That was pure guesswork: he could have got it anywhere, but the look on his face told me that I'd scored. 'So don't start giving me a load of bullshit. You were found by police in Max Forbes's house, which you had entered illegally, as a trespasser. So, right now you stand in grave danger of being charged with burglary, to say nothing of indecently assaulting a prostitute. And, depending on the reason for your entering Max Forbes's house, you may even be charged with *aggravated* burglary.' I gazed sternly at the soldier. 'And that can carry a maximum penalty of life imprisonment.' I didn't bother to tell him that I'd never, in all my career, known such a sentence to be imposed for aggravated burglary.

But my little précis of that bit of the Theft Act did the trick.

'That bastard was screwing my missus,' Hockley exclaimed, his fists clenching and unclenching on the table.

'What bastard?' I asked mildly.

'Max bloody Forbes, that's who.'

179

'How did you know that?'

'She told me. Boasted about it, she did, the slag. All up front and in yer face, like.'

I offered up a silent prayer that my English-graduate sergeant would not make one of his acerbic comments about clichés, particularly those that appeared to be inapposite.

'When did she tell you?' I hoped that he would slip up and say it was yesterday. But he didn't.

'Before I got posted to Belize.'

'You didn't mention that when we spoke last week.'

'Yeah, well, I wasn't too chuffed about it. Anyway, it's got sod all to do with you lot. I was going to sort the bastard out myself.'

'Why shouldn't Max have given Karen a seeing-to? After all, you said that you and Alex Forbes had had it off. Seems only fair.'

'That was different. That was when Karen was there,' Hockley said, as though that somehow made the arrangement acceptable to him.

'Did your wife tell you where this took place?'

'Yeah, she reckoned she went down his pad – the one where I got nicked – and did it. And she done it with his missus, Alex, an' all.'

'So you decided that you'd sort him out, is that the up and down of it, to coin a phrase?'

'Well, wouldn't you?'

'Where's your wife now?'

Hockley shrugged. 'I don't know,' he said, 'and I couldn't care less.'

'Then why are you so concerned about what she allegedly got up to with Max Forbes?'

'I was going to teach the bastard a lesson, that's all. And I'm going to teach her one when I find her.'

I forwent the pleasure of telling him about the offences of threatening to kill or inflict grievous bodily harm. He was in enough bother already.

'Have you any idea where Karen might be now?'

'No. All I know is that she took off while I was in Belize. No note, no nothing. She just upped and went.'

'Has she ever previously left home without telling you?'

'Once or twice,' Hockley admitted, 'but she always come back.'

'D'you think she might be with this Max Forbes?'

'Your guess is as good as mine,' said Hockley with a shrug. 'But I'd put money on it.'

'Have you any idea where Forbes might be, then?' I didn't for one moment think that Hockley would know, and he confirmed it.

'How could I?'

'Had your wife had other affairs?' I asked.

'No,' said Hockley a little too quickly.

'Oh? What about the sergeant-major you found in bed with her? The one you thumped, as a result of which you lost the first of your three stripes.'

'How d'you know about that?' Hockley seemed surprised at just how much we did know about him.

'I'm investigating the murder of Alex Forbes, Hockley, and, when I investigate a murder, I find out all sorts of things. Anyway, it was you who told me.'

Hockley had obviously forgotten most of our last conversation. 'Yeah, well, he asked for it,' he said bitterly.

'And have *you* had any affairs, apart from your one-night stand with Alex?'

Hockley remained silent for a while, concentrating his gaze on the tabletop, and tracing a mark with his finger. Then he looked up. 'One or two, yeah. Well, if she was at it, why shouldn't I?'

'The officers who arrested you have told me that you were smashing the place up.'

'Well, serve the bastard right. It was him I was after, but he wasn't there. I never went there meaning to do it over, but when I got into his front room, I walked into this bloody great frame and it fell over. I never turned on the lights, see.' Hockley grinned. 'Made a hell of a bloody crash, that did.

But when I got me torch on it, I guessed what he used it for, the sick bastard, and I just saw red, I suppose.'

So, why was the frame in the sitting room? It was usually kept in the cellar. Evidence of recent use maybe, and if so with whom? Sydney Gill, I suppose.

'Where did you get the key to Max Forbes's house?' asked Dave.

'Who said I'd got a key?' demanded Hockley churlishly.

Dave leaned across the table, menacingly face to face with Hockley. 'Don't piss me about, soldier,' he said. 'When you were nicked you had it in your possession.'

Hockley moved back sharply. 'Found it at home, didn't I? Down Aldershot.'

'How did you know it was the right key?'

'I never. But I found it hidden in one of the kitchen cupboards. It's where Karen always puts stuff she don't want me to find. I knew it wasn't one of ours – well, it never fitted nothing we'd got – so I guessed it must have been for that bastard's house.'

I decided that there was little to be gained from questioning Hockley any further. He could go on the sheet for burglary, but he was unlikely to be able to tell me anything helpful about the murder of Alex Forbes.

'You'll probably be charged with aggravated burglary,' I said, 'and doubtless detained in custody pending your appearance before a court.' It wasn't my job, but I was pretty certain that's what would happen to him.

'What about bail? I'm entitled to bail.'

'Not if there's a chance that you won't appear in court to answer to that bail,' I said, 'and I'll have no difficulty in persuading the custody sergeant that you'll probably abscond. After all, you've gone absent from the army twice. In any case, even if you were bailed, we'd have to hand you over to the military police, and I doubt that they'd give you bail. Probably lock you up and throw away the key.'

*   *   *

Saturday morning. And twenty-five days since the discovery of Alex Forbes's body. I presumed that Dan Hockley had appeared before the district judge at South-Western Court, but quite frankly I wasn't greatly concerned with the outcome. I didn't anticipate questioning him again.

But it was now of paramount importance to find Max Forbes. That he was a violent man had been confirmed by Melissa Watson, the young woman who had bravely come forward to tell us of the ordeal she had suffered at the hands of Forbes and his wife. There was little doubt in my mind that he was capable of murder, and I was now strongly of the opinion that he'd killed his wife before vanishing with Karen Hockley. Although what the Battersea artist and the bawdy army wife from Aldershot had in common – apart from the obvious – baffled me.

The telephone calls resulting from the publication of Forbes's photograph had now ceased, but even those that we had received proved useless.

'I reckon he's done a Lucan,' said Dave, referring to the disappearance of Lord Lucan following the death of his family's nanny. 'Either he's gone to ground or he's gone abroad again. Probably taking all his clothes off in the Black Forest as we speak.'

'We've done that check, Dave. *Hauptkommissarin* Heidi Stolpe told us that there was no one at the camp fitting Forbes's description.'

Dave ferreted about in a sort of canvas bag affair that he thought was the in thing to use as a briefcase, and extracted an orange. 'But we didn't tell her what *Madame* Garnier told us, did we, guv? That Max Forbes called himself Victor Smith when he was there the last time.'

'Bloody hell, neither did we. Why didn't I think of that?'

'Because you've got me here to think of it for you,' said Dave, surgically dissecting his orange with a pocket knife that appeared to have about twenty-seven different gadgets on it.

It was *Hauptkommissarin* Heidi Stolpe's day off. The man who answered the phone introduced himself as

Oberkommissar Walter Bohl, Stolpe's deputy, and politely enquired how he could help.

It was not until after lunch that Bohl rang back. 'I have made enquiries, *Herr* Chief Inspector Brock,' he began, 'and there is a *Herr* Victor Smith at the Beck *Nacktkulturlager* here in Karlsruhe. Also, he is with a woman who he calls his wife. Her name is Gail Smith.'

'Got the bastard,' I muttered in English.

'*Wie, bitte?*' Bohl said, not grasping my colloquialism.

'I was just expressing my satisfaction at the outcome of your enquiry, *Herr* Bohl,' I said, rapidly transposing my comment into understandable German.

'Ah, good. What are you wanting us to do about this man? Are you thinking of extradition? Is there an Interpol red-corner circular for him?' Bohl asked, querying whether an international arrest warrant had been issued.

'No, there isn't,' I said. And, if I had my way, one wasn't going to be issued. Extradition is much too complicated. 'Thank you very much for your assistance, *Herr* Bohl. Oh, did you happen to find out when Smith arrived at this nudist camp, and how long he intended to stay?'

'He arrived on Friday the twenty-third of August, but did not make a specific booking. He paid in cash for one week, and told the manager that he would probably stay for longer. But his wife did not arrive until yesterday. I thought it was not a good idea to speak personally to *Herr* Smith. However, one of my officers covertly obtained digital photographs of him and his wife, which I will transmit to you by email. If you can give me your email address it will be with you in minutes.'

I thanked Bohl once again for his help and explained that email was a mystery to me. I passed him over to Colin Wilberforce, because he and Bohl spoke the same language. And I didn't mean German.

For the next ten minutes I pondered how we could tempt Forbes, alias Smith, back to the UK.

And then the photographs arrived. One was undoubtedly of Max Forbes and the other of a woman with short blonde hair. Unfortunately the definition in the photograph of the woman called Gail Smith was not as sharp as in Max's, and was taken at such an angle that it was not possible to see if she had a butterfly tattooed on her left shoulder.

'It tallies, Dave,' I said. 'Max Forbes, also known as Victor Smith, arrived there the day after the Madisons saw him leaving Crouch Road, and the woman calling herself Gail Smith arrived the day after Dominic Kelly claims to have met Karen Hockley in a club in Fulham. It must be her and she probably went straight to the airport after she left Kelly at East Putney Underground station.'

'Hadn't we better do a double check, guv?' asked Dave.

'How?'

'Well, we've only ever seen a photograph of Karen Hockley. We've never seen her in the flesh.'

'You have now,' I said, waving the photograph of a naked Gail Smith.

Dave ignored this facetious comment. 'Be a good idea to show it to someone who's met her, wouldn't it?'

'Good thinking, Dave. Find out what they've done with Dan Hockley.'

A couple of phone calls later, Dave imparted the unwelcome news that Hockley had been remanded into military custody by the cunning cost-conscious beak at South-Western Court and carted off to Aldershot for an eight-day lay down.

'So, where does that leave us?' I asked.

'Driving to Aldershot, guv, I guess,' said Dave mournfully. He was not happy.

As we were encroaching on another constabulary's bailiwick, courtesy demanded that we tell them. Apart from that, we needed Jock Ferguson to oil the wheels. I have to admit that the army's arcane procedures are a foreign country to me.

Jock was at home, watching cricket on the television, and I'd had to pass a message through the station officer at Aldershot nick. But we made contact at last.

'Working on a Saturday, Harry? Oh dear!' said Jock when he rang me back.

After we'd exchanged the customary sarcastic badinage, I explained the problem, and Jock promised to telephone the military while we were on our way to Hampshire. And he offered to assign a detective sergeant to take us from Aldershot police station to the barracks where Hockley was incarcerated.

It was six o'clock that evening by the time we had driven the forty miles to Aldershot. Jock's young DS jumped into the back of our car and directed us to a guardroom somewhere in that labyrinth they call the military town.

The sergeant of the guard had been advised of our visit and, after a considerable amount of unnecessary stamping and shouting – without which the military machine seems incapable of operating – Dan Hockley was produced. He was wearing denim overalls and plimsolls and looked to be very sorry for himself, but it was in the character of the man that he was probably blaming everyone but himself for his present predicament.

'Is that your wife Karen?' Dave asked, showing him the photograph. 'It was taken at a nudist camp in Germany where Max Forbes is known to be staying.'

Hockley stared at it for some time. 'Definitely not,' he said angrily.

But I was far from sure that Hockley was telling the truth. On reflection, it had probably been counter-productive to show him a photograph of a naked woman, covertly taken by police, and ask him if it was his wife. Particularly when we'd added that she was with a man he had threatened with physical harm.

'Is it anyone you know?'

'No.' Hockley's reply was surly. 'Don't know any birds with short blonde hair.'

'Did your wife have a butterfly tattooed on her left shoulder?' Dave asked.

'Not the last time I saw her,' said Hockley, 'but she was always going on about getting one done.'

'Well, sod it,' I said, once Hockley had been put back in his cell. 'Any decent pubs in Aldershot?' I asked Jock's DS.

'There's about sixty pubs altogether, sir.'

'But less than half of 'em are decent,' chipped in the sergeant of the guard. 'And all of 'em will probably be full of drunken squaddies.'

Nineteen

I had intended to spend this Sunday with Sarah. Nothing special, just a run out to the country and lunch in a pub. A lazy day.

At eleven o'clock, just as we were preparing to leave Sarah's flat, my mobile rang.

'Don't you dare answer it,' said Sarah, in one of her threatening modes.

But I did answer it, always a foolish thing to do on your day off. It was force of habit.

'It's Colin Wilberforce, sir.'

'Are you at work?' I asked, mentally logging a reminder to check Colin's overtime return. It wasn't the money that concerned me – good luck to him – but more his welfare and his marriage. I knew he had a wife and a couple of children, and I didn't want him spending every day at the office, murder or no murder.

'Yes, sir. Karen Hockley was arrested at Heathrow, twenty minutes ago. On her way in from Stuttgart. Apparently one of the immigration officers wasn't too happy about her appearance. Her photograph showed her with long, blonde hair, but, when she arrived, her hair had been cut short, and she was wearing glasses, so he called a Special Branch officer over. And the SB guy did a check against the PNC.'

I immediately took back all the nasty things I'd ever said about the immigration service.

'Where is she now, Colin?'

'Heathrow Airport police station, sir.'

'Well, I'm not traipsing all the way out there on a Sunday.

Arrange for an escort to pick her up and take her to Charing Cross nick.'

'On a Sunday, sir?' asked a dubious Colin. 'Might be diffi-cult.'

He was right, of course. Coppers are an endangered species, particularly on a Sunday.

'Oh, come on, Colin, you can fix it,' I said encouragingly. 'And get hold of Dave Poole if you can, and ask him to meet me at Charing Cross when she's arrived.'

'Good as done, sir,' said Colin with more confidence than I suspect he felt.

Following the usual apologies to Sarah – who by now was more than accustomed to such disappointments – a deep-pan pizza was substituted for our country-pub lunch while I waited for Colin's next call. It came at one o'clock.

'Karen Hockley's now at Charing Cross police station, sir,' he said. 'I managed to get hold of Dave and he'll meet you there.' There was a pause. 'But I don't think you're Madeleine's flavour of the month, sir,' he added.

'I'm not Sarah's either,' I said.

I snatched a last mouthful of pizza, kissed Sarah and apol-ogized once again.

Despite the poor quality of the print that *Oberkommissar* Walter Bohl had emailed to Curtis Green, there was little doubt in my mind that it was of the woman now seated in the interview room.

'Mrs Hockley, I'm Detective Chief Inspector Brock, and this is Detective Sergeant Poole.'

Karen Hockley afforded the pair of us a cool glance of appraisal. 'Are you the person responsible for my being arrested like some common criminal in front of all those passengers and then brought here in a police van?' she asked.

'Yes, I am.'

'Well, perhaps you'd care to explain yourself, either to me or to my solicitor when he gets here.'

I was baffled by this woman. Clearly well educated and

articulate, I wondered how on earth she'd finished up being married to Private Dan Hockley, who, by anyone's reckoning, was not the brightest of men. I could only assume that, in Karen's view, his sexual prowess outweighed his coarseness.

'I am investigating the murder of Alexandra Forbes, late wife of Max Forbes,' I said. 'I understand that you had a sexual liaison with both of them.'

'And what if I did?'

'And that you spent the last few days with Max Forbes at a nudist colony in the Black Forest near Karlsruhe, where the pair of you masqueraded as Victor and Gail Smith.' I wasn't going to tell her that Forbes was my top suspect for the murder of his wife. That could make for difficulties later on.

'Is that a crime, then? Some new directive from Brussels that you can't take your clothes off if you want to, is that it?' The sarcasm flowed unabated.

There are two sorts of suspects . . . well, three actually. There are those who are arrogantly confident that they can outwit the bumbling police, and those who just crumble immediately and confess all. The third sort, of course, comprises those who didn't commit the crime anyway. Right now I was rapidly coming to the conclusion that Karen Hockley was in either the first or the third of those categories.

'Your husband, Private Hockley, is now in custody at Aldershot, awaiting trial for breaking into Max Forbes's house at Battersea and committing acts of criminal damage. He may also be charged with assaulting a prostitute at King's Cross last Wednesday.'

'Really?' Karen showed no surprise at her husband's reduction in rank or that he'd been arrested for burglary. She didn't even raise an eyebrow at the news that he was back from Belize. And she certainly didn't seem fazed that he'd been consorting with professional whores. 'Are you suggesting that I may have had something to do with these distasteful matters?'

'No.'

'Then what precisely am I doing here?'

'Why did you leave him?'

'Who says that I did?'

'He does. We have interviewed your husband and he tells us that, while he was abroad on duty, you left the marital home, but gave him no explanation. He spoke to his commanding officer about his concern, and was sent home on compassionate leave to try to find you.'

'More fool him,' said Karen.

'Why did you leave him, Mrs Hockley?' I repeated.

'If you'll forgive me for asking, what the hell's that got to do with you? You had me brought here to talk about Alex Forbes's murder, so you said, but all you've talked about so far is my marriage to Dan.'

'You left your husband to go away with Max Forbes, didn't you?'

'So?'

'Why, then, did you return on your own?'

'Because Max and I had a row,' snapped Karen. For the first time since the interview had begun, I noticed that she was showing signs of anger with Forbes. Odd that, considering that she'd displaced his wife in bed, presumably intending it to be a permanent arrangement.

'Max Forbes went to the Black Forest a week ago last Friday,' I continued. 'Why did you not go until the day before yesterday?'

Curiously, she didn't ask how I knew that she'd gone there the day before yesterday. 'I didn't know where he was and I was upset and anxious. Actually, I was bloody furious.' Karen looked down and started plucking at a piece of fluff on her skirt. 'I was waiting for a call, but it wasn't until Thursday that I heard from him. But, when I got there, he just laughed it off. In fact, he was scathing. He called me a stupid bitch for worrying.'

'And so you came straight back again.'

'Yes. Well, almost straight away. I told him in no uncertain terms that I wasn't going to have anything more to do with him. We're finished.'

There was an undisguised bitterness in Karen's statement, and I reckoned that it must have been one hell of a row. It was yet another revealing aspect of the female psyche, that she was so concerned not to have heard from her lover. As a man, I'd've expected her to say that she'd found him in bed with another woman, and that that's why she'd walked out on him. There again, knowing what Karen Hockley's morals were like – according to her husband, anyway – perhaps not.

'Did Max Forbes ever mention anything about the murder of his wife?'

'Not to me, no. Apart from telling me that she *had* been murdered. He was very upset about it at first, but I'd hoped that he was going to get over it and settle down with me after a while.'

'Why did you cut your hair and dye it blonde?' Dave asked, apropos of nothing in particular.

'Er, he . . .' Karen was obviously confused by the question and took a moment to recover. But recover she did. 'Max said I reminded him too much of Alex. She had long black hair and so did I. He asked me to shorten it and change the colour.'

'Did Forbes ever beat you, Mrs Hockley?' I asked. 'Practise sado-masochism?'

'Once or twice, yes. In fact, we would whip each other, although I don't know what that has to do with you. It was mutually satisfying. Lots of people do it, and there's nothing wrong in it.' Karen did not seem at all embarrassed at talking about her sexual practices, as though they were a commonplace.

'How often did you go to Battersea?' I asked.

'Battersea?' Karen sounded as though she'd never heard of the place.

'Yes, number sixteen Crouch Road.'

'Er, once or twice, I suppose.' She was sounding less confident now.

'And did you, Alex and Max indulge in group sex? Three in a bed, for example.'

'Yes, sometimes.'

'And did you ever whip Alex Forbes?'

'I don't see why I should answer that. It's not illegal, is it?'

'Then why not answer it?'

But still Karen Hockley made no reply, and it was apparent that we now had nothing to lose. From her reticence, I came to the conclusion that she had been involved in the death of Alex Forbes. And that it had happened at Crouch Road and the body had been stored in the freezer there – the freezer where we had found traces of Alex's hair – until Forbes and Karen could decide what the hell to do with it. For what that was worth.

'Read the caution to Mrs Hockley, Sergeant Poole,' I said.

Dave didn't have a little card, but the clever bugger knew it by heart anyway. Karen Hockley looked decidedly apprehensive by the time he'd finished.

'I put it to you, Mrs Hockley, that you and Max Forbes murdered Alex Forbes and subsequently disposed of her body in Richmond Park. And I suggest that you did it for no better reason than that you and he were infatuated with each other, but that Alex objected strongly and may even have threatened to kill you. Or Max.' I was way out on a limb with all this, but somehow I had to get a reaction that would justify my keeping this woman in custody for a while. I knew that if she was released, she'd disappear again. Even so, there could be some substance in my allegations.

'That's absolute rubbish,' said Karen hotly. 'If you think you can prove that, then I suggest you try.'

But then Dave came up with the crippler. 'Have you got a tattoo on your left shoulder?' he asked, looking up from his notes. 'A tattoo of a butterfly?'

'Yes. Why?'

'When did you have that done?'

'About a year ago.' Karen seemed a little disconcerted by Dave's question, and I wondered why.

'And where did you have it done?'

'Er, in Aldershot somewhere, I think.'

'Whereabouts in Aldershot?'

'I can't remember. But why? Why all this interest in my tattoo? And how did you know about it, anyway?'

'Dominic Kelly told us.'

Karen Hockley smiled. 'Oh, Dominic, yes. A sweet boy. Not really very good in bed, but he tried hard.' She crossed her legs and yawned. 'And now, if you don't mind, I'd like to go home to bed. I had a tiring flight and I—'

'And where is your home now, Mrs Hockley? Battersea? Or do you intend to return to your husband at Gort Road?'

'How d'you know where he lives?' Karen asked sharply.

'Because we've been there. But he's not living there at the moment. He's living in a guardroom somewhere in Aldershot.' I was interested that Karen was already saying that *he* lived there, rather than *we* live there. 'As a matter of interest, where were you living after you left your husband?'

'Er, with a friend at first, and then with Max.'

'Who was this friend?'

'I'm not saying. I don't want to get her involved.'

'Her or him?' I asked.

'That was a cheap shot,' said Karen.

And there we left it. 'Pending further enquiries, Mrs Hockley, you will be detained here.' I'd already noted that there was no sign of the threatened solicitor, and put it down to bravado. Despite her sophistication, I couldn't imagine the Hockleys ever having had dealings with a lawyer. And, living in army quarters, they wouldn't even have ventured into the legal minefield of buying a house.

'But this is outrageous,' protested Karen. 'I've done nothing wrong and you can't prove that I have.'

I knew that, if she pushed it, I really had no grounds for detaining her. She was right: there wasn't any evidence. OK, she'd run away from her husband and shacked up with a widower. So what? Nevertheless, after her initial outburst she seemed resigned to being kept in custody.

I terminated the interview and arranged for her to have a meal.

Outside, Dave was bursting with new ideas. Thank God!

'What's on your mind, Dave?' I asked.

'It's this business of the tattoo, guv. Hockley reckoned that, when he went to Belize, Karen didn't have a tattoo. But she says she had it done about a year ago. I don't know how many tattooists there are in Aldershot, but I'm not prepared to have a go at finding them all. You can bet that some of them are dodgy anyway, and they're not going to keep books. Not with VAT inspectors waiting in the wings, that's for sure.'

'Doubtless you've thought of a shortcut.' I knew that Dave was the king of shortcut detectives.

'Yeah, but you'll probably think I'm off the planet,' Dave said, and then explained his theory.

At exactly five minutes to nine the following morning, I rang Melissa Watson's mobile. The same hesitant voice answered.

'Mrs Watson, it's Detective Chief Inspector Brock. I need to speak to you again, urgently. Would you be able to come to Belgravia police station at about twenty to one? It's rather important and I think you may be able to help me.'

Although she sounded unhappy about my request, Melissa Watson kept the appointment.

'Was there a woman called Karen Hockley at Crouch Road when you met Alex Forbes there, Mrs Watson?' I asked.

'No, it was just Alex and me, and later Max came in, as I told you before.'

'Did you hear either of them mention a Karen Hockley during the time you were there?'

'No, I've never heard the name before. Oh, just a minute though. Wasn't there a photograph of her in the paper the other day?'

'Yes, there was,' I said, 'but it was me who had it placed there. We were anxious to trace her, you see.'

'Oh, and you're still looking for her, I suppose.'

'No, we've found her.'

Melissa looked distinctly puzzled by all this police mumbo-jumbo, and was probably wondering why the hell we'd asked her to come here.

'The reason I asked to see you again, Mrs Watson, is that I have an important question to ask you.' I glanced at Dave who was concentrating on the ceiling. I think he may have been pleading with his particular God for Melissa Watson to come up with the right answer.

At two o'clock, I rang Jock Ferguson at Aldershot and explained what we wanted of him and why. He agreed at once.

Dave and I were already at the mortuary when the army prison van arrived. Private Dan Hockley, now correctly dressed in uniform, was escorted by two beefy regimental policemen.

As quickly as possible he was conducted into the viewing room.

It didn't take long.

'Oh, God Almighty!' he exclaimed. 'It's Karen.' He paused. 'But she never had black hair before. She must've dyed it.'

'You're a clever bugger, Dave,' I said.

'It was the business of the tattoo, guv. The moment that the woman we've got in Charing Cross nick said that she'd had the butterfly tattoo done a year ago, I wondered if she really was Karen Hockley. And when Melissa Watson told us that Alex Forbes had a tattoo of a butterfly on her left shoulder, I knew we'd got her. And the fact that she used Karen Hockley's passport when she arrived at Heathrow clinched it in my book.'

And there went the kaleidoscope again. No one had murdered Alex Forbes, because it looked very much as though she was still alive. And, if I was right, she was in custody at Charing Cross police station.

But someone had murdered Karen Hockley.

And, being the detective I am, I knew that very soon we'd have to feel Max Forbes's collar.

Twenty

The astonishing revelation that the body in the Horseferry Road mortuary was Dan Hockley's wife Karen, and not Alex Forbes, had turned my enquiry on its head and had caused me to waste nearly a month going in the wrong direction. All along we'd believed that the fingerprints we thought were Alex's were, in fact, those of Karen. And vice versa.

Dave and I went straight to Charing Cross police station, and found a worried custody sergeant who was very pleased to see us.

'I've been trying to get hold of you, sir,' he said. 'This Karen Hockley is really kicking up. She's threatening civil action for wrongful arrest and false imprisonment. She's even been talking about a writ of habeas corpus. I've really no justification for holding her. I've spoken to the superintendent and he agrees.'

'Fear not, Sergeant. I have good news for you,' I said. 'You don't have a prisoner called Karen Hockley at all.'

'I don't, sir?' The sergeant adopted the hunted look of a man who thought that the whole scenario had suddenly changed for the worse: that a prisoner in his custody had escaped.

'Her real name is Alex Forbes. And, before the day's out, I'll probably charge her with murder.'

'Oh!' said the sergeant, with a sigh of relief, and began amending the large form on his desk.

The prisoner was still maintaining an aggressive confidence when she was brought into the interview room.

'I wish to protest in the strongest possible terms,' she began.

I held up my hand. 'You're still under caution,' I said, 'but just to make sure that you're under no illusion about that, I'll get Sergeant Poole to repeat it.' I nodded to Dave and he recited, once more, the sonorous prose of the Judges' Rules caution – as those of us at the sharp end still call it – before doing the necessary with the tape recorder. It wasn't really essential, but we'd cautioned someone we thought was Karen Hockley. No doubt defence counsel would make a big thing of it if we didn't do it all over again in respect of someone we now knew to be Alexandra Forbes.

'I want a solicitor,' was the woman's only response.

'I'd go further than that,' I said mildly. 'You actually *need* a solicitor.'

That disconcerted her, but she said nothing.

'My enquiries have revealed that you are in fact Mrs Alexandra Forbes and I put it to you that, in concert with your husband Max, you murdered Karen Hockley.'

Alex Forbes's face drained of colour and for a moment I thought she was going to faint. She certainly collapsed rather heavily into a chair. 'That's absolute nonsense,' she said eventually, her voice rising. 'How can you say such a thing?'

'You can deny it as much as you like, Mrs Forbes,' I said, 'but the evidence is overwhelming. A woman has come forward who alleges that you and your husband savagely beat her at your house in Battersea, and who is prepared to identify you.' But even as I said it, I doubted that Melissa Watson would be willing to go into the witness box. 'And, less than half an hour ago, Private Dan Hockley, with whom you also had a sexual relationship, positively identified the body found in Richmond Park as that of his wife, Karen Hockley.' Then, as a risky afterthought, I added, 'And Bill Griffin saw you in the West End on the tenth of August.'

It was a guess, of course. I was by no means certain that Griffin *had* seen her – in fact, was still convinced that he'd made a mistake.

But Alex didn't deny it. 'I want a solicitor,' she said again, and this time she meant it.

That, I suppose, was the inevitable outcome of telling her she could have one, but that's the law for you.

'You may call a solicitor of your own choosing, or one can be provided for you under the duty solicitor scheme,' I told her.

'I don't care where he comes from so long as he's a solic-itor.' Suddenly the fight had ebbed. Within seconds she appeared to have aged, and her face was now drawn and haggard.

It took an hour, but eventually a young man wearing wire-rimmed glasses turned up at the nick. I suspected that he was newly admitted to the profession: he still had that knight-in-shining-armour look about him that said he was ready and willing to save this particular damsel in distress.

But you'll have to go some this time, sport.

When we resumed the interview, it was apparent that, during the time she had spent waiting for the lawyer, Alex Forbes had been thinking about her predicament. And her strategy. As a result the attendance of the solicitor turned out to be an unnecessary drain on the public purse.

'All right, I'll tell you what happened,' was Alex's opening statement.

'I must remind you that you're still under caution,' I was obliged to tell her. I didn't want anything going wrong at this stage. 'I take it you're willing to make a statement?'

'Yes.'

'And are you willing to answer questions?'

'Yes.'

'Would you like Sergeant Poole to write down what you are about to say, or do you want to write it yourself?'

'He can write it,' said Alex, waving a nonchalant hand in Dave's direction.

Having gone through all that legal hocus-pocus, Dave prepared the forms, obtained the woman's signature to the written caution and glanced up with pen poised.

'Go on then, Mrs Forbes,' I said.

'It was Max.'

'What was?'

'It was Max who killed her.'

'D'you wish to expand on that?'

Alex paused for a moment, seemingly collecting her thoughts. 'I made contact with Karen through one of the SM magazines we took. She came to the house several times.'

'Was Max there?'

'Not at first, no.'

'And you went to Aldershot, didn't you?'

'Yes.'

'Let's get this straight. It was actually you who made the contact and it was you who went to Aldershot before Karen came to Battersea and met Max, wasn't it?'

'I shouldn't have thought it mattered which way round it was. But yes, you're right,' said Alex. 'Anyway, I went to Aldershot and met Karen, and she was great fun. She, Dan and I had some good times down there, but then I made the mistake of telling Max about her. He suggested inviting her to Crouch Road when he was there and could join in. I told Karen that we'd got some good kit at our place: the frame, all sorts of specially made restraints, and a variety of whips. Much better than the stuff she'd got in her crummy little army house in Aldershot. The best she could come up with was a selection of webbing equipment that the army had issued to her husband. Including a belt that hurt like hell.' She forced a smile. 'But it was a real turn-on.'

'And so Karen agreed to come to London,' I prompted.

'She was all for it, and the first few times we enjoyed ourselves. We used to take it in turns on the frame while the other two inflicted the punishment. We always called it that. It made it more fun.'

What a strange idea of fun this woman did have.

'Did your husband ever have sexual intercourse with Karen Hockley?'

The young solicitor blinked furiously and coughed

affectedly. 'Mrs Forbes, I really don't think that you should answer—'

'Oh, shut up,' said Alex, turning on him, her eyes blazing. 'Who's doing this?' And for the rest of the interview, the lawyer didn't say another word. Facing me again, Alex said, 'Yes, we all had sex, after every session. Max with Karen, Max with me, and Karen with me.'

So much for Max Forbes saying that he and his wife didn't enjoy a sexual relationship. There again, perhaps he didn't enjoy it.

'When we interviewed Bill Griffin—'

'Why did you go to see him?'

'When we interviewed Bill Griffin, he said that you'd arrived at his houseboat the night that you supposedly left your husband.'

'That's right. I did. Found him screwing some toffee-nosed bitch on the floor. Very embarrassing.' Alex gave a weak smile. 'For them.'

'Griffin claims that you told him you'd left your husband Max because he was homosexual.'

Alex laughed at that. 'Max gay? Not a chance. Bill's making that up, but God knows why.'

I certainly hadn't a clue. 'Didn't you mind your husband having sex with Karen while you were there?' I asked, getting back to the mainstream of the interrogation. 'I presume you were there.'

'I told you I was, and of course I didn't mind. What was there to object to? We had an open marriage. I had my lovers and he had his.'

Exactly what Madame *Garnier had said, but what a world of difference in the two women's approach to their respective affairs.*

'Would you like to tell me what you know about Karen's death?'

'We always shared a bottle of champagne as a preamble to our games,' Alex began, 'and I'd gone out to the kitchen to get one.'

I wasn't quite sure what this had to do with Karen Hockley's death, but I didn't interrupt now that the woman was beginning to open up.

'We had a firm rule that we would only play when all three of us were in the room,' Alex continued, 'so Max knew not to start until I got back. But on this occasion – it was about the fourth or fifth time Karen came to Battersea – there wasn't any champagne in the fridge, so I had to go down to the cellar, where we had some more. But, by the time I got back, Karen was already naked and strapped to the frame, and Max had started laying into her.' She reached for a glass of water and took a sip.

'Your husband told me that he didn't drink. That he was a reformed alcoholic.'

Alex hesitated. 'Yes, he was. But he didn't think that champagne would do any harm. I suppose it's possible that on this occasion he'd had something stronger when I wasn't looking. You know how deceitful alcoholics can be.'

'Yes,' I said, 'but do go on.'

'He'd put the leather hood on her and had done the straps up really tight, much tighter than usual, and he was beating hell out of her, really hard, much harder than we normally did. Karen was screaming and sobbing, but of course it was muffled by the hood. It was obvious that she wasn't enjoying it and I shouted to Max to stop, but he was in a sort of frenzy and, when I tried to pull him away, he hit me with the back of his hand, really hard. I fell over and banged my head on the coffee table as I went down, and that stunned me for a moment or two. But then I started to get really frightened. He'd gone completely berserk. I'd never seen him behave so viciously before and I was sure that any moment he'd turn on me.' Alex paused and there was silence in the room, save for the slight hum of the tape recorder. 'But then I noticed that Karen had stopped making a noise and I shouted to Max again to stop, and to get the hood off her. Then we found that she'd stopped breathing too. We got her out of the restraints as fast as we could and put her on the floor. I tried mouth-to-mouth, but it was no good. She was dead.'

'What did you do next?'

'What d'you think we did? We panicked.' Alex's mood had lightened a little, probably because she thought I was believing all this. 'We'd got a dead woman on our hands. Then Max came up with the idea of putting her body in the chest freezer we'd got in the cellar, while we worked out how to get rid of it.'

'What happened then?' I asked.

'We went on holiday.'

'*You went on holiday?*' Despite all the years I'd been a CID officer, the sheer callousness of that statement amazed me.

'Well, we had to think about what we were going to do. We knew that Dan had been sent to Belize for six months, so there was plenty of time before he found out that his wife was missing.' Alex was becoming more confident now, presuming, I suppose, that she was convincing me of her innocence. 'Then Max came up with this brilliant idea: he would report me missing, and I would pretend to be Karen. And, when her body was found, as we knew it would be, Max identified her as me. We dyed Karen's hair black, so that she'd look more like me.'

'And the point of all that?' I asked.

'We thought that you'd suspect Karen of murdering me,' Alex continued, 'but after a few weeks I'd stop being Karen and she would disappear, so to speak.' Then, with a sneer, she added, 'And so it would become another of your unsolved murders. I went into shops and deliberately gave the name of Karen Hockley, and I told Dominic that was my name on the day her picture was in the papers, so that he'd obligingly go running to the police, bursting with his news, which I presume he did, poor naïve little boy.'

'And going on holiday was part of this grand plan, was it?'

'We had to give ourselves time to think. To plan what we were going to do with Karen's body.'

'When exactly did she die?'

Alex thought about that for a moment. 'It was a Thursday. Yes, the eleventh of July. I'm not likely to forget it.'

'But you went to Aldershot after that. Why?'

'We wanted to make sure that there was nothing in the Hockleys' house that would connect us with Karen.'

But you missed Karen's secret address book.

'Why did you bother with this business of the postcards?' I asked.

Alex shrugged. 'Max thought it would be a good idea to lay a few false trails,' she said. 'He made the phone call to Skinner, too, and told him I was ill.'

Max seemed to have had a lot of ideas but, as it was turning out, none of them very good ones.

'Max thought that to send the postcards in Karen's hand-writing, but to the addresses of my men friends, and to Skinner, would eventually make you think that Karen was the killer and was on the run,' Alex continued. 'Max is an artist, you know, and he's very good at copying other people's writing. We'd grabbed a sample of Karen's writing from Aldershot and took it with us.'

'Except that it was a sample of Dan Hockley's handwriting you took,' I said, 'not Karen's.'

'What?' Alex raised her eyebrows in surprise.

'Not as clever as you thought, were you?'

'It was Max who took it. He was very careful, too. He wore rubber gloves the whole time he was there.'

So, that's why Jock's team didn't find Max Forbes's finger-prints at Gort Road.

Alex obviously didn't attach too much importance to the serious blunder that her husband had made, probably because she was so desperately intent on shifting all the blame on to him. She probably imagined that Max – being in the Black Forest – was beyond our reach, and that, having convinced us that she was an innocent party in the murder, she would shortly walk out of the police station scot-free.

'Where did you go, on this holiday?'

'We went to the nudist colony in the Black Forest for a fortnight.'

'When was this?'

'Max reported me missing on the Monday after Karen's death, and the next day we drove to Dover, crossed to Calais and went on from there. We'd been to the camp before, a few years ago, but this time we called ourselves Victor and Gail Smith and paid in cash so there'd be no record of our stay as Max and Alex Forbes.'

'But the postcards were sent from Belgium.'

'I know that,' Alex said dismissively. 'When we arrived in Calais, we drove straight from there to Ostend to post them. It's not far, less than a hundred kilometres, I should think, and wasn't much out of our way. Then we went on down to the Black Forest.'

'When did you come back?'

'The end of the month, the thirty-first of July. We waited for a week after we got home, and one night we put Karen's body in the boot of the Mercedes and next day we drove to Richmond Park. I thought it was a crazy idea, but Max told me not to worry, that it would be OK. We had to drive around for quite a while until there was no one about, then we dumped it in a dip near the Richmond Gate. I was amazed that we'd got away with it.'

'You haven't,' I said.

But they damn near had. To think that the Forbeses were able to carry a body out to their car in a Battersea street, unnoticed by anyone, surprised me. No it didn't. On reflection, it didn't surprise me at all.

'Where is your husband now, Mrs Forbes? Still at the nudist colony?'

'I very much doubt it,' said Alex, probably hoping that he wouldn't be found and would not, therefore, be able to contradict her story.

'Incidentally, how did you know he would be there this time?'

'I guessed that's where he'd have gone. I kept ringing him

and eventually he answered his mobile. He probably thought it was one of his fancy women. Anyway, he said he was leaving there, but didn't tell me where he'd be going, and frankly I don't really care what happens to him any more. What I said yesterday was true. He wasn't in the least bit bothered about me. He just took off without telling me where he'd gone, until I managed to contact him. But, when I did get there and complained, he just ridiculed me for worrying, laughed at me, in fact. But I've told you all that. What really decided me to leave him was the streak of viciousness he displayed when he killed Karen. I knew I could never trust him again. That what he'd done to Karen he could as easily do to me. But we had to stay together while we disposed of the body. I can see now that he's a sadist, and we're finished, done. It's all over.'

Well, if that didn't beat cockfighting. After what we'd heard from Melissa Watson, it beggared belief that Alex could accuse Max of being a sadist.

'Yes, go on.'

'All he was bothered about was saving his own skin,' Alex continued. 'After all, it was his fault that Karen died.' She paused for a moment. 'I think he was jealous that I'd got it on with her.'

'Or was he more annoyed at you doing it with Mike Farrell, Bill Griffin, Clive Parish, Peter Morton and Rory Simpson, to name but a few?' It wasn't a very professional thing to say, but I couldn't resist it.

Alex flushed with anger, her mouth opened slightly and she tensed in her chair. 'How the hell d'you know about all of them?' she asked, her voice rising a pitch or two.

'Your husband very obligingly gave us your private address book.'

'The unspeakable bastard.' Alex was clearly furious at this latest act of betrayal.

I reckon I'd just given her yet another reason for leaving him.

'Why did you choose Richmond Park to dispose of the body, Mrs Forbes?'

'I don't know. It was Max's idea.'

Of course it was.

'Would it have anything to do with the fact that one of your less intelligent lovers lived very near there, and your husband hoped to cast suspicion on him?'

'I don't know what you're talking about.'

'I'm talking about Jamie Ryan, Mrs Forbes. Tennis and swimming coach, and part-time actor, so he claims.'

'I've never heard of him,' said Alex. But I don't know why she bothered to deny it, unless I'd hit on the truth.

'Well, he's heard of you. And he reckons you threw him over because of his lack of sexual prowess.'

Alex smiled but said nothing.

Dave finished writing and gave her the statement to read. She signed it without comment.

But I hadn't believed a word of her story, probably because Melissa Watson's sincere account of her ordeal at the hands of the Forbeses led me to believe that Alex Forbes was just as much of a sadist as she claimed her husband was.

'I shall shortly charge you with the murder of Karen Hockley,' I said.

Alex Forbes went ashen. 'But you can't. I told you, it was Max. It wasn't me, it was him!' she screamed. 'I'm not going to prison for something he did.' Suddenly she leaped up and flew at me like some wild thing, fists flying. It took a while for Dave and me to restrain her, but eventually she calmed down.

Back at Curtis Green, there was a report on my desk telling me that none of the fingerprints found at Crouch Road matched those of Alex Forbes's five known lovers. But it no longer mattered. The need for that had been overtaken by events.

Far more important right now was that somehow or other we had to find a simple way of getting Max Forbes back to this country. If we embarked on the palaver of extradition proceedings, it would probably take years to get him within the jurisdiction of the British courts.

It was Dave who came up with a bright, if not entirely legal, stratagem for dealing with the problem.

I was extremely dubious about the morality of what he suggested, but I soon talked myself out of those doubts. Anyway, it seemed the only quick way.

I just hoped to God that the commander didn't find out. In his view, any course of action that wasn't catered for in the rule book was automatically a disciplinary offence. There was no middle ground as far as he was concerned.

I got the telephone number of the Beck *Nacktkulturlager* in the Black Forest from international directory enquiries and rang it. Eventually I was put through to the director.

'This is the police in London, England,' I said. 'Can you pass a message to Mr Victor Smith, who is staying at the camp?'

'Of course, sir,' said the director. 'What is the message?'

'Would you please tell him that a close friend of his, a Mrs Karen Hockley, was killed in a car accident this morning.'

Well, it was half true, wasn't it?

Twenty-One

I had to admit that I was on tenterhooks for the next thirty-six hours. I didn't believe Alex Forbes's self-serving statement that Max had probably moved on from the nudist colony, and I wondered what his reaction was going to be to the spurious information I had passed to the director.

Was there anyone – unknown to us – whom he could have telephoned to verify it? I hoped not. I'd primed the incident room and Jock Ferguson to confirm my deception. But, in the unlikely event that Forbes had discovered it to be false, would he lodge an official complaint? Somehow I didn't think so. He was now my chief suspect for the murder of Karen Hockley, and was hardly in a position to complain.

On the other hand – assuming we went to trial – would defence counsel make a big thing of the trickery involved in bringing him back to this country? Or, worse still, would the judge have a bitch about it? Knowing the detached way in which some of today's judiciary interpreted the law, I could well be in for some heavy criticism from that quarter.

That, however, was all in the future.

The situation was partly resolved by a phone call at midday telling me that Max Forbes had been detained by Special Branch officers at Heathrow Airport.

I breathed a qualified sigh of relief and directed that he be transferred from the airport to Belgravia police station. I didn't want there to be the remotest chance of him catching sight of his wife at Charing Cross police station. Such unfortunate accidents do happen, and have happened in the past. And that would upset everything.

'Oh, it's you,' said Forbes, when at last we came face to face.

'Yes, it's me, Mr Forbes.'

'Perhaps you'd explain why I was arrested when I arrived from Stuttgart this morning.' There was an insufferably superior air of truculence about the man, a supreme confidence that indicated this was not going to be an easy interview.

So, for a start, let's hit him with the incontrovertible facts.

'Yesterday afternoon, at Horseferry Road mortuary, Dan Hockley positively identified the body of his wife Karen,' I said.

Forbes slumped in his chair, beads of sweat breaking out on his forehead. 'Oh, God!' he said. 'So, it's true. She has been killed.'

'Of course it's true,' I said. 'But it was the same body that you positively identified as that of *your* wife, Alex Forbes. And it was no accident.'

An expression of shock mixed with anger crossed Max Forbes's face. He grasped the edges of the table and half rose from his chair. 'What on earth are you talking about?'

It was a masterful performance. For artist read artiste.

'Sit down, Mr Forbes, and listen. Your wife Alex is in custody at Charing Cross police station, charged with the murder of Karen Hockley.'

'What? You can't mean she's still alive.'

'You can cut the crap, Forbes,' I said, 'You know damn well she is. And she's told us everything.'

Forbes slumped back into his chair, chin on chest, and absorbed that piece of treacherous information without comment.

'Furthermore,' I continued, 'she has made a statement in which she accuses you of the murder of Karen Hockley.'

'But that's ridiculous. Has she gone mad?'

'I have here a copy of her statement,' I went on, 'which you are entitled to have.'

That was one aspect of the law that often worked to the

advantage of the police, frequently resulting in accusations being bandied back and forth between the co-accused. But it also often created further difficulties.

Dave thumbed through the pile of paper in front of him, extracted a photocopy of Alex's statement and handed it to Max.

For the next ten minutes, he read through the closely written document, a document which effectively damned him. And then he read it again.

Finally tossing aside the several sheets of paper, he looked up. 'It's worthless,' he protested. 'A tissue of lies. Everything in this document that Alex ascribes to me was her doing. It was me who went down to the cellar to get the champagne—'

'Your wife said in her statement that you always had champagne as a preamble to these sessions of yours. She also hinted that, without her knowledge, you may well have had something stronger on the day that Karen Hockley was killed. Yet when I first interviewed you, you said you didn't drink, because you were an alcoholic.'

'She can think what she likes, but I never drink. Never. The champagne was for Alex and whoever else was taking part in our game.'

Nice one, Max. Whether it was true or not didn't matter, but he had just inadvertently ruled out any sort of defence of not knowing what he was doing through drunkenness. *And it had been tape-recorded.*

'Yes, go on. You were saying that you'd just been down to the cellar.'

'Yes, and it was Alex who was whipping Karen when I got back. It was me who had to restrain Alex and get Karen off the frame, and it was me who gave her mouth-to-mouth resuscitation.'

I was in a difficult position here. All I had was an allegation against Max Forbes by someone who was not only, on the face of it, a co-conspirator, but also the wife of the man she was accusing. And that meant that, if she stood trial, she would not be a competent witness. But, that aside, she would not be a compellable one anyway.

And there weren't any independent witnesses either. I knew from other cases where it was uncertain which of the parties inflicted the fatal blows, that a jury was unlikely to convict either of them. As things stood at the moment, the best we could hope for was to charge the Forbeses separately with concealing a dead body with a view to preventing an inquest. And that, believe me, was definitely a non-starter.

I was going to need more. And it was Dave, appreciating the dilemma, who supplied it.

'Can I have a word, sir? Outside.'

I suspended the interview and Dave and I went into the corridor.

'What's on your mind, Dave?' I asked.

Dave outlined his theory, backing it up with what he had observed when we'd interviewed Alex Forbes and Max Forbes.

Got the bastard. Ye Gods! The boy's a bloody genius and undoubtedly worthy of promotion. But, if I get him promoted, I'll lose him.

'It's a possibility, Dave, I suppose,' I said, 'but it all hinges on whether Henry Mortlock can back it up.'

Henry Mortlock was one of the best forensic pathologists I'd ever worked with. He would never be rushed into formulating an opinion, but once he had done so he stuck by it, and although defence counsel always attempted to discredit his evidence, they rarely succeeded.

Fortunately, Henry was at the mortuary, doing another post-mortem. I put Dave's hypothesis to him and his response was immediate.

'From my examination of the body, there is no doubt whatsoever, Harry,' Mortlock said. 'Sergeant Poole is absolutely right.' He nodded at Dave and smiled, as if wondering why *he* wasn't the chief inspector.

'And you'd be prepared to testify to that at the trial, Henry?' I asked.

Mortlock gave me the pitiful sort of look that suggested it was a rather naïve question. 'Naturally, dear boy,' he said, with an air of disdain. 'That's what I do for a living. That's why I'm called a forensic pathologist.'

'Yeah, all right, Henry, all right. I've got the message.'

I was convinced that Max Forbes would maintain that his version of the events surrounding Karen Hockley's death was the right one, just as I was equally certain that Alex would swear that her account was the truth.

That one or other of them had killed Karen was beyond doubt, thus it would all depend on Henry Mortlock's testimony. But I had no worries about that.

It was six o'clock that evening when Dave and I returned to Belgravia police station and continued our interview with Max Forbes. It would, I knew, be an unproductive formality. Forbes wasn't going to budge.

'I suppose you've come to tell me that I'm free to go,' said Forbes, his air of condescension undiminished.

'We have a little problem, Mr Forbes,' I said.

'I'm sure you have,' said Forbes with something approaching a sneer. 'One that my solicitor will doubtless resolve for you when he starts proceedings for wrongful arrest.'

'In a sense, your version of what occurred is a mirror image of your wife's. Each of you, it would appear, is adamant that the other murdered Karen Hockley.'

'Well, Alex would say that, but it was she who actually killed the woman.'

'I wouldn't have expected you to say anything else. In the circumstances, however, I have no alternative but to charge you both with murder.'

It was obvious from his alarmed reaction that Max Forbes thought I'd accepted his tale, and that he was about to walk away from the whole sordid affair. Just as his wife had believed she would.

'But that's bloody scandalous. I've told you what happened,' he said, his face working with anguish.

'So has Alex,' I said calmly. 'It will, therefore, be a matter for the jury to decide.'

I certainly wasn't going to tell him what Henry Mortlock proposed to say at the trial. That, with any luck, would only be revealed when Henry came to give his evidence-in-chief. And I was content to allow Max to find it out when his counsel took a deep breath and wondered how the hell he was going to counter it.

The venue of the offence had been Battersea, and the first hearing would be at South-Western Magistrates Court. And, given the Forbeses' predilection for running away, I didn't foresee any problem in securing a remand in custody.

'It would appear that your enquiry has been drawn to a satisfactory conclusion, Mr Brock,' said the commander, once I'd acquainted him with the latest on the Karen Hockley murder. He looked at me over his glasses and primped his pocket handkerchief.

Most real detectives would have said that I'd got a result, but the only person who believed that the commander was a real detective was the commander himself.

'There are still one or two problems though, sir,' I said, and attempted to explain in laymen's terms the difficulties of proving which of the Forbeses had killed the woman.

'Yes, I see,' mused the commander, not really seeing at all. 'And Dr Mortlock will be prepared to say that, will he?'

'Without a doubt, sir.'

'In that case, I shall be interested to cast my eye over the report for the Crown Prosecution Service.'

Which meant he wanted to see it before I started negotiations with that band of inadequate lawyers.

But, for a change, the CPS lawyer who handled the case was quite a switched-on guy. Wearing a startlingly loud pinstriped suit, he lounged back in his chair, feet propped on an open bottom drawer of his desk, and, contrary to all the office rules, lit a cigar.

'Alex Forbes can't be compelled to give evidence against her husband, nor he against her,' he began.

'Yes, I know,' I said.

'And she'd only be competent if we didn't charge her with the murder, or if she pleaded guilty, or was found guilty first.'

'I know that too,' I said.

'So . . .' The lawyer put his feet on the ground and shot forward in his chair. He thumbed through the report to that part containing a summary of the pathologist's statement. 'D'you reckon Mortlock will be all right in the box?' he asked, looking up at me.

'Henry Mortlock will be rock solid,' I said. 'He always is.'

'Then the safest thing we can do is to indict the pair of them and let them throw accusations at each other across the courtroom.' He grinned. 'Ain't that grand?'

'What about concealment of the body?'

'Forget it,' said the lawyer. 'Murderers always try to conceal the body. It's what makes it exciting for them.'

It was some weeks before Dave and I were required to attend the Central Criminal Court at the Old Bailey. The usual cardboard boxes of statements and exhibits were unloaded from a police van, but it was the large metal frame upon which Karen Hockley had died that excited particular interest among the ranks of the journalists and photographers who hovered at the main entrance. The next day's tabloids were full of it, together with appropriately lurid headlines that came within a whisker of breaching the sub judice rule.

In the confines of the dock in Number Three Court, Max and Alex Forbes somehow looked smaller than they did in real life. That was understandable, I suppose: there was nothing real about what went on here.

The serried ranks of bewigged barristers, a couple of QCs

among them, bowed to the judge and the whole lumbering process of the law got under way. At its usual snail's pace.

The Forbeses each pleaded not guilty to the indictment that they had murdered Karen Hockley, and prosecuting counsel launched into his opening address.

The trial opened with the customary sort of formal evidence that sets the scene, but the highlight was, as I'd anticipated, Henry Mortlock's evidence.

After a straightforward – and unchallenged – exposition of his findings, he came up with the coup de grâce.

'In my professional opinion,' he began, 'the marks on the back and buttocks of the deceased's body are consistent with her having been assaulted with a whip or some similar instrument, and were inflicted by a person who was left-handed.'

Prosecuting counsel faced the judge. 'Evidence will later be adduced that will prove the accused, Maxwell Forbes, is left-handed, My Lady,' he said, 'and that his co-accused, Alexandra Forbes, is right-handed.' And, returning to his examination of Mortlock, he asked, 'And are you absolutely adamant that the injuries were not inflicted by a right-handed person, Doctor?'

'Most certainly,' said Mortlock.

And despite Max Forbes's barrister indulging in all manner of pathological jargon, and citing opinions from learned medical works, Henry Mortlock remained unshaken in his assertion that the injuries on the woman's back had been inflicted by a left-handed person.

And for once even the judge was on my side. When defence counsel tried to make capital out of the ruse I'd employed to bring Max Forbes back to England, there was a sharp interruption from the bench.

'We are not concerned with the manner in which the accused was brought before the court,' said the judge. 'Suffice it to say that he is here. That's all that matters.' Unfortunately, they don't seem to make judges like her any more.

And so it panned out exactly as I'd anticipated. Max Forbes was found guilty and sentenced to life imprisonment for the murder of Karen Hockley, even though, at one stage, I thought that the judge was going to convert it to manslaughter.

Alex Forbes was acquitted, even of the subsidiary offence of assisting an offender. Personally I thought that her acquittal was diabolical, but that's juries for you.

It was fortunate that, on the one occasion we had visited Max Forbes at his studio, Dave had observed that he was using his left hand to draw a sketch on a storyboard. It was also fortunate that Dave had noticed, later, that Alex Forbes had signed her statement with her right hand. And it was even more fortunate that Henry Mortlock had been able to confirm that the blows that contributed to the death of Karen Hockley had been inflicted by a left-handed assailant. And from that the jury had inferred that the assailant had also restrained her and fastened the leather hood over her head. Much too tightly.

Upon such minor observations are convictions for murder so often secured. Aren't juries wonderful?

As Dave drily commented, it was a case of not letting the right-handed know what the left-handed had been doing. At least, not until the trial.

And then, just as I thought the case was over, the judge looked down into the well of the court.

'Is Detective Chief Inspector Brock still here?' she enquired. It was a rhetorical question; she knew damned well I was still there.

'Yes, My Lady,' I said, rising to my feet. Here we go, I thought. Now for the judicial bollocking.

'The court wishes to commend you for your detective ability in the investigation of a very difficult and complex case,' she said. And, leaning forward to address the clerk of the court, she added, 'Please convey that commendation to the Commissioner of Police.'

'Thank you, My Lady,' I said, breathing a hefty sigh of relief.

Dave and I retired to the Magpie and Stump and rapidly consumed a couple of pints of best bitter.

'I've got two spare tickets for the ballet tonight, guv,' said Dave. 'Madeleine's appearing in *Coppelia*. D'you think Sarah would fancy it?'

'I'll give her a ring,' I said.

Dave's face split into a huge grin. 'D'you mean that at long last you're going to marry the girl, guv?'